CALLIE
& THE DEALER
& A DOG
NAMED JAKE

Oak Tree Press

Oak Tree Books may be purchased for educational, business, or
sales   promotional use. Contact Publisher for quantity dis-
counts.

This book is intended for entertainment purposes only, and all
the characters and situations are purely the invention of the author. Any similarity to real persons, living or dead, is purely
coincidental.

First Edition, July 2001

Cover Design by Yvet

Cover Photograph by Mary Montague Sikes

10 9 8 7 6 5 4 3 2 1

Library of Congress Cataloging-in-Publication Data
Mills, Wendy Howell, 1975-
Callie & the Dealer and a Dog Named Jake / by Wendy Howell
Mills. — 1st edition
P. cm.

CALLIE
& the DEALER
& a DOG
NAMED JAKE

WENDY HOWELL MILLS

Oak Tree Press
Claremont CA

ACKNOWLEDGEMENTS

When I sat down to write this acknowledgment, I realized that I had so many people to thank that I could write a book just thanking people for all the encouragement and support that I have received over the years to finally make it to this point. For the reader's sake, I'll make it short, but I could never have done it without all of you, and you know who you are.

To Jamie Jamison, who introduced me to "Della and the Dealer" and who still makes me cry whenever he sings it.

To everybody at the Ramada Inn and Peppercorns, who allowed me to "borrow" their hotel. I'm giving it back to you now, a little changed, more than a little fictionalized, but thank you for the loan. All the good bits are real; all the bad are purely a figment of my imagination.

Thanks to Erik Speer, Robin Rector, Mark Pennington, and Joan Pittman for their expert restaurant advice. I would also like to thank Steve Clinard of the Nags Head Police for his help. Any mistakes are entirely my own, not theirs.

I am indebted to Alan Ross, and Will and Emily Robertson for their close reading of this manuscript, and whose suggestions have been invaluable.

On a personal level, thank you, Eddie for putting up with me all these years. You always believed. Thank you, Mom, for teaching me the love of reading and writing.

Thank you Billie Johnson, for giving me a chance.

And finally, this book never could have happened without all of the zany, wonderful people on the Outer Banks whose lives have given me inspiration.

*Della and the dealer and a dog named Jake
and a cat named Kalamazoo
Left Tucson in a pickup truck
Goin' to make some dreams come true*

Hoyt Axton
"Della and the Dealer"

We wish to salute the long and rich career of Hoyt Axton whose words, music and spirit have enriched us for many years, and, we trust, will continue to do so for decades to come.

Mr. Axton is memorialized on numerous Internet sites, some of which contain his complete discography. We encourage everyone to take a moment to view these sites and discover — or rediscover — this American legend.

Dead Men and French Fries

There was a dead man in the freezer.

I had quite enough on my plate already, thank you, with a hurricane blowing and fifty journalists hungry for stories and filet mignon sitting upstairs in my restaurant. But it's pretty hard to ignore a dead body stuck to the floor of your walk-in freezer.

Sprawled in wide-eyed abandon, the man looked, if anything, surprised. I didn't blame him. I was pretty surprised myself. I stepped back, choking down a surge of hot bile that flooded the back of my throat. And sorrow, because I knew the man. I worked with him. *Had* worked with him. How had this happened?

All I had wanted was a box of French fries. I suddenly wished I had told the pushy journalists that we were out of French fries, but we've got some real nice long-grain rice. It's better for you.

This wasn't getting me anywhere. I stepped forward into the swirling mist of the sub-zero freezer, kicking an empty box aside as I went. I leaned down to check the pulse of the dead man. I knew he was dead, there were bloody icicles hanging from his nose, for God's sake, but I had to be sure. His skin was ice cold. He was dead.

I moved back, and accidentally brushed against one of his legs. I heard a crackling noise as the leg came unstuck from the floor. *Oh Jesus.*

I suddenly felt the intense cold of the freezer, especially on my exposed hands and face. My stomach was flip-flopping, and I closed my eyes as I swayed. *I will not pass out, and I will not cry,* I told myself sternly. *No way.*

The dizziness passed, and I opened my eyes to find that the body was still there, dammit. He lay stretched out on the cold metal floor, one frozen hand grasping the side of an upturned steak box lying beside his head. Incongruously, individually packaged frozen steaks lay scattered around his body.

The box of French fries was on a shelf right beside my head. I looked down at the body stuck to the floor of the freezer, and then thought about the fifty people sitting in my restaurant, probably banging their forks on their tables by now.

So I did what any self-respecting restaurant manager in my situation would do. I grabbed the box of French fries, and got out of there, making sure I locked the door behind me.

Then I went upstairs to face my hungry customers.

Nine Days Prior

CHAPTER ONE

You Don't Have to Go Home But You Can't Stay Here

"I think you're certifiable," I said.

"Without a doubt," Chef said cheerfully. "I'm certifiably neurotic, paranoid, obsessive, and at the moment, very, very drunk. Are you just figuring this out?"

I shook my head and took another swig of my Tanqueray and tonic. There wasn't much you could do with a man who readily admitted he was crazy as a loon. Fortunately, he wasn't *my* man, so I didn't have to put up with him day and night, but he was a coworker. He was CHEF (drum roll, please) the executive chef in charge of the restaurant and banquet rooms inside the Holiday House Hotel, and as the restaurant manager, I had to work with him closely. Not as closely as Chef would have liked, judging from the lascivious leer and the intent stare he was now bestowing on me (though his eyes seemed to be longingly lingering on my nose).

"I don't understand why you just won't talk to him," I said, for what seemed like the fifteenth time.

"Why not?"

"Ugh," I said in disgust and looked around the dimly-lit bar. Sharkey's was a narrow dark room with bright neon signs and mariner relics on the walls. The core of the people who came here were locals, and Sharkey's was their home away from home. They arrived right after work and often stayed until closing. One regular had a special kind of chardonnay that he drank, and the owner ordered a case just for him every month. Another regular, a local bank teller, had a special chair emblazoned with her name. Sharkey's took care of the locals in the summer, and the locals took care of Sharkey's in the winter, when business could drop to a standstill.

It was just past two a.m., when the bars closed their doors and the bartenders began stocking their beer and ignoring their customers. I had just gotten off work, so I was a lot more sober than the majority of the remaining bar customers.

"I wish I'd known you were deranged when I took this job," I muttered to myself.

"But it makes the job so much more *interesting!*" Chef proclaimed, sweeping his arms wide and hitting Elizabeth, a woman in a very short mini-skirt sitting next to him.

"Chef," she said, fixing him with a glare only an eighty-year-old drunk lady can bestow. "If you wanted my wig, why didn't you just say so?" She whipped off her hair, revealing her bald head underneath, and cackling, tried to hand it to Chef.

"Whoa," Chef said, giving her a sneering look and turning back to me. "And you're calling me crazy? She just tried to give me her hair."

Over his shoulder, I saw Elizabeth calmly put the wig back on her head and take another large swig of her drink. A group of expensively dressed, searingly-red tourists stared at us in disbelief and began whispering among themselves.

There are three very distinct groups of people who inhabit the Outer Banks of North Carolina. You have your locals, who have moved to the Outer Banks from somewhere else, and are highly individualistic, enjoy the numbing effects of alcohol, and are usually running from something or someone. Even though I had only been on the beach for two months, I fit right in.

Then there are the natives, who were born on the Outer Banks, and whose lives are rich with local lore and fishermen instincts.

And then you have the tourists, or "tourons" as they are sometimes affectionately called. The tourons are a faceless mass of people from points north who breeze into town for a week at a time, and ask silly questions like "Why don't you people mow the dunes? It looks so messy," and "What do you mean you don't have a real mall? I came all the way from a big mall-blighted city for some peace and quiet and you don't even have a mall?" But despite the silly questions, without the tourists most of us could not afford to live here.

Chef pushed his drink to the edge of the bar and called loudly for Melissa to bring him another one. She ignored him, of course, because it was after two a.m., as he knew very well.

"I'll go home with you again if you give me another drink," he said in a wheedling voice, and the blond bartender gave him a withering look.

"It wasn't that good," she said.

"Oh, don't lie," Chef said. "How about you Callie?" He flicked back his long gray hair and tried to look sexy and pouty, but only succeeded in looking like a drunk, sleepy sheep dog.

I shook my head, trying not to laugh.

Chef looked around, his eyes fixing on Elizabeth, the elderly barfly sitting beside him.

"Now I know you've lost it," I said, and he grinned.

But I had known that almost as soon as I started my new job and had introduced myself to Chef. Chef, who had been perfectly sober *that* day, had turned to Mac, one of the line cooks, and asked derisively, "Is she talking to me?"

Mac answered: "Yes, Boss."

"What does she want?"

"She's the new restaurant manager, Boss."

"Uck," Chef had said and disdainfully held out his hand to shake mine. "I hope you last longer than the last one."

"Steve! Knock it off, we're closed!" Melissa the bartender yelled at the musician, who was singing an off-key melody about truck drivers and alien lesbians who love K.D. Lang.

He ignored her and polished off one of the line of full shot glasses sitting in front of him.

"So why won't you talk to Luigi?" I asked for the sixteenth time.

"He's so *horrid,*" Chef said, and picked up Elizabeth's drink while she wasn't looking and took a swig. "Such an overbearing wait person."

"Luigi says you haven't spoken to him for the past three days," I persisted. "He says you've been writing him notes and pointing to your throat like you have laryngitis."

Chef was patently uninterested.

"Chef, you don't *have* laryngitis," I told him, as if maybe in his drunken state he had forgotten.

Chef was gazing toward the front door of Sharkey's where a tall, pretty girl was just entering. He half stood, and then sank back onto his stool. He was tall, at least 6'1, but at 5'4 most people looked tall to me, even when I wore my detested heels. He wore his luxuriant mane of silver hair long, in the old eighties style with wings and curling up in the back. His mustache was also a tad too long, drooping around his mouth.

From what I had gathered, Chef thought he was irresistible to women. He came on to almost every woman that he met: young or old, pretty or ugly, rich or poor.

"So, how come you haven't been speaking to Luigi?" I asked.

He smiled, his brown eyes as milky as a Hershey's Chocolate Bar. He took a deep breath and held it in his cheeks before gently blowing it out. Then he deigned to answer me.

"He kept telling me his special orders instead of writing them down, the skinny pig-head. Like I'm supposed to remember twenty special orders in my head and cook at the same time. So I made the little spaghetti noodle write everything down, so he had to write his special orders down too. It worked, didn't it?"

Typical for Chef. No one said you couldn't get anywhere in this world being passive aggressive. I shook my head, and dropped the subject. Chef was a source of constant irritation to my staff, *and* to me, but sometimes I couldn't help but admire his sheer audacity.

"Took you a while to finish inventory tonight," he said pleasantly, his eyes roaming the bar for likely pickup material

"And I'm not done," I said. I did not want to think about inventory. From what I had completed so far, I knew already that we were missing items. A *lot.* But thoughts of a skewed inventory would have to wait until tomorrow.

Chef launched into a description of a particularly ugly customer that night who had sent her steak back three times and then had marched into the kitchen and handed the steak to Chef himself, demanding that he cook the steak right, since "Obviously my server is not understanding my instructions."

"Chef!" The tall girl with long brown hair and platform shoes hugged Chef from behind.

"Daisy!" he said delightedly. "Gotta go," he said to me. "Been wonderful talking to you. Don't call me, I'll call you. Why can't we just be friends, and all that?" He delivered this in a rapid-fire monotone, and gulping the remainder of my drink, got up and followed the girl.

I smiled and shook my head. After two months of living on

the beach, I had gotten used to finding my company in strange places. Chef might be certifiable but he was fun to talk to, and at two in the morning who could be picky?

I'm not much of a drinker, but I have trouble sleeping and would rather be at a bar with people I knew than staring at the ceiling as the clock ticked away. And it was certainly interesting to see my new work mates out of the restaurant, when everybody loosened up and showed their true colors.

P.m. restaurant people are a different breed from most people. They don't like a lot of structure, they don't like getting up early, and they usually enjoy other people's company. They are not antisocial animals.

When the rest of the world is enjoying the Fourth of July, Thanksgiving and New Year's Eve, we are working. When the rest of the world is getting up every morning at seven o'clock, we are sleeping. When the rest of the world is watching Jay Leno and getting ready for bed, we are just getting off work and are ready to raise a little hell.

I stretched and yawned. I had raised enough hell for this evening, and tomorrow I had to finish the inventory, figure out why we were missing glasses and plates, and start planning for the Fourth of July holiday which was only days away.

Melissa turned the lights all the way up and announced at the top of her lungs,   "You don't have to go home, but you can't stay here..."

I went home, dreading my cold, empty bed, and the nightmares that would follow me into sleep.

HOLIDAY HOUSE HOTEL

Memo

April 6
To: Lily Thomas, General Manager
From: Darryl Menden, Restaurant Manager
Re: High Food Costs

I would like to speak with you about a matter that is of the utmost importance to the fiscal health of the restaurant. The food costs are dangerously close to that limit which will preclude the managers from receiving their bonuses at the end of the year. I am doing everything in my power to lower the food costs on my end. Thus, I feel that the rising food costs must be blamed on the back of the house.

As far as Michael, I am seriously concerned about his performance as executive chef. Over the last six months, he has been unduly distracted and inattentive.

I do not mean to be an alarmist, but I feel that there may be a very serious underlying problem causing these symptoms. I am looking into it and will be seeking a meeting with you by the end of the week to inform you of my findings.

Darryl

CHAPTER TWO

Bearding the Lion

The memo was tucked into a folder marked "Easter."

It figured. My predecessor, Darryl Menden, had been a piece of work. After two months of trying to decipher his cryptic management decisions and notes, I was fed-up with almost everything about the man, even though I had never met him.

I had been curious to see what the restaurant had done in the past for the Fourth of July holiday, three days away, and had remembered seeing a folder marked "Fourth of July." Finding a plethora of folders marked with varying holidays, I had been leafing through them all, to get an idea of what my new job would entail over the upcoming months.

I was happy that Darryl had seen fit to leave all of his notes from the years that he had worked here, but I wondered again why he had left so many personal effects. Pictures of his wife and certificates of achievement had still been in place when I had taken over his desk.

I shook my head. From comments I had heard, Darryl had been a strange bird all the way around.

The memo in the "Easter" folder was disturbing. What "underlying problem" was leading to high food costs? How close were the monthly food costs to that cap that would cost the managers their bonuses?

The food and beverage bonuses at the Holiday House Hotel were based on volume and food costs: i.e. the department had to keep restaurant volume above a certain level and food costs below a certain level for the year to get our bonuses. As I naturally had reason to be concerned about the bonuses, I had asked how the department was doing when I was hired. From what Lily had said we were still within acceptable limits to receive the bonuses at the end of the year.

So why had Darryl been so concerned?

The memo was disturbing in another way, as well. Darryl had left his job a week after the memo was dated.

Sighing, I put the memo on my desk and put the file back in the file cabinet. I would have to deal with it later.

I found the Fourth of July folder and leafed through menus and notes from the last several years. The Fourth of July had been busy last year, and Darryl had kept the deck bar open until eight. I pondered that, and then picked up the phone, thumbing through my Rolodex.

I tried not to think of the million other things I was supposed to do today, finishing the inventory of the restaurant's glassware and silverware foremost. I had already been here since six this morning, and it was after one in the afternoon.

"Len, hi, this is Callie McKinley," I said into the receiver. "How are you?"

The deep resonant voice answered cheerfully, "Never better. How's Kalamazoo?"

I winced and smiled. "I'm fine."

Lenny Marks was a local musician who had been working the Seahorse Cafe crowds for the past five years. Before that, he had played the Nashville scene and had a band that was pretty well known. Now, he was simply legend. He played mostly western; his deep raspy voice, thickened with whisky and cigarettes, was perfectly suited to Waylon Jennings and Willie Nelson.

"You got any plans, say from five to eight on the fourth of July?"

He paused. "I got a gig at the Jolly Roger," he said, "but I don't start until ten."

"How would you like to play the deck bar, usual terms?"

"Sounds good," he answered, and we discussed details.

"How's the voice?" he asked just before we hung up.

"Hasn't gone anywhere," I answered with a smile.

One thing to do down, only twenty thousand to go. I stood

up from my desk and stretched. The food and beverage office was empty on this early Saturday afternoon, but as usual, it looked as if a whirlwind had danced through the five cramped desks.

A man appeared at the door, his eyes slightly unfocused, and he headed for one of the desks. He looked young, with toffee-colored hair pulled back under a baseball cap, cherubic face unlined and innocent. "Salmon mousse and lobster," he muttered, sitting down and grabbing a pad of paper.

On closer inspection, he was closer to forty than twenty, streaks of gray touching the amber of his long straight hair. "Hi Jerry," I said, used to his distracted manner.

"Callie," said Jerry, the restaurant chef, not to be confused with "Chef" who was the executive chef. He did not turn around from where he was still furiously scribbling. "The waits are scooping again, not piping."

I tried not to smile, amused despite his faintly scolding tone. "Well, Jerry, the servers tell me that it's a pain in the butt to pipe out a week's worth of butter on sheet pans and that by the end of the week a quarter of the butter is squished and unusable. I think scooping would eliminate that wastage."

He turned and looked at me with eyes the royal blue of a letter jacket. "Cranberry chutney and ostrich," he said, and turned to scribble again on his notepad. "They aren't letting the butter freeze properly before putting it in the storage container. I'll show Margie."

I left him, deep in his creative fugue, and went toward the elevator. Inventory awaited.

The inventory was screwier than a corkscrew.

I sat at my desk, staring at the numbers as if somehow they would magically flicker and add up to what they were supposed to.

It wasn't happening.

According to my numbers, we were missing an entire rack of water glasses, twenty-five plates, two boxes of silverware and at least fifteen steak knives.

From tradition at the Holiday House Hotel, it was the restaurant manager's duty to do inventory for both the restaurant and the banquet department. I had done an inventory when I had first started, and it had been off, but as in everything I couldn't be sure how diligent my predecessor had been. But I knew how diligent *I* had been, and the numbers this month were definitely off.

"Hey Janet," I said, leaning back in my chair to look at the desk on the other side of the computer terminal.

"Hey what?" she said irritably, flipping down her headphones and glaring at me.

I hadn't decided how to take Janet, the hotel's banquet/cater manager. Most of the time she seemed stressed out and didn't want to be disturbed. Every once in a while, she waxed garrulous and I couldn't shut her up. Obviously, the "Do not disturb" sign was out today.

"Just wondering if you've been hiding racks of water glasses, silverware, anything like that."

She reached into her bag of trail mix and popped a handful into her mouth. Janet was fitness personified, short and lithe and stacked, with a great tan contrasting with her subtly bleached hair. "Darryl complained about that," she said around a mouthful of raisins and nuts.

"Yeah?"

"He was always complaining that stuff was missing. At least for the last six months or so. But you had to know Darryl; he was a real strange one. He started lurking around in the middle of the night trying to catch someone stealing. He was pretty paranoid, and a whiner to boot. We never took him serious. " She shrugged and turned back to her desk, flexing her shoulders.

"What about this? Anybody take this seriously?" I handed her the memo I had found in the Easter folder.

"Never heard anything about it," she said slowly. "But like I said, nobody, including Lily, took Darryl seriously. He was always whining, scribbling little notes on manila folders. You always got the feeling he was taking notes so he could tell Lily on you, like he was in the third grade."

Great. They never took him seriously. So what was I supposed to do? Reveal myself as another whiner, or ignore the fact that glassware and silverware were sliding out of the Holiday House Hotel faster than sand through a sieve?

"But what if he had a point?" I asked doggedly.

"Let me tell you a story about Darryl," Janet said, leaning back in her chair to look at me. "I went on vacation this spring, and Darryl had to take over some of my functions. I get back, and I find out that he's trying to change the menu for my Easter Brunch for Born Again Christians, a menu they've had for *years*, mind you, and he's managed to piss off all the chefs. I left him alone for two weeks, for God's sake! I didn't care what he did in the restaurant, but when he started messing with banquets... he was a shmuck, plain and simple."

"What about Chef? Has he been 'inattentive'?"

"You know him. He's weird. He took over the executive chef position about a year ago, and we've all been trying to adjust to him. He's well qualified, of course, came from some fancy five-star restaurant in New York, and is CIA certified. He's a big believer in 'delegating,' maybe that's what Darryl had a problem with. But I figure Jerry and Noel know what they're doing, so why mess with them? I haven't had any major problems with him."

I grimaced, and then forced my face into smooth lines. Someone had once told me I looked like an elf when I wrinkled up my nose in a grimace. The fact that I was small, with a little face and snub nose with black hair that lay flat and short around my skull didn't help either.

I had an appointment to interview yet another waitress. I stood up, grabbing my little gold glasses off the desk and perching them on my nose. Janet was rocking in her chair, singing an off-tune version of The Rolling Stone's "Under My Thumb." Inventory would have to wait while I figured out what to do. I had the very bad feeling I knew what it would be. I would have to beard the lion in her own den, face the stampeding bull with the wrong color cape.

I would have to go see the general manager of the Holiday House Hotel, Lily Thomas.

Ugh.

But first, my interview.

"I've been waitressing practically *all* my life," said the smoothly pretty blond, fluttering her blue-coated eyelashes. I tried to avoid staring at them, but they waggled up and down like a pair of iridescent blue butterfly wings.

"Um, yes," I said, shifting in my seat.

We were in the three-story lobby of the hotel, my interview room, as all the conference rooms were being used, and it didn't seem fair to interview someone in the cramped confines of the food and beverage office. Potted trees shimmered as someone came in the front doors, and a blast of hot air washed across my face.

"Were you looking for a permanent position, or will you be leaving to go back to school at the end of the summer?" I asked, in my very best professional voice.

"I just need something through August," she said. "Then I'll be going back to ECU."

"Ah," I said, scribbling stars and smiley faces on my notepad. Blond Linda with the blue eyelashes was a carbon copy of the other five applicants I had interviewed over the past week. I would have to lower my standards.

A strange and wonderful thing happened on the Outer Banks every summer. Just when the tourists are due to arrive, and employers are looking around at their meager winter staffs in dismay, a knock sounds at the door, and about a million and one eager, fresh college students are at the door, wanting a job for the summer. They aren't particularly reliable, and they are very clear on their priorities, party first, and work a very distant second, but they are warm bodies.

"What I need right now is morning help, with an eye to maybe moving up to p.m. in a couple weeks. Can you work mornings?"

"Sure," she said, but her enthusiasm had dampened, and she avoided my gaze.

"Okay," I said. "I'll give you a call in a couple of days."

I watched her as she left, probably on her way to another interview. She fluttered her eyelashes at Ray, the totally gorgeous front desk manager, and sashayed out in her tight red dress.

"Oh well," I said, settling back on the flowery cushions of the wicker couch. A man with corpse-white legs and fuschia pants wandered by, leading his wife and three kids like a mamma duckling leading her chicks to water. Kitty, the hotel cat, jumped up beside me and announced that he was ready to be petted.

"You want to work for me?" I said to Kitty, a long-haired tabby who was friendly and dead to the world in turns, as the mood struck him.

"Yeow," he commented and I nodded agreement.

"Yeah, it would be a shame to mess up our wonderful relationship."

I glanced at my watch. It was almost five, and if I wanted to talk to our glorious leader, I had to do it now before she left to go home. I headed for the front desk, and the door beside the counter leading to the back offices, sketching a wave at Ray, the totally gorgeous gay front desk guy. His fine brown hair was damply mussed, as if he had just gotten out of bed, but I knew that he had been running his hands through his hair frenziedly, stressed out about one thing or another.

"Hi Callie," he said. "Great outfit."

I barely refrained from saying "What, this old thing?" because I had always wanted to say that. Instead, I smoothed my hands over the crisp blue lines of my summer suit and thanked him, aware of his envious eyes on me as I went into the back.

The general manager's office was directly behind the front desk, at the head of the offices that marched down the front of the building, ending with the food and beverage office.

"Kelly, honey, I appreciate what you're telling me, now appreciate what *I* have to say to *you.*"

The lion was definitely in her den. I could see the walls shaking from where I stood.

"The mattresses were ripped and torn by the time they got here. I don't know whose fault it was, but it definitely wasn't *mine.* I expect those mattresses to disappear by Friday, and new ones to appear to take their place. I don't even want to hear anything else about it. Are we hearing each other? Good. I'm glad. You have a nice Fourth of July, you hear?"

I poked my head around the side of the door, just as Lily slammed down the phone.

"Callie, get in here, I want to talk to you."

Oh wonderful. I smiled calmly, and went inside to sit at the desk across from her.

Lily Thomas was a big woman. About 5'10, two hundred pounds, she overflowed the big leather executive armchair. Lily Thomas was also a *loud* woman. Everything about her, from her brassy curly red hair the color of a copper pot, to her kiwi green suit, to the jaunty tiger orange scarf around her neck.

"Callie-girl, I've been talking to Sales. You're causing problems. Why did you veto the use of the restaurant for the Nark's meeting?"

I steeled myself against the blaring voice and gathered my thoughts. I had been expecting this, but not quite so soon. "The Narks wanted to have their meeting at nine o'clock in the morning, right in the middle of my breakfast rush, and they refused to order any food. I do not think it is a good idea to section off half of the restaurant for thirty-five people who are not going to eat, and who are only willing to pay a nominal fee for the space. I would lose considerable breakfast revenue. Also, I checked, and there was a cancellation, so there is a banquet room open."

Lily stared at me, her honey-dew eyes hard. She reached into a water-filled cup and extracted cut celery, which she savagely bit. Lily was trying to quit smoking, and someone had told her that celery was a good pacifier. She chomped away, staring at me as she apparently thought of seven different ways to eviscerate me.

"Okay," she said suddenly. "Makes sense."

I held myself tightly and refused to sag in relief. I had known I was right, but I had expected to have to fight. I had won a major battle over the sales department, who had ridden roughshod over me since I had arrived.

"So what did you want?" She regarded another piece of celery and then bit off a large bite, as if she wished it were someone's head she was biting off.

"The inventory. Several items are missing."

Lily's interest was hard and rapid. "Such as?"

I detailed to her the missing items and she sank back in her seat, chewing loudly on her celery. "So, so, so," she said. "Why didn't you catch this last month?"

"I did," I said, "but I wasn't sure how– ah, diligent Darryl Menden had been when it came to inventory."

She laughed, her double chins swinging. "Very diplomatic. So what are you going to do about it?"

"Change the locks on the doors. Restrict keys to essential personnel. Check inventory twice a month," I answered.

"Okay," she said, swiveling her chair back to the computer screen, and reaching with a grimace of distaste for another piece of celery. "Anything else?" She was impatient.

I glanced down at the noteboard on my lap and made my decision.

"Yes. I found this in Darryl Menden's files. I wondered if I should worry about it." I unclipped the April 6th memo from Darryl to Lily and handed it to her.

Lily read the memo expressionlessly, biting another hunk out of her celery.

"Yeah?" she said aggressively.

"It just seemed– odd," I said carefully. Frankly the memo had disturbed me deeply. I didn't like the hint of controversy between the chefs and the previous restaurant manager. I didn't like his implications.

"I looked into this at the time," Lily said, crumpling up the memo and throwing it at the trash can.

It missed.

"I talked to the three chefs, I looked at the numbers. Volume is definitely within the acceptable parameters, if maybe a little low. The food and beverage department is having a great year, you know that. As far as pricing, the chefs decide the pricing, based on their ordering. It wasn't Darryl's business."

"And the food costs?"

"Thirty-nine percent for the year. It's between thirty-five and forty percent, which is what ya'lls bonuses are based on. Oh, it could be a little lower, but we could serve cheeseburgers and fries like McDonald's if we were really worried about it. I've talked to the chefs and they are working on getting it back down to a more acceptable level."

"Did Darryl tell you what 'underlying problem' he thought was affecting the food costs?" I felt as if I were dancing through a minefield. Lily was sending out clear signals that she was tired of this conversation, and you ignored Lily's signals at your own peril.

"Darryl Menden was a crybaby. He was always scribbling notes and running to me every time he had a spat with the chefs. Which was often. I called him in here a couple of days after he gave me that memo and he acted like he didn't know what I was talking about. Denied that there was any 'underlying problem.' I think the man was beginning to lose it, honestly. Finally he ruffled too many feathers and now he's gone." She stared at me.

I nodded, smiled and took my leave. Her implication was obvious, and I had never been slow. I better be careful not to ruffle too many feathers.

I could hear Lily bellowing into the telephone as I walked down the hall toward my office. I wondered if anyone would notice my knees shaking.

I glanced down at the copy of Darryl's memo, which I had made before I went into Lily's office. I folded my interview notes over top of it and pasted a smile on my face.

CHAPTER THREE

Shriners and Hell

Two hours later, I entered the kitchen, which resembled a picture-book version of what hell would look like if it were constructed solely for those in the restaurant business.

Okay, to the trained eye, it was an *organized* hell, but it was still hell.

A banquet for two hundred seventy Shriners was taking place in an hour downstairs in the banquet ballroom, and the kitchen was in chaos. Chef, in an immaculate white chef's coat, waved a spoon as if it was a baton and he was directing a symphony. Prep guys slaved over a tilt skillet filled with twenty-five gallons of French onion soup, chopped vegetables, and pulled hotel pans of rosemary chicken from the ovens. The kitchen thermometer wavered between 111 and 112 degrees, and settled decisively on 112.

The servers, or "waits" as they were more commonly known, were wearing their "black and whites"— black pants and white tuxedo shirts— and prepping salad dressings and butter and monopolizing the slicer to turn out two hundred and seventy wheels of lemon for the ice water.

"I thought you were off tonight," Chef said to me, piling petit fours and strawberries on glass seabreeze plates.

"I am," I said, catching a strawberry before it fell to the floor.

"I must be finally going over the edge, because it seems to me that you are still here. Or am I just dreaming about you again?" Chef smoothed a hand over his thick, perfectly groomed hair.

I shrugged and helped him for several minutes by opening the boxes of petit fours, and handing him the seabreeze plates. This was my first Saturday night off since I had started my new job and I was at loose ends.

"I *told* him," someone yelled from the other side of the kitchen, "that it is *impossible* to substitute fries for the rice in the risotto. Jesus, who trained these people?"

I winced as a plate hit the floor, and peered over at the other side of the kitchen.

Thank God it was a big kitchen, because besides the Shriners we were serving downstairs in the banquet rooms, we had a full restaurant. Three restaurant waits in khaki shorts and Hawaiian shirts rushed in and out of the kitchen laden with trays full of steaming food. Another plate crashed to the floor, and I turned to see Jerry, the restaurant chef, baseball hat askew, cherubic face screwed up in fury, throw yet another plate to the floor.

I looked at Chef for support, but he was sedately arranging petit fours. "I told you," he said, "that the waits don't know the menu. Wonderfully trained."

I snorted with disgust and marched over to Jerry. He saw me coming and looked me in the eye. "That wait is the stupidest person on the planet earth," he said sweetly. "Aren't you supposed to be off tonight?"

After several minutes of yelling, it was established that the wait was an idiot and that Jerry was Restaurant God. I smoothed feathers, threw oil on the waters and thankfully escaped.

"Can you tell Noel that I've got somewhere to go and more rolls are on their way down? And then, would you please leave? All your aimless wandering is making me nervous," Chef called to me as I headed down the wide staircase that connected the main kitchen to the prep kitchen of the banquet rooms. More chaos here, though on a lower key.

In the banquet prep kitchen was a sweating Santa Claus sans beard in a chef hat calmly directing the prep guys with a cigarette clamped in his mouth. I watched in wonderment as the inch-long ash wavered and held together over the full pan of rice he was inspecting. Ugh. Smoking in the kitchen was a definite no-no, but try telling that to Noel.

"Tell them I'm going to need fifty more rolls," he said in his mellow, phlegmatic voice. A boy of about sixteen in a chef coat took off running before I had a chance to tell him the rolls were on their way.

"Hiya Callie," Noel Landrum called out, flapping a large hand in my direction. "What are you doing here?"

"Wandering," I said absently, and passed on the message from Chef.

"He's leaving in the middle of a function?" Noel roared. "Imagine that!"

Of the three chefs, Noel, the banquet/cater chef, was the most laid-back. He was always cheerful, never stressed out even in the midst of chaos. In his late fifties, his chef coat was always splattered with undefinable stains and his face always sported at least a three day's growth of beard. His hair was pure white and thick, despite a receding hairline, and his nose was squished across his face like a biscuit and was shot through with broken purple blood vessels.

"Seen my new Suburban?" he yelled in my direction, flicking ashes toward a nearby sink.

From the upstairs kitchen, "I Love Rock N' Roll" pounded down the stairs; Noel had his own radio in the prep kitchen, which was oozing classical music. I felt schizophrenic.

"Is that yours? The mile-long red monstrosity in the parking lot? I thought it was a fire truck!" I called back, flattening myself against a wall as a huge metal box was wheeled by me.

"Ha!" he said, opening the door of the box and not flinching as waves of heat rolled past him to singe my hair. "They won't let me drive a fire truck, so I got the next best thing. That'll teach those bastards in Mary-land!"

With that cryptic statement, he wheeled away and cheerfully roared at one of his disciples for more sternos, more sternos!

When I had first met Noel I had been confused by his repeated references to "those bastards in Mary-land." It didn't seem to matter what the circumstances, somehow it was the fault of the bastards in Maryland. I had finally gotten an explanation from Janet in one of her good moods, and she explained to me that Noel had been an accountant in Maryland for some thirty years, and one year before his lucrative retirement he was let go. Noel had moved to the Outer Banks, sworn hatred for everything Maryland and corporate, and had gone back to his roots as a cook.

To his credit he had worked his way up to banquet/cater

chef in just a few years, and Noel was a happy man. He had a lovely wife, some twenty years younger, whom he worshipped. He was a volunteer fire department deputy — he loved it when his beeper went off and he had to race away to a fire, sirens singing.

"Noel," I said after a moment.

"What's up, sweetheart?" Noel looked around.

"Did Darryl Menden ever talk to you about rising food costs?"

It wasn't the most ideal time to ask the question, but the question just surfaced to the top of my mind. It was a pretty good indication of where my mind was.

Noel took a long drag of his cigarette and squinted at me. "You never met old Darryl, did you?"

I shook my head.

"I liked Darryl. I might have been the only one around here who did. Oh, he could be aggravating, don't get me wrong. But he was very serious about his job, and that's why he asked the questions and pissed people off, not because he was *trying* to be annoying, if you know what I mean. Yeah, he talked with me about the food costs. Asked me some questions, showed me some figures. He was overreacting as far as I could tell. Seriously, I think he was one of those fellows that was wound so tight that it was inevitable that one day he would start to come apart. That last month, he was pissing off everyone, as far as I could tell." He shrugged and turned back to his pans.

I said good-bye and went back upstairs to check on my baby, the Seahorse Cafe. I was having trouble leaving tonight, as if the moment I left disaster would strike. The depleted inventory and Darryl's strange memo were disturbing me more than I expected. It was a red flag in an otherwise almost perfect job. It was probably nothing, but somehow I could not help but worry.

I made my way through the kitchen without colliding with anyone and went out into the restaurant.

I moved slowly through the tables, stopping here and there to chat with the customers and to fill up a water glass or a coffee cup. Everything was running smoothly. Nobody was searching angrily for an absent waiter, or mumbling under their breath about undercooked chicken. It was one of those wonderful nights when everybody was actually happy.

There weren't many of them.

I looked around, trying to see the restaurant through an

unbiased eye. The room was a large square, with windows stretching across the ocean-facing wall. The bar area was on a platform at the back of the room, raised up about three feet so the bar customers had a good view of the ocean, and separated from the diners by a wooden corral. The bar itself was a horseshoe, with the closed end of the U facing the ocean and tables on either side.

The Seahorse Cafe was on the fifth floor of the Holiday House Hotel, accessible by an elevator from the lobby, so it was a given that the views from the numerous windows were spectacular. From where I stood I could see sailboats and other pleasure boats dotting the dark blue ocean.

The restaurant had a pleasant enough atmosphere, but I thought it looked too much like a Denny's. Brown carpet with green designs, wood tables and large pale green booth chairs clashed with the multicolored carnival blinds. I had already vowed that as soon as I could, I was going to do something about the restaurant's decor.

I stood, lost in thought, until Kate, the p.m. supervisor, came over to me.

"Callie, are you okay?"

"Kate, what did you think about Darryl leaving?"

"Darryl was a strange one. Talked like a dictionary and thought like a calculator. Absolutely no people skills. But he was an okay guy, just uptight. That last month, with Janet out of town, he really seemed to lose it. I don't know what was going on with him. Why?" She waved at the hostess to indicate that a window table was clean and ready for the next couple on the waiting list.

I shrugged. It wasn't something I could explain, just a feeling that things weren't quite right.

"Callie," she said gently. "Go home. You haven't had a night off in ages. Get away from this place." She swung her stylish brown mane over her shoulder as she arranged the menus on the table and twitched a napkin into shape.

I nodded, and took her advice.

CHAPTER FOUR

Conversation at Sharkey's

It was a perfect Outer Banks sunset, calm and clear, the sun setting in a blaze of crimson, orange and pink in the west, over the sound. The air was as warm as heated honey and tasted of salt and suntan lotion. I swung into my topless black Jeep and pulled out onto the Beach Road, the thirty-five mph sand-swept road that ran right beside the ocean.

The Outer Banks, a string of islands stretching down the coast of North Carolina, were basically windswept sand dunes and scrubby pines with man's mark sketched in the sand in the shape of cottages, hotels and restaurants.

The Beach Road was crowded with frantic tourists hungry and tired after a day on the beach, searching for that perfect restaurant.

Unfortunately, all the perfect restaurants were running on a wait at least forty minutes long. I passed The Wharf, an Outer Banks tradition, and saw a line of people patiently waiting for their turn at the plentiful seafood buffet inside, assuaged only by small paper cups of lemonade.

I thought about the Florida Keys, which were so different but in many ways so similar to the Outer Banks. I had lived in the Keys for the last year, basking in the healing gaze of the benevolent summer sun. But when I had needed a place to start again, I had naturally been drawn to the Outer Banks, where I had spent the summers of my youth. I had grown up one hundred miles north of here, in southern Virginia, and the Outer

Banks had always seemed magical to me.

The inevitable cop passed me on the Beach Road and I saw his brake lights flash in my rearview mirror as he checked me out. The police were always looking for drunk drivers. The expression, "Came on vacation, leave on probation" was true for many of the tourists who came to the beach and forgot that the police had very little violent crime on which to focus, and a lot of time to devote to DWIs. After what I had been through, I could live with that.

I slowed down as I neared Sharkey's, debating whether I should go in. But the prospect of a lonely evening with my memories was not a pleasant one. I pulled into the parking lot.

Once inside, I made my way to the end of the bar and saw that Lily Thomas was here.

I considered turning around and leaving, but Melissa the bartender had already handed me my Tanqueray and tonic. I smiled my thanks and leaned against the wall at the back of the bar.

Not that it was unusual to see Lily here, she was a regular. I could see the container of celery in water that Melissa had sat in front of Lily, right next to her drink.

I was scared of Lily.

There was no rhyme or reason for my feeling, except that Lily talked normally at the top of her lungs, and the volume went up with every sip she took. Except that Lily had a disconcerting habit of finding something about me or my actions to criticize and insisting on dissecting it with me, blow by blow. Except that she had a disturbing bent toward confrontation, and if I sat with her I would find myself embroiled in a political discussion with a Ross Perot disciple, or an argument with a Hell's Angel about Japanese motorcycles vs. Harley-Davidsons.

"Hey, you look familiar. Have we met somewhere before?" My heart pounded at those familiar words, and I wondered who could have recognized me in this backwater of North Carolina, thousands of miles from California.

When I turned, relief flooded through me as I saw a familiar face, and then irritation. "What a pick up line," I snapped. It was Kyle Tyler, the owner of Sharkey's.

"Oh, oh, we're irritable tonight," he said, laughing at me. Kyle was in his early thirties, young to be the sole owner of the profitable Sharkey's. From what I understood, he had worked his way up from line cook, until finally he had gotten financial backing and bought the old owner out. He was tall and lean, with dark curly hair, dimples and a goatee, and attractive, though I was loath to admit it.

He was also extremely irritating. I hadn't been able to put my finger on why he bothered me so much, but every time we met, he managed to rub me the wrong way.

"So who was the Japanese admiral who commanded the fleet that attacked Pearl Harbor?" he asked, leaning an arm against the counter at my back.

See, there's a good example. When we had first met, he had asked me what college I had attended and my major. Ever since I had told him I was a history major, he had been drilling me with history questions. I had made the further mistake of telling him that I was particularly interested in the history of World War Two, and he had made a point of testing my knowledge of that period ever since. I think that he had some kind of chip on his shoulder because he had not gone to college, and he was bound and determined to prove his intelligence.

"Chuiki Nagumo," I said smugly. "He committed suicide later in the war." I thought quickly. "What was the name of the plane that dropped the atom bomb on Hiroshima?"

"Jesus Christ, and you call yourself a history major," he mocked. "Enola Gay, a B-twenty-nine. On August sixth, nineteen forty-five, nine days before Japan surrendered, incidentally. Talk about easy. Good thing you're in the restaurant business, and not a history professor."

I smiled thinly and turned away slightly to study the crowd, hoping he would take the message and disappear. I wouldn't let him know that his barb had stung. I *had* wanted to be a history professor, but somehow life had interfered. Straight out of college, when I should have been looking for a place to get my masters, I had accepted a corporate position in the restaurant where I had worked all through college. And seven years later, here I was.

Kyle saw my eyes wander in Lily's direction.

"Oh ho," he said. "The boss is here. Are you on your best behavior?"

"I can't figure out whether to slit my wrists now or do it after she gets hold of me," I said, without thinking.

"Knowing you, you'll figure it out." He smiled at me, dimples twinkling, and I found myself grinning inanely back. The man was annoying, but boy did he have a sexy smile.

"Ugh," I said as he walked away.

I elbowed my way over to Lily, who was talking to Susan,

another regular, and said hello.

"Callie," said Susan, smiling her grandmotherly smile at me through a haze of blue smoke. "We were just talking about you." Susan was the local bank teller who was such a regular at Sharkey's that she rated her own chair. She was a plump, friendly woman with frosted gray hair in a bun, and a softly-lined face that crinkled up when she smiled. She reminded me of my grandma, until she took a big belt of her Jim Beam and soda and lit up a mile-long cigarette.

Oh great. "Really?" I inquired sweetly, balancing my glass on the bar and eyeing Susan's cigarettes. I smoked a cigarette now and again when I drank or when I got nervous, and suddenly I was craving one badly.

"Yes," Susan continued blithely, though I could see the mischievous gleam in her eye.

Lily was disturbingly quiet.

"I was just telling Lily here that I thought you might be the teensiest-weensiest bit afraid of her. Lily said no, that you're almost as ballsy as she is. So fill us in."

I glanced over at Lily and found her grinning, large teeth clamped around a celery stick. "So Callie," she bellowed, pounding me on the back. "It's not true, is it? You're not scared of me, are you?"

"No," I said, frankly lying.

Susan shook her head. "I guess I was wrong. Melissa, bring Lily another drink. And bring Callie one too, on my tab."

I protested faintly, especially since I had been lying, but then the drinks arrived and Lily insisted on a toast. As my first glass was mysteriously empty, I took a long swallow of my cold, faintly bitter drink.

"Callie's a good girl," Lily informed the bar, though she was looking at Susan, and patted my back. I put my hand out to prevent myself going face first into the bar. "I like her, that's why I hired her. I thought she had the guts to stand up to those jerks in the kitchen."

I carefully controlled my expression.

"Oh, I like them all right," she said, leaning close and blasting me with her whisper, "but I have no control over them, do you see, honey? I'm a general manager with no control over half of the food and beverage department. It's infuriating."

"I've told you, Lily," Susan said, her lined face earnest. "I don't mean no harm, but if they're that bad, just fire them."

"Yeah!" Lily snorted, and downed the rest of her drink in

one gulp. "I wish it were that simple. But Peterson won't hear of it, so that's that. And who am I to gainsay the owner of the hotel?"

And apparently, that was the end of the subject.

We fell into easy conversation. Elizabeth, who was Susan's best friend, was sitting on the other side of her. She wore a long blond wig tonight, and sparkling spandex leggings that proved that her eighty-year-old legs looked better than my twenty-eight year-old ones. She merrily chimed in with highly irrelevant tidbits of information about the population of India and the illiteracy rate in Japan. Where she got this stuff, I don't know.

"Who cares how cold it was in Siberia last night?" Susan finally asked, giving Elizabeth a disgusted look.

"I thought you might want to keep informed about the world outside of this narrow strip of sand," Elizabeth said in a hurt voice.

Susan sighed, and I tried not to smile. If Susan and Elizabeth hadn't been best friends, they would have hated each other.

I changed the subject to the latest gossip, which I knew would take their minds off their differences. The Outer Banks' grapevine was the size of a sequoia, and we chatted merrily about the girl who worked at Sharkey's who had had a breast enlargement, but didn't think anyone knew, the tourist who had been driving illegally on the beach at night and had sunk his 4Runner into the ocean and the local fire chief who had been fired by a power-hungry city manager.

Being a local in a small resort town where tourists throng by the thousands is like being in a secret society. I was new, but I felt like I belonged here. Some people were like that, and some people never fit in even after years. I was at a disadvantage, because I didn't know most of the people that they talked about, but they would always find a connection that I could follow.

"Lisa Myers, you know her, the big red-head, always in here with a different guy but everybody thinks she's a transsexual. Her." or "You know Mike Tyler, he's the no-good brother of Kyle Tyler."

So I listened, and soaked up the knowledge that would one day make me a true Outer Banker. And the crazy thing was, I craved it, like a girl longs to join a sorority for the acceptance and companionship, and the little bit of snobbery.

Lily flung her arm around me and insisted on singing along to Tom Petty's "Free Falling" and I sang with her in a quiet voice, itching to hold a microphone.

"What a pretty voice she has," I heard Susan say to Elizabeth, and I stopped singing.

"My Callie's a good girl," Lily was telling the guy on her right, a German tourist who was nodding and beaming. "Even if she lied on her resume."

I kept my smile in place, as if I hadn't heard what she said, and glanced around the restaurant. A few minutes ago, Kyle had been bussing a table. Now he had donned a green apron and was in the kitchen, sliding plates out of the open window for pickup.

No help there.

I decided my best defense was pretended ignorance, so I gave Lily a wide smile, and she grinned back with a gleam of malice in her eye.

The German tourist nodded and beamed, probably wondering what in the hell the crazy Americans were grinning at.

I was half-tipsy as I stamped around my kitchen, dropping pots on the floor and generally making enough noise to raise the dead.

"Hey– what?" said Kim, my sleepy-eyed roommate, opening her bedroom door.

"Oh, hi Kim," I said cheerily, banging a skillet on the stove and turning the dial to high. "How are you doing?"

"Sleeping," she said grumpily, tossing her shoulder length-blond hair. "It's eleven o'clock."

"Oh, I'm sorry, did I wake you?" I opened a cabinet, grabbed a plate, and slammed the door. Hard. "I'm just making myself some dinner."

"I get it," she mumbled, swiping at her eyes. "You're getting back at me." She stumbled back to her room.

"Bingo," I said to the closed door.

Kim and I were on opposite schedules. What had seemed like a match made in heaven when she had answered the ad– she liked animals, didn't smoke and wasn't moody– had turned into the match from hell. Every morning at seven o'clock, Kim was up, stomping around, playing the Morning Show until the walls shook, singing cheerily in the shower.

I had been polite, I had asked her nicely, I had drawn funny little cartoons showing me sleeping with a sign hung on the door reading "Quiet please!" Nothing worked.

My cat wandered into the kitchen, which he always did

when I opened the refrigerator. He sashayed over to me and reared up on his hind legs to put his front paws on my thigh.

"Hello Ice," I said, leaning down to pick him up.

He rubbed his silvery white head against my chin, purring.

I turned off the stove, now that I had made my point, and grabbed a stack of mail as I went upstairs to my bedroom, my bare and quiet bedroom with the colorful quilt my grandmother had made for me. The single mattress was on the floor, and my clothes were in crates around the room.

I flipped through the mail, throwing aside the bills and credit card offers until I got to a post card.

It was a picture of the Pacific Ocean and the stucco, red-roofed houses of a small California seaside town. On the back, in a childish scrawl:

Dear Laurie-
I miss you, I wish you didn't have to move away. I got your letter and am glad you are happy in North Carolina. I have to go back for another operation tomorrow, so don't be scared if I don't write for a while. I hope you don't forget about me.
Love,
Andy Gray

I hugged Ice to me and blinked back the tears, picturing the quiet dark-haired boy in my mind. I loved the boy as if he had been my little brother. I stood up and went into the bathroom. I set Ice down on the sink and he mumbled a protest.

Taking a deep breath, I lifted up my shirt and stared at the purple scar that dug a crater into the right side of my stomach.

No, I wouldn't be forgetting Andy Gray anytime soon.

Dreaming...

I could not move. It was as if I existed solely in my head, and had no contact with the rest of my body. I could not even feel the rest of my body, much less try to force it to move.

I could see the bullet- a long dark oblong object- moving in slow motion toward me. I could hear Andy Gray behind me, and I could see one of the men out of the corner of my eye.

"Don't shoot the chick, man," he said, in extreme slow motion. I could see down his throat as he shouted, a long dark hole surrounded by black stumps of teeth and bits of tobacco chew spewed from his mouth as he spoke.

And still I could not move. I had forgotten how. The will, the intention was there, Move, move, move, move, *a monotonous drone in my head, over and over again with no effect. And still the bullet spun toward me, growing bigger with a laughable lack of speed. I had time to dance a jig and do somersaults before this bullet arrived. If only I could move.*

"Mooommmaaa," Andy Gray said, as if someone had taken the words from his mouth and drawn them out in a long stream of syllables, and then snapped them back so they jammed in his throat as the sound ended with a guttural, strangled sob. He still lay sprawled on the floor behind me, where I had pushed him. I could hear his legs sliding on the floor as he struggled to get up, and one of his booted feet hit me in the back of the leg. Andy Gray was having no trouble moving.

"No, no, no, no, no," someone chanted, probably the woman cashier, and her words became one with the word in my mind.

Move, move, move, move, move.

And still the bullet came.

CHAPTER FIVE

Ruffling Feathers

I was being fried alive.

Waves of heat penetrated my skin, down to the deepest part of me which hadn't been warm since I woke up this morning. The slow roasting of the sun on my bare flesh had finally thawed the inner core of ice.

I opened my eyes and stared upward at the pale blue sky, the molten blaze of the sun forcing me to keep my eyes closed. I was half-dozing, listening to the chatter of the people around me on the beach. A mother told her toddler son to stay under the umbrella, the sun was bad, bad, bad for him.

You're gonna die some day.

A radio was rocking to old beach music, couples whispered lazily sensuous pleas in each other's ears, surfers boasted of the great rides they'd had, recalcitrant husbands snapped that they *know* their backs are as red as a lobster, lifeguards whistled people out of the water, teenage girls giggled sweetly over the surfers.

And above it all was the somnolent hush of the ocean, flinging foam-flecked waves at the shore, and then sucking the waves back in a gurgling rush. The smell of salt, decaying marine life and coconut suntan lotion was almost overpowering.

The Beach Boys faded away and the radio announcer gave the local weather forecast, 86 degrees, increasing chance of afternoon thunderstorms. Low tide at 7:44 a.m. and high tide at 1:14 p.m. at Oregon Inlet. Outlook for tomorrow: pretty much the same. And finally, meteorologists were watching a large wave that had rolled off the African coast and had shown signs of developing into a tropical depression, which was unusual so early in the season.

I listened halfheartedly, appreciating the Outer Bank's obsession with hurricanes– after all, we lived on a thin strip of sand on the edge of the mighty Atlantic. A sneeze, and the Outer Banks would be gone.

During the summer, the Weather Channel was the station of choice, especially if something happened to be brewing in the Atlantic or Caribbean, which was often the case. During the year that I had lived in the Florida Keys, I had tracked three full-fledged hurricanes as they spun toward St. Thomas and the Gulf Coast, and one that had gone right up the Atlantic seaboard to bombard North Carolina. However, I had yet to live through a hurricane season on the Outer Banks. I wasn't sure what to expect.

I thought about Florida, and the Keys, which I had only left two months ago. I had lived on Big Pine Key, an island about halfway down the island chain, staying at a small hotel that Debbie, one of my best friends from college, now owned.

The Keys had been a refuge from the horror that I had experienced and wanted to leave behind forever. I knew I could not stay forever, and when I was searching for a place to go, to pick up the pieces of my life and go forward, the Outer Banks had automatically come to mind.

It hadn't been my idea to fudge on my application. Debbie was a big Internet buff, and she had been the one to find me the job ad over the Internet for the Seahorse Cafe. She was a good enough friend that even if she didn't want me to go, she realized that for my own sanity I had to leave.

Debbie had filled out most of the application for me, because I still hadn't shaken the melancholy which was threatening to drown me.

When it came to the question about present employer, Debbie listed herself, even though I had been anything but a help to her for the last year. And she had made up a restaurant for me to manage, because her small hotel didn't have one.

She did all of this because she was afraid the fact that I hadn't been working for over a year would count against me. It wouldn't have, I knew now, but by that time it was too late to change Debbie's well-meaning fib.

And apparently Lily had found out.

A shadow passed over me, touching me with a chill, and I opened my eyes. Wispy gray clouds were tickling their way across the sky. Over the green sheen of the ocean, a line of dark clouds was advancing slowly.

I sat up and glanced at my watch. It was after one, and I had to be at work at four o'clock. I stood up, wincing as my feet sank into the burning sand, and stretched, my crimson one piece pulling tight over my stomach and breasts. The beach was clearing rapidly as the clouds rumbled closer, and I saw lightening flicker across the sky.

As I pulled on my shorts, I saw a dog nosing his way up the beach, carrying something in his mouth. He found a piece of a fish washed up on shore and pounced on it with tail wagging madly. He was a brown Lab, skinny and young, not yet through his puppyish first year, judging from his long legs and huge paws that had temporarily outgrown the rest of his body. The lifeguard was eyeing him narrowly, and I clucked gently at the dog to get his attention.

His ears perked up, and he turned to face me with such an expression of longing and hope that I clucked again softly and gestured him over. He picked up whatever he had been carrying and ran toward me, all tangled gangly legs and flopping ears. One of his eyes was blue, one brown, giving his face a strangely lopsided look, and he was limping noticeably, favoring his right rear hip.

He dropped a piece of cardboard at my feet. I noticed that it was part of a cardboard box, with "seaf" in bold letters across the scrap. I let him sniff my fingers and then fed him the remains of my ham sandwich. He wolfed it down easily, and looked up for more. I scanned the beach, but no one was paying any attention to the dog. He was collarless and filthy, and I wondered where his owners were.

Raindrops hit the ground, digging wet holes into the coarse yellow sand. I grabbed my towel and my bag and made my way to the stairs over the dune, wondering what to do with the dog. The lifeguard was too busy closing down his station to worry about a stray dog, and no one else seemed to be paying him any mind as they packed up, holding towels over their heads against the large raindrops.

A piercing whistle floated over the beach. I looked up and saw that a man was standing at the edge of the water, whistling for his two daughters to come in. Hearing the whistle, the dog cocked his head, and then took off running down the beach.

I watched him for a moment, but he showed no signs of stopping. Mentally shrugging, I went up the stairs, down the walkway past the outside pool to the deck bar.

The deck bar was full as people crowded under its shelter, and the bartender gave me a thumbs up when I asked him if he was okay. The rain was coming down harder now, gusts of wind whipping sheets of rain around the side of the hotel and I dashed for the safety of the sliding glass doors into the indoor pool, enclosed in a sloping glass structure very similar to a greenhouse. Both the hot tub and the pool were jam-packed with people as the rain streamed down the glass, and the wind picked up a plastic deck chair and threw it across the deck.

I had left my keys in the food and beverage, or F & B, office and I clumped down the stairs in my sandals, through the lobby to my office. All the offices were closed and dark on this early Sunday afternoon. Lily rarely came in on Sunday unless there was an emergency, and I was thankful for that. I still wasn't sure what to say to her.

I heard the clanking of the walk-in doors opening, and stuck my head down the back hallway to see who was making all that noise. Mac, one of the young line cooks, and Noel were discussing the placement of some boxes in the walk-in freezer.

"Hey Callie, are you in the mood to fall in love?" Mac called, his voice teasing, but I could tell he was high (his normal state from what I could tell) from the anxious flicker of his eyes.

I waved at him and ducked back into my office.

There was a note on my desk next to my keys: Luigi had called in dead, or something to that effect. I sighed and reached for the phone. Three calls later, I had found another wait to re-place him.

I had also found Darryl Menden's phone number in the F & B communal Rolodex.

I stared at the number, tapping my fingers on the desk. Then I pulled my clipboard out of the drawer and flipped to the memo.

I was re-evaluating what I had heard about Darryl Menden, and what I knew about Darryl Menden. Everybody said he was a whiner, and that I could believe. But was he incompetent?

Of that I wasn't sure.

After all, he had realized that stuff was disappearing out of the restaurant, even if nobody took him seriously. Perhaps his complaints about inflated pricing and high food costs had been right on, but again no one took him seriously.

He ruffled too many feathers and now he's gone.

I thought about 39% food costs. That was well within the range of what most decent restaurants considered acceptable, but still on the high end. Chef, Jerry and Noel ran an extremely tight kitchen, meticulously accounting for each portion of food that went out of the kitchen, keeping a very accurate waste report listing food that had gone bad, and refusing to let any employees eat without paying. This was fairly unusual in a business where free dinner was considered a fringe benefit.

Food cost was an intangible number reached each month, reflecting how much food was bought, how much was sold, and how much remained to be accounted for at the end of the month. The basic rule of thumb for pricing a menu was the "33% Rule", which meant that the menu price of an item equaled the cost of an item divided by .33. For instance, if you had bought one steak for $4, then $4 divided by .33 equals $12.12. Add a few bucks for salad, vegetables and starch, which was called the "Q factor" and you came up with a menu price of $14.12. The price on the actual menu would probably be $14.25, a more even number.

Of course, this was very simplistic. It was a very complicated formula, and I only had a basic understanding of the process.

But if you priced your menu using the 33% rule, your food costs should be close to 33%. Of course, no one was perfect and some food would always be wasted, so a more realistic number would be 35% or 36%. A 39% food cost was not out of line for many restaurants, but it did seem strange at the Seahorse Cafe, where the menu prices were high, and the chefs policed food wastage as if every morsel wasted was a penny out of their pockets. Which it was, in a very real way. If the food costs were too high, all of the managers would be out of their substantial bonuses at the end of the year.

I picked up the phone and dialed Darryl Menden's number. A recorded voice informed me that the number I had dialed had been disconnected. Please check the number and try again, or call the operator for assistance. No forwarding number.

I sat and tapped my fingers some more, and looked out the window. Rain still dripped slowly down the window, and wet tourists fought with recalcitrant umbrellas in the parking lot.

None of this was any of my business. I couldn't see that it had any effect on me, besides the bonuses that the chefs had every reason to want as much as I did. But I was conscious of the fact that I, like Darryl had been, was in a unique position to see discrepancies that no one else would see outside the kitchen.

Don't ruffle any feathers.

I was treading on thin ground with Lily already. I should forget my traitorous thoughts and throw away that memo.

Tap, tap, tap went my fingers.

I pulled open the file cabinet. In shorts and T-shirt, reeking of Coppertone, I methodically searched through Darryl's files.

I found a cornucopia of useless and trivial information– old applications, old menus, floor plans for functions, and every schedule that Darryl Menden had ever completed– and threw it all in the trash.

Darryl Menden had been a pack rat, and he had evidently believed in leaving a paper trail. Every memo he had ever fired off to Lily, Chef, Jerry, Noel or Janet, was duly copied and filed in a folder ostentatiously marked "Office Correspondence." I wondered why the April 6th memo had been in the "Easter" folder. Was it because he had been working on the upcoming Easter brunch and he had come across some information that made him question the food costs and write the memo?

I saw what Lily had meant about Darryl being a crybaby. Memo after memo he complained about one thing or another. Eventually it all started to run together. I wasn't surprised that no one took him seriously when he had a legitimate complaint– he had cried wolf once too often.

But I also realized that Darryl was a very methodical person. He had his own personal short hand– thus my difficulty in deciphering his inventory sheets– but he had diligently kept notes and inventories, and I saw that things had started disappearing about six months ago. Locks had been changed to no avail. Twice, as a matter of fact. Why hadn't Lily mentioned that to me?

I kept the pile of memos and the back inventories. I would go through them more carefully when I had the time.

I pulled the Easter folder out again, and flipped through the entire folder, but there was nothing else of interest. What had been going through Darryl's convoluted mind when he had been working on the Easter menu?

I tried to put the folder back, and tutted impatiently because the folder was backward. As I pulled it out to turn it around, I noticed "SS" written in faint pencil on the back of one of the folders. Numbers and letters followed in Darryl's indecipherable shorthand.

SS
430-j
4899-j
6591-a
7542-s
8289-o
7845-n
9102-d
8611-j
9680-f
10421-m

And that was all.

I had noticed Darryl's meaningless scribbles on the back of manila folders before. I stared at the numbers. What had he been thinking when he wrote those numbers? Did the fact that they were written on the back of the Easter folder where he had kept that last memo have any significance?

Thoughtfully, I grabbed an empty folder from the stack beside my chair and wrote "Easter" on the label. I transferred the contents of Darryl's Easter folder to the new one and put it in the file cabinet. I added the empty Easter folder to the memos and inventory and took the entire stack with me as I left the office.

CHAPTER SIX

Going to Make Some Dreams Come True

It was cheap diner night, Margie informed me.

"Didn't you know? I put that on the sign," I said.

Margie, her brown curly ponytail swinging, laughed over her shoulder at me. She was my head wait and had been at the Seahorse Cafe for more than two years. She had the uncanny knack of getting along with everyone — even the kitchen — and knowing everything about everyone.

"Do you think you could put the fact that I only make $2.13 an hour on the sign?"

I watched as she cruised off to her section, deftly snagging empty plates and chatting with guests. Margie had come here on summer break between her junior and senior year in college and never left. She was a good wait and a nice person, and hadn't shown any resentment toward me for taking over.

It was a busy Sunday night, two days before the Fourth of July holiday, and I was filling in for Kate on her night off.

"That dog's still at the back door," Chris said as he headed toward a new table. Chris was big and blond and friendly, with a placid expression and sweet smile.

I glanced at the glass doors leading out onto the back deck and sure enough the brown Lab I had seen on the beach was sitting forlornly at the door. It was still raining, and when he saw me looking at him, he put a paw gingerly on the glass door. On my way to the door, I was intercepted by Margie.

"Could you please talk to forty-one? They sent back their calamari, said it was greasy — it wasn't — and now they're complaining about the Tucson Tuna being dry, but they won't let me take it back. I think they just want to bitch." She breezed off to the service bar to pick up three strawberry daiquiris.

I sat another table, and then headed toward table 41, and saw the older couple with identical disgruntled expressions on their faces. I groaned inwardly. This was the couple who had blamed me personally for the fact that the rain and clouds obstructed their ocean view. Silly me, and I thought I was just a restaurant manager; all this time I've been God.

I smiled brightly as I approached the table. "How is everything tonight?"

The man ignored me, digging intently into his tuna. His wife, heavy face framed by long black hair shot with silver, scowled at me. "She served us used tarter sauce," she announced, holding out the half filled two ounce soufflé cup.

"Ma'am?" I said, kneeling beside their table.

"It was only half full. It was used. We usually go to Owen's, you know, but it's our thirty-year anniversary, and Joey said, 'Let's go somewhere different.' So we came here, though I wished we had gone to Owen's, they never would have served us used tarter sauce!" Her eyes were full of hate as she looked at me, sure she had been cheated or maligned in some way. It always amazed me how normally pleasant people could turn into ogres went they sat down in a restaurant.

"Well, actually ma'am," I said, inwardly cursing the mix-up in the ordering that had delivered two ounce soufflé cups instead of one ounce. "The waiters have been instructed to only fill the cups halfway to prevent wastage."

"Humph," the husband said distastefully.

The woman swung her heavy head in Margie's direction, who was tickling a toddler and laughing.

"She hasn't paid any attention to us," the woman said. "She's a horrible waitress, not like the girls at Owen's. And I don't believe you. I think you're lying." Her voice had risen, and near-by tables were beginning to watch us uneasily. From the corner of my eye I could see that the hostess, Jen, was getting backed up on seating people, and Chris was waving a frantic hand at me from the wait station.

"No, ma'am, I wouldn't do that," I said cheerfully, standing up. As the woman opened her mouth to disagree, I said smoothly, "Thirty-year anniversary? How wonderful. I'd like to give you two pieces of our famous home-made Mississippi Mud Pie, on the house of course, just to let you know how happy we are that you came in on such a special day."

The pie was neither famous nor homemade, but it did the trick. The man grunted his approval. His wife sat back, mollified.

Or partially, anyway.

"I still think it was used," she said clearly when I was half-way across the room.

I made my way up to the hostess stand and helped Jen seat the crowd that had accumulated at the door, and then went to the wait station where Chris had disappeared.

"He's weeded," Margie said, fingers moving lightening quick over the computer as she put in an order. "I had to pick up the last table for him. What did Grandma and Grandpa say?"

"The tuna was fine, and you are a lovely, talented waitress," I said. "I'll comp them two pieces of the Mississippi Mud Pie."

I passed through the kitchen, wincing at the deafening roar of music, banging pots, clanging dish machine and shouting of Lee the dishwasher– who recited Shakespeare at the top of his voice as he worked.

"'Over hill, over dale, over park, over pale, through flood, through fire, I do wander everywhere, swifter than the moon's sphere,'" yelled Lee as he pulled a rack of dishes down and fed them through the washer.

"Chhhhr-is," shouted Jerry. "Oooorder-uuuup! It's drying out, we wouldn't want that to happen." He stared at me through the window, and I saw that the intricate patterns he had drawn on the side of the plates in oyster sauce and colored sour cream were beginning to run.

I pulled Chris's plates and set them up on a tray for him. As usual, he had forgotten to put a table number in, so I had no idea where to take the food. He rushed in, face red, fine blond hair damp with sweat.

"I'm weeded," he wailed when he saw the tray.

"Just tell me where it goes," I said.

"I have no idea." He ruffled through his wait book, drop-ping bits of paper on the floor. "Thirty-four, I think."

It was actually table twenty-four, but in the end the food got where it was going. I went back into the kitchen to retrieve bread for another of Chris's tables.

"Hey Callie," Mac yelled over the din.

"Hey what?" I said back, pulling out the bread drawer and fishing out a loaf of bread.

"Will you go home with me tonight?"

I laughed and waved him off. Mac was a terrible flirt. He was twenty-one, tanned and lean with a shaved head and a modified mohawk of long bleached white hair and the ever-present brilliant green baseball cap emblazoned with a bright red pot leaf. He had more tattoos than I had even seen on a body, and the body rings to match: one in his tongue, his nose, plugs in his ears, rings in his nipples, and the rumor was other places as well. But despite his exterior, Mac and I hit it off immediately when I found a poem he had written for me on my desk.

As I left, Mac began wolf-whistling, and the entire kitchen crew began whistling with him as loud as they could. I looked back and saw Jerry whistling the loudest of all, his face turning red as he tenderly rolled a roulade.

The night passed quickly. I finished the cashier check out and nodded when Margie said they were done with their side-work — setting up for breakfast, cleaning the wait side of the kitchen, polishing silverware, refilling salt, pepper and sugar containers — myriad other nightly tasks. When Margie worked, I rarely went behind the waits to check their thoroughness.

"I think I'm going to hang out for a while," Margie said, peering at me shyly. "Are you staying?"

I nodded, and she and Chris went up the stairs to the bar. Lenny Marks had started playing, crooning out a country western tune. He smiled when he saw me looking at him.

Lenny was thin with skin the color of oak and gray-brown hair braided down his back. His face was creased with deep lines around his mouth and eyes, a cigarette burned in the ash tray beside him as he stroked Jennifer, his beloved guitar.

I made my way up to the bar and sat with Margie and Chris and Jerry and Mac as Lenny said, "This one is for a special friend," and flashed a smile in my direction.

He broke into "Della and the Dealer" by Hoyt Axton which features a saucy cat named Kalamazoo. I sang softly, feeling my throat close up at the familiar words:

Della and the dealer and a dog named Jake and a cat named Kalamazoo,

Left Tucson in a pickup truck, going to make some dreams come true."

I would not cry, I would not start thinking about California and the horror and the terror and all that I had left behind, when I had packed up everything I could fit in my Jeep and had gone without looking back. On the way to Florida this song had come on, a song my grandfather had used to sing to me. He always used to call me Kalamazoo, Callie for short, because he said I reminded him of his favorite character in his favorite song, the wily cat named Kalamazoo who never said a mumbling word. I had decided to go by my old nickname "Callie" when I needed the anonymity of a different name.

"You've got a beautiful voice," Jerry told me, and I smiled at him, hoping he wouldn't see the tears I blinked back, tears for myself and for my grandfather.

"Why don't you get up there and sing with Lenny?" Mac yelled at me from the other side of Jerry, scribbling a poem on a beverage napkin. Already, napkins lay scattered around him as he finished one poem and started another.

"Nope," I said firmly, and Matt delivered my Tanqueray and tonic, cutting off the conversation. It had been a year and a half since I sang in public, and I wasn't going to start now.

Jerry was in a good mood, ordering drinks for all of us, doing a shot of tequila with Mac. As usual, Mac's eyes were a bit blurred, probably from pot, though I had caught him inhaling oven cleaner one day trying to get a buzz.

Jerry was talking about "the little shit town" where he had grown up. "I swear to God, the big hangout was the Laundromat. Nobody had anything better to do than go down there every afternoon. It was across the street from the police station, and we used to watch Gus, the sheriff, drag in the DWIs around eight o'clock. That's when Buddy's, the only bar in town, would close, and Gus would set up a road block and pick up the three or four tourists who had come all the way to Lee Town to fish for bass," he said, shaking his head. "God, I was glad to get out of there. Won me my scholarship, and good-bye Lee Town."

Jerry ordered another shot of tequila for himself and Mac, and I watched as they solemnly licked the salt from their hands, threw back the shot of tequila, and then bit quickly into the lemon. I laughed at their identical expressions of "ugh."

"And here I am, living only an hour from them, those panhandling freaks. Let me tell you, families suck. You pick your friends wisely, because you sure as hell can't choose your family. My friends are my life."

I had never seen Jerry so garrulous. I had never seen him so drunk. Matter of fact, I had rarely seen Jerry drink. Tonight, he looked like a fallen angel, apple cheeks red with tequila, eyes bright and hot, long hair loose around his face. Only the hard-ness around his mouth, and the gray in his hair belied his age.

"So what's your story, Callie?" Jerry asked. "You go around watching everyone, and your little brain's ticking away behind those gold glasses, making judgments about us, but you never say anything about yourself. Where are you from originally?"

"Southern Virginia," I said. "Virginia Beach. I used to come to the Outer Banks all the time on my summer vacations."

"But you're what, twenty-eight, twenty-nine? What have you done since then?" Jerry was gazing at me intently, leaning forward as if my answer was of extreme importance.

"Well," I said easily, taking a sip of my drink. "I went to school in Northern Virginia, I'm a history major. But I got of-fered a corporate position with the restaurant where I had been working all through college, so I moved to Palo Alto, Cali-fornia. After a couple of years, I got tired of the corporate life, and moved to the Florida Keys, and that's where I was before I came here." It sounded so mundane, not representative of the way my life had really gone, even if the facts were correct.

"Hmmm," Jerry said drowsily. "Matt, could you call me a cab?" He turned to me. "I don't usually drink like this. Not since I was hooked on heroin and I was thumbing across the country to get back to school. But not anymore. Have you ever been married?" His thoughts were disjointed. I struggled to keep up.

"Yes," I said, and amazingly, the pain wasn't as bad, wasn't clawing through my chest and ribcage to reach my heart.

Jerry must have seen something on my face, because his face twisted in concern. "He didn't die, did he?"

"No, he's still around somewhere," I said, forcing myself to smile. "Have you ever been married?"

"Never have, never will," he said, and not for the first time I wondered if perhaps he was gay. But he didn't enlighten me. "Are you going to the food show tomorrow night?"

"Oh joy," I answered. "I'll be there with bells on."

"Come on, Mac," Jerry said, throwing an arm around the younger man. "Let's go home. I need to take Jesse out."

Mac shrugged, and said good-bye to Margie, who he had been hitting on. Jerry and Mac made funny room-mates, but necessity made funny bedfellows, no pun intended. The cost of living on the Outer Banks was pretty high.

"Good night Callie," Mac said to me, playing with one of his ear plugs. "You sure you don't want to see my Prince Albert?"

I shook my head, mock regretfully. "Not tonight, Mac."

Once the chefs left, Margie and Chris moved over a seat and we chatted about work. "Darryl used to follow us around with white gloves," Margie said. "You're strict, but at least you're fair." The two Long Island Ice Teas had loosened her tongue and she leaned toward me conspiratorially. "Darryl was nice, I guess, but he was always so uptight. He used to document *everything*, and you had to wonder what he was writing about you, you know? It just made you kind of uncomfortable."

"What happened to him?" I said casually. "He move away?"

"Well, I heard he was bartending at Fishbones up in Duck. I never go up there, so I don't know."

"Hey look, it's the dog again," Chris said suddenly, pointing toward the back door.

I turned around, and sure enough, the brown Lab was back. I went to the door, and called him softly. He was limping and moaning softly as he came to me.

"Come here boy, good boy, it's all right," I said quietly. He let me pick up his paw and I saw that he had a bur stuck in it. He whined under his breath as I gently yanked it out, Then licked my face and put his chin trustingly in my palm.

"Where're your people?" I rubbed his head, and he thumped his tail. Rain was still blowing, and I was getting wet.

"Okay, boy," I said, standing up. "You can go home with me, but only until we find your owner." He twisted his head, staring up at me as he listened to the tone of my voice. "Stay right here. I'll be back."

I went inside and paid my tab, and said good-bye to everyone. Lenny was playing Willie Nelson's "Georgia on my Mind" when I left by the back door.

"Come on," I told the dog, and he followed me willingly down the back steps, dark and slippery in the rainy night. As we clattered down the stairs, I heard a door slam and someone run around the side of the hotel.

"Stop!" I yelled, even though I had no idea why the person was running. "Stop right there!"

The dog barked and danced around my feet, almost slipping down the steps.

I went down the stairs carefully, and saw the door leading under the decks to maintenance. Was that the door that had slammed shut? It was normally locked and the maintenance staff who would use that door had gone home for the evening.

Then I saw what was spilled on the sidewalk in front of the door. It was a box of steak knives.

CHAPTER SEVEN

Memos, Inventories
and Phone Calls

The dog had fallen in love, and the cat had sworn never to speak to me again by the time I had got home and settled.

I had spent ten minutes in futile chase over the dunes after the shadowy figure. Then, I had to go upstairs and ensure that the kitchen and restaurant were locked up. It was, as was banquets. The storeroom, a room near the ballroom where we kept tables and chairs on racks, as well as linen and tablecloths up above in the loft, was also locked. The box of steak knives had come from the storeroom. I remembered distinctly counting five boxes yesterday and now there were only four.

I put the box back where it was supposed to be.

I locked the storeroom securely behind me, little good that it would do, and made my way through the dark, shadowy ballroom to the back service elevator. Once downstairs, I asked Dowell, the front desk clerk, if he had seen anybody unusual.

"Oh, just Jerry and Mac, stumbling drunk, let me tell you. They must have waited for that cab for thirty minutes. Kept making me call back, but everybody on this beach wants to be going somewhere else right now." Dowell's wide face was perky after several cups of coffee. By three in the morning, though, he would most likely turn off the phones and lean back in Lily's chair for some shut-eye.

"Can you keep an eye out for anybody suspicious? I just caught someone trying to steal a box of knives."

"Those kids, Jesus Christ, they've pulled fire alarms, spray-painted the elevator and poured food dye in the hot tub. We've called the police about them, but they disappear so fast you don't get a chance to grab 'em." He leaned across the counter, winking conspiratorially. "Did you hear? The Petes came in last night with some friends and raised a little hey. I sure would have liked to see Mr. Peterson out on the dance floor at Kelly's boogying away."

"I heard," I said, moving away from the desk. "I'll talk to you later, Dowell."

"Oh, all right," he said, clearly disappointed that I wouldn't be staying and gossiping with him.

The Petes were Mr. and Mrs. Peterson, the owners of the Holiday House. From what I understood, Mr. Peterson got his money from a dog food corporation that his father had started. When Mr. Peterson had sold the corporation for some unbelievable amount of money, he decided to "invest" in other projects. Thus, the hotel, and a charter boat in Florida, and a restaurant on the west coast. He and his wife spent only a short time each year on the Outer Banks, though they had a huge house on five acres of oceanfront.

The dog was still waiting patiently for me outside and I coaxed him into the Jeep, and drove to South Nags Head, where I lived. After I had given him a quick wash with the hose and soap downstairs, which strangely enough, he loved, we went upstairs to meet The Cat.

The Cat was not pleased.

The dog, on the other hand, thought Ice was the bomb. He followed the cat around, sniffing at Ice's bushy silvery tail, snuffling in the delicate feline ear and sloppily cleaning the cat's face with his wet tongue.

Ice was thinking about doggy homicide, it was obvious. He also knew exactly whose fault it was that this was happening. All mine. He refused to come to me, and whenever I came near him, he would walk haughtily away with tail raised.

"It's only for a little while," I told Ice, where he sat aloofly indifferent to the fact that the dog was wolfing down several bowls of his Cat Chow. "I just need to find his owners."

He did not deign to look at me.

Sighing, I went upstairs, whistling for the dog to follow me. Apparently, Kim was not coming home tonight, which she did sporadically when the mood struck her. Of course, it did not occur to her to call me, so I would not worry about her in the middle of the night. Of course not.

The house that Kim and I rented was what was called a "salt box," basically a square on stilts with one side of the roof sloping steeply downward. The result was two bedrooms and a bath downstairs, kitchen with breakfast bar, which was open to the dining space and the living room with fireplace. The living room was open two stories up, where, once you went upstairs, a loft overlooked the living room. The loft, my office.

Thankfully, Kim had some furniture when we moved in, enough to put in the living room, at least. My two rooms were spare. The office was a nice executive office chair, which I had splurged on when I got my first paycheck, in front of a desk made of plywood over two file cabinets.

I sat down at the desk, and switched the light on. The dog flopped on his side in the middle of the otherwise empty room, and fell instantly asleep. He was thin to the point of emaciation, and he was still favoring his right back leg.

"Good boy," I said softly. He thumped his tail sleepily.

I had dragged my leather briefcase upstairs and I pulled out the sheets that I had pilfered from Darryl's files. First I pulled out the memos and spread them across the long table. I knew that Darryl had worked at the Seahorse Cafe for over three years, and I was looking at three years worth of complaints. The most virulent had been written over the last year and he was very thorough about his complaints, listing people and specific dates.

Chef's name, or Michael, as Darryl insisted in calling him, came up most frequently. November 17- *Michael used foul language to me because he said it was my fault that a wait took food to the wrong table.* January 5- *Michael insists on speaking gobbledy-gook every time I approach him about the New Year's Eve fiasco. Literally, gobbledy-gook, I think he's speaking Russian.* February 15- *Jerry attacked me verbally in front of the waits because he did not feel I had put enough time and effort into the Valentine's Day advertising.* March 15- *I checked in the SS order, and the invoice was wrong, but when I said something to Noel he said I shouldn't have taken it upon myself to check the order in.* March 28- *Michael and the dishwasher turned up the radio very loud, and flicked the lights on and off like strobe lights in the middle of our dinner rush."*

I giggled at that one. I couldn't help myself, it sounded so much like Chef. He was such a strange combination of intense, ferocious professionalism and then malicious indifference. The fact that he was very passive aggressive, and would not speak any criticism unless it was veiled or behind your back, made matters worse.

Unfortunately, from what I read, I saw that Darryl was a perfect victim for Chef's barbs. He reacted so nicely! Those big glowing buttons on his forehead that Chef knew exactly how to push for the best effect. And Chef was not the only one to get the edge of Darryl's vituperative tongue. Jerry was too un-realistic about his plates, throwing a fit if they sat in the window for more than thirty seconds. Noel wouldn't use his, Darryl's, well-meaning suggestions. Mac was dirty and loud and all those earrings had to be unsanitary. It seemed that Darryl found fault with everybody around him. Of course, Darryl was perfection personified.

I found several things strange about the memos. First, that he would take the time to record this magnitude of petty of-fenses, and then actually send them to his boss, Lily, as if she were the school teacher and she would punish the prankster with a dunce hat.

Second, I found it interesting that there were no replies from Lily. Not one direct reply from Lily, though there were other general memos that Lily had put out to the hotel at large. But on second thought, Lily was the type of person who would deal with the Darryls of the world face to face. She never could avoid a confrontation, if she could at all manage it.

The third thing I found strange about the memos was that Darryl's final April 6th memo had been in a separate folder, the folder marked Easter. Why?

The dog was twitching and moaning in his sleep, and came awake with a jerk, eyes staring wide at some internal night-mare. He got up stiffly and lay down under my chair, his nose touching my feet.

Ice had ventured upstairs, because he always loved it when I sat at my desk, and he could sit beside me and bat at my pen. He royally walked by the dog and jumped up onto the desk, skidding slightly on some loose papers. He ignored me disdain-fully when I tried to scratch him under the chin, still pissed about the dog, but he sat and looked over my papers with a scholarly air.

He was the most unusually colored cat I had ever seen, a mutt, but a long-haired Persian father had left him with long hair and a bushy tail. Some strange mix-up in the genetic stew had given him snow-white hair, tinged with a gray and black that was almost blue. His fur was the color of a windswept ice-covered lake in the late afternoon, when trees were throwing long blue-black shadows over the frozen water. He was from a litter that my mother-in-law's cat had had on the sly, and had been a birthday present from Karen to me. That reminded me that I needed to call her, and tell her where I was. I trusted her enough to know that she would not tell Dave, my husband, who was still in California. For that matter, I needed to call my own mother.

Ice gazed at me with eyes the color of yellow silk, and allowed me to stroke his head. "Meow," he said, forgiving me, and squirmed over on his back to present the snowy underside of his belly.

I heard fumbling with the lock downstairs, and watched as Kim came in the door. She was wind-swept and drunk, and waved a hand at me when she saw me.

"Damn, I'm going to be hating myself tomorrow," she moaned, kicking off her sandals and collapsing in the love seat where she could look up at me in the loft.

"I figured you wouldn't be coming home," I said.

"Yeah, me too," Kim said. "I packed my overnight bag, but it didn't work out. Guess what I heard in Kelly's?"

Kelly's was a local hot spot, a bit of a meat market, but fun nonetheless.

"Yeah?" I asked, not real interested in what she had heard at Kelly's.

"The kitchen manager at the White Gull got busted for selling coke out of the kitchen. I didn't recognize his name, but Patty said that she had a friend who used to date him, and he was going away for a while." Kim sprawled back in the chair and looked up at me. "I also heard, that Lucky Lucy, you know Lucky Lucy– big, blond and beautiful, used to work at Hurricane Alley?– she got busted drinking behind the bar again. Apparently she was passed out on the back prep table with an empty bottle of Jaeger next to her when the other bartender found her. Can you believe that?" She rattled on, and I mostly tuned her out, glancing over the inventory sheets that I had snagged from Darryl's files.

According to his records, things had begun disappearing in January. It wasn't real noticeable at first, just silverware and old platters that the hotel didn't use any more. Then it stopped the month of March. In April's report, the thief had grown bolder; three entire racks of glasses had disappeared.

More likely than not, the culprit was an ex-employee of the Holiday House Hotel and was stealing for another restaurant. That would explain how the person knew where everything was stored, and was able to get in and out unnoticed. What I didn't understand was how this person had managed to get a key, when the locks had been changed twice in the last six months.

I put the sheets aside and picked up the folder with the numbers scribbled on the back.

"What the hell is that?"

I saw that Kim was staring up at me with drunken puzzlement on her face. Something knocked against my leg and I looked down to see that the dog had stood up and was wagging a friendly tail at Kim.

"It's a dog."

"No kidding. Where did he come from?"

"He's lost. I'm going to try to find his owners tomorrow."

Kim sighed and got up, muttering something about a menagerie in the making, and then stumbled off to bed.

The dog put his chin on my knee and I stroked his head softly, and his eyes slowly dropped closed as he fell asleep standing up.

The phone rang and I snatched it up. It was after one o'clock, and I was finally starting to feel tired, though I knew I probably wouldn't be able to get to sleep if I got in bed.

"Hello," I said.

"Laurie, how's it going?"

I smiled at the familiar voice flowing over the line. "Debbie. I'm doing good. How are you?" I didn't bother to ask what she was doing up so late; she was as much of an insomniac as I was.

"I'm good. The motel's falling into the ocean, but I'm doing fine." Debbie was constantly bemoaning the state of the motel she ran in the Florida Keys, even though she kept it in tip-top shape. Debbie was my best friend from college, and the person I had run to after the disaster.

"Listen Lor, I don't have much time, I just want you to know that Dave called here the other day looking for you. Of course I said I didn't know where you were, but I told him if I talked to you I would pass on his number."

She read out the number, dropping the numbers in the

pool of my silence. I hadn't spoken to my husband in over a year. The only thing I could think of that he would want to talk to me about was a divorce, which we had never bothered to do.

"Are you going to call him?"

"I don't know, Debbie. How's Chuck?"

She laughed, a deep rich chuckle. "Oh, he's doing fine, hon. You need to find yourself another man. One more thing before I go. I know you don't want to know, but there was an article in *People* about Henry Gray's new movie. It recaps the whole incident in Palo Alto, and there's a picture of you and that kid Andy. I just thought you might want to know." Her voice was hesitant and concerned. I didn't like that she felt unsure around me and I wondered what the hell my problem was.

"Thanks Debbie," I said, injecting real warmth in my voice and when she spoke again, I could hear that she felt on safer ground.

"I know you've been incognito and all, but it's a pretty good picture of you. I just wanted to warn you. But with that cute new name of yours– what is it, Cat? Cathy?– I'm sure no one will make the connection. You look a lot different. Oh, shoot, I got to go, Chuck's got dinner ready."

"Yeah," I said, not finding it at all strange that they were eating dinner at one in the morning. Those wacky night people, you never know what they're going to do next. "Thanks for calling. Call back when you have more time to talk."

We hung up, and I sat staring at the folder in front of me. As much as I loved Debbie, talking to her brought back so many memories. What did Dave want? Did I care? Would anyone recognize me from the picture in *People*, when I had been twenty pounds heavier with longer hair and a different name?

Ice batted a gentle paw toward my glasses, a feather-light love caress on the side of my face. I scratched him behind the ears, and then scratched the dog's chin. Poor dog, abandoned and all by himself.

After a few minutes, I realized that I was staring down at the string of numbers on the back of the empty Easter folder.

SS
430-j
4899-j
6591-a
7542-s
8289-o

7845-n
9102-d
8611-j
9680-f
10421-m

It was obvious that Darryl had been listing months, in order from June to March, but what were the numbers? SS...

That triggered a memory and I picked up the memos and leafed through them. Ah, here it was: March 15- *I checked in the SS order, and the invoice was wrong...*

SS? Oh... It must be Smith's Seafood, which was a seafood purveyor out of Virginia Beach. I had seen the truck outside the loading dock delivering seafood at least once a week. But why had Darryl written SS on the back of the Easter folder? And what did the numbers mean?

CHAPTER EIGHT

Duck, Duck, Goose

The Outer Banks are different from other resort communities. We have no towering hotels, no "strip" of hotels and eateries, no boardwalk. I personally preferred the languorous pace of the Outer Banks, as opposed to the frantic energy of the resort cities like Virginia Beach and Ocean City.

As a resort area, the Outer Banks had had a shaky start. Scrubby, sand-swept islands swarming with mosquitoes and unreachable except by ferry were not on the top of anybody's list of favorite vacation spots. But by 1840, the first hotel was established on the sound side of Nags Head, and Carolinians began to flock to the Outer Banks to escape their stifling plantations in the heat of the summer and to enjoy the sea breezes. The tourist industry had been born.

Of course, the Outer Banks has a long and rich history which has nothing to do with ten bedroom vacation cottages and putt-putt courses. Native Americans frequented the area long before Sir Walter Raleigh's famous doomed colony disappeared on Roanoke Island, leaving behind the mysterious "Croatoan" carved on a tree. Blackbeard roamed the waters which would come to be known as "The Graveyard of the Atlantic" because of the numerous ships lost forever beneath the roiling waves. Wilbur and Orville Wright chose the Outer Banks to make history with their first flight.

But when people decide to shell out several thousand dollars a week for an ocean-front cottage with a pool and five wetbars, I'm pretty sure they are paying for the wide beaches and beautiful water, not the history.

So here we were today, cottages and hotels clinging to a narrow band of sand which was washing away at an astonishing rate. Nobody said humans weren't tenacious.

It was a sunny, warm morning as I made my way to Duck, a small town on the northern Outer Banks.

There were two main roads on the Outer Banks, both running parallel to the ocean. Route 12 or the "Beach Road" was the older road that ran by the ocean from Corolla all the way down to Ocracoke, via bridges and ferry. The Bypass, or US 158, was the five-lane "big road" that ran from Kitty Hawk to Nags Head, the most crowded of the Outer Banks towns.

Old one-story cottages painted blue and pink with flat roofs lined the road after I turned off the Bypass and onto hot, crowded Route 12 which took me north. These gave way to the expensive cottages on stilts that were being built every day on the Outer Banks at a frenzied rate. The road swooped and turned from ocean to sound and then crawled at twenty-five miles per hour through loblolly pines. Soundside restaurants, boat rentals, shops and realty companies lined the road, as well as a small gas station and convenience store called "Wee Winks." Streets named after birds turned randomly off the main road.

Fishbones in the Scarborough Lane shopping center was a long narrow room with a tiki hut over the bar and lots of polished wood surfaces, fake palm trees and bright neon beer signs. It was just 11:00, and the bar was empty except for a woman with frizzed hair and jeans miniskirt and fingers wrapped with silver rings. She was setting clean glasses on the shelf behind the bar and looked up at me with a crooked smile.

"Hi honey," she greeted me. "What can I get you?"

"I'll have coffee and Baileys please," I said, not used to drinking this early, but not wanting to order a coke.

Without comment she poured a shot of Baileys Irish Cream into a coffee cup and topped it with coffee. "You want to look at the menu?"

"No," I said, sipping the sweet, delicious coffee. "I was just walking around the shops and decided to stop in."

She smiled, and went back to wiping glasses, and I sipped my coffee. A talk show was on and we watched in companionable silence as the twins who were pregnant with twins by the same man bared their souls. Where do they find these people?

During a commercial break, I said casually, "Darryl Menden works in here, doesn't he? Is he working today?"

The bartender gave me a strange look, and started messing with her rail liquor bottles. "You know Darryl?"

"I work at Holiday House Hotel," I said, neglecting to mention that I had started work after he had left.

"Oh," she said, and I could tell by the look on her face that she had known that Darryl was from Holiday House. "No, he left last week, as a matter of fact. He went back to Virginia." We sat in silence as the show came back on, but the bartender was antsy now, and she kept staring at me out of the corner of her eye.

Finally she leaned forward across the bar, giving up on the talk show. "Listen, can you give me the scoop on Darryl? We all wondered about him." Her eyes were avid with curiosity and I could practically see her salivating at the prospect of some good gossip.

I took a sip of my drink. "What do you mean?" I asked nonchalantly, playing it cool.

"I mean, he goes from restaurant manager to bartender. And he acted so strange whenever anybody asked him about Holiday House. I mean, he quit, right? That's what he said. But Jesus, the man was weird. I mean, he was *paranoid*. He left early one day because he said someone was watching him. He got so upset, I told him sure, leave, even though it was my day off, and I had only come in for a Bloody Mary."

"Did you see the person he thought was watching him?" I did not have to fake my interest in her story.

"No, but he said it was someone he used to work with. He even said something about, 'If I don't come in tomorrow, call the police.' All melodramatic like. Of course he came in the next day, and he blew me off when I asked him about it. Said he was taking diet pills and they made him jittery. So what's the scoop? What, was he having an affair with the boss or something?"

"Well," I said. "You probably noticed how anal he was about everything. He really just got on everybody's nerves after a while."

"Oh Jesus yes, I noticed. I had to share a bar with him. He was a pain. I probably would have killed him if he had stayed much longer. But he up and quit one day, called in and said he was going to Virginia. Okay," she said, stopping to light a cigarette and leaning toward me. "Tell me this. What really happened to the tips of his fingers? He said something about frostbite, but how the hell do you get frostbite in the middle of the summer?"

"His fingers?" I asked.

"Oh come on, when he first came here, he wore little bandages on the tips of three of four of his fingers, and when he took them off, they were all blistered and raw-looking. You don't know anything about it?"

"No," I said. "It must have happened after he left." *Frostbite?*

"Anyway, he left me high and dry as far as shifts. He could have given two weeks, you know?"

"That's a shame," I said. "As much of a pain as he was, I kinda liked the guy. I was hoping to see him. You wouldn't happen to know where he moved to?"

"Nah," she said, losing interest in the conversation when she realized I didn't have anything juicy to contribute.

I asked for my tab and paid it, giving her a ten-dollar tip as I finished my coffee. As I got up, the bartender slipped me a napkin. "He left a forwarding address for his last paycheck," she said, and winked at me. I think she thought that Darryl was an old flame of mine, or maybe she was just impressed by the tip. Either way, she had come through for me.

I went back out into the hot sun and climbed into my Jeep. I had the bikini top on, which shaded me from the sun, but the seat and steering wheel had absorbed heat like a frying pan.

I opened the napkin. In a round curling hand, the bartender had written down a Virginia Beach address. No phone number, but I should be able to find that. Humming happily, I set out for the Holiday House, dodging gleaming Buicks with tinted windows and New Jersey plates, and the boiled lobsters posing as human beings who were walking in flimsy sandals beside the road.

The Holiday House Catering truck was pulled up to the loading dock when I entered the downstairs hallway. Chef and Noel were supervising the loading up of chairs, tables, glass racks, silverware, linen, trays and last but not least, food.

Holiday House Catering was Chef and Noel's brainchild, started about a year ago. It had been pretty successful. Several times a month, the big blue and white truck loaded up with supplies and went off to a wedding reception, a birthday party or retirement party.

"Hey Callie," Noel yelled, sucking on his cigarette. "Some guy is looking for you. He's probably still in the F & B office."

"Said he had an appointment with you. Just as late," Chef said cattily. He held a checklist, on which he was carefully checking off items as they were loaded. He looked tired, circles under his eyes, and I could smell the reek of stale alcohol from him from where I stood.

"He's early," I said shortly, hot and tired from the drive. The locksmith had been scheduled for two o'clock, and it was only one-fifteen. I went through the door into the offices, and saw a heavy balding man examining the lock on the office door.

"This the one you want changed?" he asked, chewing on a paper clip.

"No," I said. "They're upstairs. Come on."

I wanted him to change the banquet and restaurant locks, all of them. And so my work day began. While the man was changing the locks, I took the two keys, which was all I had asked the locksmith to bring, and went to Lily's office. I explained to her what I wanted to do.

"You got balls, girl," she bawled, laughing. She was in violent violet today, with a red headband holding back her copper curls. "They'll eat you alive, but might as well give it a try. I don't want to have to hire a security guard. Frankly, we're not losing enough money to warrant that. Too bad he can't change the master key for all the room locks too, lately we've been losing lamps and stuff out of the rooms."

She put the key in the safe, and I went to the front desk. The front desk people monitored the giving out of keys. They were kept in a locked drawer, and a person had to sign them in and out before the front desk clerk would give them out. I talked to Ray, the front desk manager, and he promised to have his clerks countersign each signing in and out of this particular key.

Then I went to face the music.

In the past, almost everybody in the food and beverage department had a key. Even when Darryl had changed the locks– twice– he had made six or seven copies of the key and distributed them to everybody. I had only made two. A backup in Lily's safe, and the key that everybody would have to sign in and out. It wasn't necessary for everybody to have his or her own personal key, it was simply convenient. And as much as they might complain, I had Lily's backing.

I went into the food and beverage office and snagged an empty manila folder from the communal stack beside my desk. We were thrifty in the food and beverage department and I was just erasing what had been written on the tab when I realized what I was erasing. "Smith's Seafood" was written in Darryl's unmistakable back-slanting handwriting.

Slowly, I turned the folder over and saw that there was a scribbled note on the back of the folder.

Frank- Miami??? 16/20?

What in the world? Who was Frank? Why had Darryl written it on the back of the Smith's folder?

As far as the 16/20, I thought I knew what it meant, if not *why* it had been written. Shaking my head, I put the folder in my briefcase and filled out another folder with the name of the locksmith company.

I was off that night so I could attend the food show. I left around five, exhausted and wanting a nap, but with twenty million things to do. I had had to put up with a temper tantrum from every one of my colleagues about the key, and I was tired.

I had put an ad in the paper today for the dog, and he was waiting eagerly for me when I got home. I petted Ice, and gave him a dose of canned cat food, and then took the puppy down the road to the beach. The beach wasn't crowded this far south, and only a few occupied towels and beach chairs adorned the sand. I figured I was safe and let the dog off the leash, and walked slowly down the water line as he ran, nose down, in circles.

The water was a clear blue today, the waves a subdued wash. The dome of the sky was a pale shimmer in the late afternoon sun, coming down to touch the ocean in the dark blue line of the horizon. I carried my shoes, and the salt water was cool on my feet, stinging blisters I didn't know I had. Sea gulls wheeled over me and screamed, apparently thinking I looked like someone with food. Sandpipers hopped energetically at the edge of the softly lapping water.

The dog was steering clear of the beach blankets, God bless him, and jumping into the waves with abandon. I resolved to bring him a ball the next time I brought him out. When I called him, he turned back toward the cottage with me.

I took a long hot bath, drinking a glass of Sauvignon Blanc as I soaked. I read books while I bathe. It's a bad habit and I admit to some nasty accidents. But I loved to read and was having trouble finding time for it. Currently, I was re-reading Herman Wouk's *War and Remembrance*, an old favorite, but I had just bought a new Dick Francis which I was looking forward to reading.

Forty minutes later, two chapters and a glass of wine finished, water cooling, I reluctantly got out of the bath. I shook water onto the dog, who had twice tried to get into the tub with me.

I stared indecisively at my closet, conscious of the fact that I was running late. This food show would be featuring products from several different purveyors, and I was anxious to arrive and see what they had. This food show was a bit different from the norm as it was rare to have a food show on the Outer Banks. Virginia Beach was close and had a much bigger population. But as the Outer Banks had grown, several of the smaller food purveyors had decided to get together and throw a mini-show just for the Outer Banks restaurants. The show was being held in the Ramada Inn in Kill Devil Hills, and most of the F&B department was going. I was meeting Janet at the Holiday House so we could drive together.

After getting dressed, a slim cream skirt and silk coral top, I went back upstairs to grab my purse off my bed. My glance fell on the memos and empty folders strewn across my desk. Ice had been using them as his bed, and silvery fur dotted the pages. What had Darryl been thinking and doing that last month?

I stood indecisively for a moment and then sat down at the desk. I was late but Janet could wait a few extra minutes. I picked up the phone and dialed the number for Virginia directory assistance.

"Virginia Beach," I said in answer to the computerized voice asking, "What city, please?" and "Darryl Menden" to the question "What listing?"

Apparently, it was not an easily found number, because a real-life operator had to come on the phone. "I don't have a listing for a Darryl Menden, but I do have one for an Eugenia Menden."

"Eugenia Menden?" I bit my lip. "Yes, okay."

The operator clicked off and I listened to the computerized voice again, reading out the area code, and then the number.

I dialed the number, and an old quavering voice answered the phone. "Hello." It sounded as if she were distrustful of the phone and was holding it far away in case it suddenly grew tentacles and wrapped them around her face.

"May I speak to Darryl, please?"

"*Darryl?*" the old voice wavered, drawing the word into roughly eight syllables.

"Yes, ma'am. Darryl Menden. Does he live there?"

The phone clanked down on the table, and I waited a good five minutes. Finally the phone was picked up, and a man's voice said impatiently, "Yes?"

"Darryl Menden?" I said doubtfully. Perhaps he was living with his mother.

"Yes, what is it? I am not interested in vacuum cleaners, credit cards or books on improving the house," he said. "Does that answer your question?"

"Actually," I said. "It doesn't. My name is Callie McKinley. I'm the new restaurant manager at the Seahorse Cafe."

Silence, as thick as a warm winter blanket sucked through the line. "Yes?" he said carefully. "What do you want?"

"Mr. Menden, some strange things have been going on in the hotel, and I was wondering if you could shed any light on it."

"No, I really don't think so," he said hurriedly.

"Real quick," I said. "Is that April sixth memo the reason you left, the one about food costs and menu pricing?"

"I don't know what you're talking about," he said, his voice thin with fear. "I really don't want to talk to you. Tell them that I'm going away, that I don't want anything else to do with that place."

"Mr. Menden, I don't know who you are talking about. I just felt like you had some answers that might help me. Who is Frank?"

"I don't know," he said hurriedly.

"I found some numbers..." I began.

"You better watch out," he said, his voice growing quieter and stretching thin as a taut rubber band. "Don't poke around, just keep your mouth shut."

I was taken aback at his words. Why did he sound so afraid? "Mr. Menden? Could you tell me what happened to your fingers?"

Silence, cold and deep, flavored with profound fear, flowed through the line. Finally, he said two words, his voice filled with such abject misery and hopelessness that tears involuntarily came to my eyes.

"*The freezer.*"

CHAPTER NINE

Cordon Bleu Balls

The mini food show was a roaring success, if you could judge success by how drunk people were getting. It looked as if perhaps the venders were making a few sales as well.

The Ramada Inn had a nice ballroom about as big as the one in the Holiday House Hotel. Booths were lined up along the edges of the room, and most of the restaurant people from the Outer Banks strolled around the room, the venders busily trying to work a deal before the kitchen manager or owner walked on.

Two bars were open on either end of the room, and I was carrying my usual gin and tonic.

Somehow I had gotten stuck with Lily.

Janet had been in one of her surly moods, and we parted company as soon as we arrived. I had run into Lily, who was munching on samples, and sipping from her drink. She was still wearing the violent violet, but had added a jazzy green, orange and red scarf to compliment the outfit. She tottered toward me on lime-green high heels and clutched my arm.

"Try this. " She stuffed a morsel of food in my mouth.

"Um, good," I said, my tongue burning. "Hot."

"Aren't they adorable? They're Cordon Bleu Balls. Wish I knew how they made them, I'd love to try them at home. I cook, you know, though I've never worked in food and beverage. You people are all crazy, did you know that?"

"I resemble that remark," I said lightly. What else was I supposed to say? I took a fast drink. "By the way, about my resume..." I had been searching for some way to explain my falsified resume, and Lily in a happy mood was too good to pass up.

"Oh, don't worry about that. I was just needling you." Lily waved a hand in dismissal, and continued where she had left off. "Of course anybody who chooses to go into management is crazy in some way. I realize that. I told myself that when Peterson approached me eight years ago about being the general manager. I'd been the front desk manager for years, but I really wasn't sure about the whole thing. But it's all worked out, and the hotel would fall apart without me now." She nodded her head in satisfaction as she steered me around the room, greeting people with a wave and a broad smile.

"So my point is this: you food and beverage people don't make sense to me. I understand the numbers, yeah, and I care heart and soul for this place, like you do, but when it comes to food and beverage..."

I nodded and smiled, because I sensed that she was paying me a compliment.

"I like you. You keep your mouth shut, but you *listen,* I know you do. You're not like me in that respect, I like to talk." She laughed, and reached into her purse for a bag of cut celery. "Damn, I want a cigarette. More than you can know. Doctor said the combination of weight and smoking was killing me and I either had to give up cigarettes or food, and preferably both. Well, I gave up the cigarettes, but I swear it's killing me faster than anything else could."

She didn't expect me to answer, so I didn't. I saw Noel in the crowd, talking to Chef, and they both turned to look at Lily and me. Noel, looking odd without his dirty chef coat, gave me a thumbs up. Chef turned away as if he hadn't seen me.

"I know something's up in that restaurant," Lily continued. "I can't figure out *what,* the numbers are okay, and I really can't complain. But something is going on, and I want to know what. Darryl was helping me out, but he finally pissed us all off with his whining. I remember when I first sat him down and told him I thought it was time for him to go. He was a stubborn little man, and he refused to go without me firing him. I wanted him to go nicely, I didn't want to have to mark up his record.

"I gave him a couple of days, and then he told me he was

ready to go, that he didn't want to work with the chefs anymore. Jesus, I think the man was losing it. He was literally shaking when he said he couldn't work here anymore. I told him fine. He wasn't fired, at least it's not on his record like that. But he just couldn't seem to get along with everyone. It wasn't just the three stooges, because God knows they're not easy to get along with. It was everybody."

She lapsed into silence, chewing her celery contemplatively.

"The memos," I said. "Darryl's reports to you on the chefs."

"Yep, but he sucked at it. All he wanted to do was complain about the trivial stuff. Nothing useful."

"But what about that last memo?" I said diffidently. I remembered well her reaction from the other day.

"I checked into it, I did, but he didn't have anything to back up his allegations. I know he was working on the Easter brunch for those Born Again Christians, and was bugging the chefs about the menu. Kept saying the distributor they were using was charging too much for the seafood, and they could do it cheaper than what they were charging. Well, yeah, the price of the menu went up, but for God's sake, it had been the same price for years and the contact was okay with the whole thing. Why did he care? He got all bent out of shape and then the chefs started complaining he was snooping through their files.

"All I want you to do is keep your eyes and ears open. No big deal. So what do you think?" She turned her face to me and fluttered eyelashes, all the world like a coquettish southern belle. Lily actually had a very pretty face., smooth and unlined; her eyes were big and green, emphasized by subtle makeup.

I wasn't sure what to make of her new attitude toward me. I didn't know whether to trust her. I remembered all too well Darryl's horrified whisper, *the freezer.* Something had happened to scare him thoroughly, and had left him with badly damaged fingers. I didn't know whom to trust. It was possible Lily was asking me to report to her, just so she could keep tabs on me for her own purposes.

"I don't understand why you don't just ask them," I said. "I don't understand all this cloak and dagger stuff. Frankly, it seems very underhanded to me."

Lily laughed, and patted me on the shoulder. "Good girl," she said. "I didn't expect anything less. But I don't have any control over it. Mr. Peterson hires the chefs, has since I started working here. He's got this idea that he's a food connoisseur, and that no one else would have the taste to pick a decent chef."

"How did he pick Chef?"

"Jerry and Noel had both been here for a couple of years when the last executive chef left. Peterson wanted to give the job to Jerry, but he didn't want it. He's all into that creative mumbo-jumbo, you know, the integrity of the dish and decorating plates. Which is great, I know, but he takes it too far. Peterson was thinking about giving the job to Noel, though he doesn't have much experience, but Jerry talked him into Chef, who was working at some fancy restaurant in New York. Jerry and Chef had been friends in college. So Peterson hired him for the executive chef position. I didn't have any say in it at all."

Lily stopped to talk to some people and introduced me.

As we exchanged small talk, I thought about what she had told me about Darryl's last month. When we were alone again, I asked carefully, "Do you remember what seafood purveyor Darryl was saying charged too much for seafood?"

Lily stopped and stared at me. "Hmmm. You know that's funny, because Darryl asked me some questions about them before he left. It was Smith's Seafood." As we walked on, she patted my back. "You think about it. I'm going to wander off now, but I'd like to hear what you think." She went toward the bar, and I continued to walk around, looking at frying oil, cheeses and spices, but my mind was racing. Smith's Seafood. Why was I not surprised?

"So are you enjoying yourself?" I looked up and saw Chef at my shoulder. He was dressed in a light-weight summer suit and carried a folder thick with promo information. He looked every inch the successful executive chef.

"Did you see the plates over there? The small seabreeze would be nice for desserts and salads. We've run low," I said.

"I'll take a look," he said. For once, he wasn't drinking and I sensed he was in his professional affable mood. "How have things been going? I haven't had a chance to touch base with you. Have you been settling in, getting all the help you need?"

"I'm getting there," I said.

"Great. Well, I want you to know, I'm always available to talk if you need to. I think communication is so important in this business, don't you agree?" he asked, as if he hadn't just refused to talk to a wait for three whole days.

"Sure," I said wryly.

"It sounds like we are on the same wavelength. Great. I saw you talking to Lily, don't let her get to you. She can be rather overwhelming for a shy person like you, can't she?"

I smiled noncommittally.

"It's going to be busy tomorrow, are you all set?"

"We're forecasting close to two hundred," I said, "and I've planned accordingly."

"Good," he said. "Look, Callie, I know I can be overbearing sometimes too." He looked at me with his haggard eyes, thick lines edged around his mouth. "I just want you to know that you are doing a good job. I have a lot of respect for the way you get things done." He was being honest, and for the first time I felt a burst of warmth toward Chef. Granted he was in a rare, pump-up-the-troops mood, but it was nice to hear it.

"Thank you," I said sincerely. "Real quick– could you tell me if Smith's Seafood has got a booth?"

"Oh sure. It's over there." He waved a desultorily hand toward the back of the room and I nodded my thanks.

I made my way toward the back of the room and saw the Smith's Seafood booth about the same time I saw Janet, hands on hips, talking to a big man, with a low swinging belly, blond hair thin at the top of his head, and a shaggy reddish beard.

"I *know* you sell quality seafood," Janet was saying, blond hair swirling around her shoulders. She was in a tight blue dress, which hugged every rolling hill of her muscular body. "But you know we had a very bad experience last New Year's Eve, and even if it wasn't your company who was responsible, I just want you to understand how important it is to me that that doesn't happen again. There's Callie. Callie, this is Frank Smith, owner of Smith's Seafood. I was just talking to Frank about our New Year's Eve disaster. Frank, this is Callie McKinley, our new restaurant manager."

I shook his big sweaty hand and he smiled at me warmly. I liked his smile, it rolled off his face in friendly honest waves. Then I did a double take. Frank Smith. Frank. Was this who Darryl had been thinking of when he wrote "Frank-Miami???"

"How are you doing?" he said, and I detected a little relief in his voice. Janet must have been on her soapbox again.

From what I had heard, the previous New Year's Eve had been a total disaster. Apparently, a box of spoiled shrimp cooked into a puff pastry had sent several customers to the medical center, much to everyone's horror.

"I'm sure you were glad that it wasn't your shrimp," I said to Frank and his eyes smiled over his big beard.

"More than you can know," he agreed. "As a matter of fact, we supply a lot of the Holiday House's seafood, but it was just bad luck Chef ordered from Deel's that week. Something like that would never happen with our seafood."

He was boasting, but it was the proud boasting of a man secure in the knowledge that his product was good.

"Deel's?" I frowned. "I don't think I've ever heard of them."

"It's not surprising," Frank said. "The hue and cry after the shrimp incident sent them right out of business."

"And up to the end they refused to admit it was their fault," Janet said. "You'd think they'd own up to it, but they never did."

Frank shook his head. "I feel for them. Smith's is not a real big company, you know, and the couple of big accounts like the Holiday House really keep us in business. Something like that would have been disastrous for us."

"Where're are you based out of?" I asked.

"Virginia Beach. My Daddy started the company thirty years ago. It's been hard competing against the big companies who can provide bulk for a cheaper price. But I still don't think there's anything that beats good fresh seafood, and friendly, personal service. That's my motto, and people like Michael, Noel and Jerry have awarded me with their business."

His speech sounded a little stilted, and I guessed that the Holiday House business meant even more to his company than he had admitted. He wanted to make sure that he kept on our good side.

"That sounds like a good policy to me," I said, even though I was aware that the convenience of the big purveyors was slowly driving the family-owned businesses into oblivion.

"I think my father would be happy to see that I've kept the old Smith's alive." His voice was cheerful, but there was a hint of a false note. Why?

I wondered why Darryl had written this man's name on the back of a folder. I didn't even know what questions to ask.

"So, do you know the chefs well?" I asked, fishing, but hoping it sounded like idle chit-chat. Janet had been talking to someone, and when she stepped aside I saw that it was Mac, looking debonair as usual in cut-offs and ratty hat with the red pot leaf emblazoned across the front. Jerry was working the restaurant tonight with another one of the line cooks. Chef had thought it would be good experience for Mac to come to a food show.

"Well, I know them all casually. They're all real good guys," Frank said, his eyes sliding off of Mac, who had joined our circle.

"And Darryl Menden? Did you know my predecessor?" I

asked, and then realized how abrupt my question must seem. I quickly added, "I guess I'm a bit curious about the man whose shoes I've filled." I could tell by the curious glances that my tone had not been convincing. *Damn!*

"Darryl? I met him a time or two, but we really didn't have much contact," Frank said, his puzzled gaze on my rapidly heating face.

"Hi, Mac," I said into the silence that had fallen. Janet looked distracted and nervous.

"Did you see that we've got a tropical depression out in the Atlantic?" she asked suddenly, turning back to the group with a wide smile, and we discussed the possibility of a hurricane for a few minutes.

"They have to evacuate us if the hurricane gets anywhere close, because there are only a couple of ways off of the islands. And an evacuation takes forever. We haven't had a bad hurricane in years, and most of us just come and stay in the hotel. They say it's one of the safest places to be. And if we get hit real bad, they won't let you back onto the islands until they clean up, which could be weeks. This way, you're already here," Janet explained to me.

"You stay in the hotel? Right on the ocean?"

"It's concrete, it's five stories tall," Mac said. "It's not going anywhere."

"Whenever there is an evacuation, we get a lot of people into Virginia Beach," Frank said. "Which is kind of ironic, because we may not be as vulnerable as the Outer Banks, but we're still on the water."

He glanced over the crowd and started making well-I-guess-I-need-to-mingle noises.

"So you deliver to us every week," I said, before he could go.

"I put away his boxes," Mac said, as if he had said something funny. Frank looked at him blankly and smiled, as if he was trying to place him.

"Well, it was nice meeting you, Callie," he said, and shook my hand. He squeezed Janet's arm gently in passing and I was surprised at the warmth in her glance. He didn't seem Janet's type, but then again, I didn't know what Janet's type was.

"What a lughead," Mac pronounced and went off to get another drink. Janet glared at his back.

"That boy needs a good smacking," she said. "Just tell me when you're ready to go."

"Frank seems like a nice guy," I said, before she walked off.

"He does, doesn't he?" Janet said warmly.

"Have you known him long?"

"Oh, we've been talking for the past several months." Janet played with a strand of her hair and smiled.

"Has he been with Smith's Seafood for a long time?" I asked. I wasn't sure what I was fishing for, but I knew something was up. Why else would Darryl have written his name on the back of the folder?

Unless he just couldn't remember the man's name. Yes, but why write "Frank- Miami???" What was in Miami?

Bingo. "Oh, he lived in Florida for a couple of years. To tell you the truth, I think he had a little trouble down there right before he moved up here about four years ago. He doesn't like to talk about it much. In the last two years since his Dad died, he's really turned Smith's around."

I stayed for another half an hour, but the room was beginning to clear and I didn't see anybody I knew. I had already marked down a few items I was interested in, and had made a couple of orders for glassware and steak knives.

Janet and I rode back to the Holiday House mostly in silence, and once there I went upstairs to check on the restaurant. It was Karaoke night, and people were packed in the bar, hoping to be a star just for the night.

Kate said it had been a busy night all the way around, which wasn't surprising as it was the night before the Fourth. She said Luigi had skipped on his sidework and that Jerry had been mean to Chris, who had gotten weeded again.

"That poor boy," she said, shaking her head, her long brown hair swinging. "He *tries*, I know."

I grimaced in sympathy, and then switched subjects. "Kate, do you know if Darryl ever lived in Miami?"

Kate gave me a strange look. "I don't think so. He grew up in Virginia Beach and kinda prided himself that he had never lived more than a hundred miles from where he grew up. Wait though. He *did* talk about a trip he took to see the Miami Dolphins. God, he was a fan of the Dolphins, let me tell you. Every time the Dolphins would play he would trot out the old story about shaking Dan Marino's hand. It was kind of sad, really."

I went to the bar and shook my head at Matt's offer of a drink. "I'm just stopping by," I said.

Jarred Kent, the handsome Karaoke man, announced the next singer, "Lisalicious, our very own rock-and-roll hoochie coochie!"

Jarred had a wicked sense of humor, and enjoyed assigning nicknames to his singers. I smothered a smile as the unassuming little senior took her place at the microphone, beaming as Jarred be-bopped along with her for a few moments. Karaoke had taken off like crazy the last year or so on the Outer Banks, and I actually enjoyed it.

Jarred worked his way across the room, encouraging a couple of people to sing, pointing out where his song books were located, and kissing his beautiful wife on the cheek.

"Hello, Callie," he said, when he reached me at the back of the bar. "Pretty good night."

I nodded.

"It would be even better if you would sing..." He raised a dark eyebrow in inquiry. I laughed at his mock-pleading look.

"I don't sing," I said, shaking my head. *Anymore.*

"Oh, come on, everybody sings. And I've heard you singing when you think no one's listening and you've got a fantastic voice. So how about it?" He kept one practiced eye on Lisalicious as he spoke, but she was belting away with no problems.

"No, I don't think so," I said firmly.

"Even Darryl used to sing. It's a tradition with you restaurant managers at the Seahorse Cafe, didn't you know?"

"Darryl used to sing?" I was surprised. From everything I had heard about Darryl, I had not expected this.

"Oh yes, he sang Frank Sinatra, *just* like the radio." Jarred smiled wryly, then suddenly raced off toward the front of the room, leaping over a chair and landing beside Lisalicious with his hands on his hips for all the world like Superman just as the song ended. I shook my head in amusement, used to Jarred's frantic departures, and decided to leave myself.

I went downstairs, and on impulse, I turned down the short hall that held the walk-in refrigerators and freezers. There were two refrigerators, and the freezer on the end. There was plenty of storage space upstairs in the huge kitchen for the food that was used every day. In the walk-ins were back-up supplies, and food for caters and banquets.

I made a mental note to ask someone from maintenance to clean up the empty paint cans, two by fours and plywood that lay piled in an alcove across from the walk-ins. I pulled out my keys and unlocked the padlock that held the metal bar across the freezer door. These locks had not been changed, because, as far as I knew, the thief had not been taking food. But if someone had been stealing food, that would explain the high food costs. I would have to ask Chef.

I stepped inside the freezer, and goose pimples immediately rose on my arms from the sub-zero temperatures. Shelves stacked three high lined the sides of the big freezer, and on the shelves were frost-covered boxes marked with identifying labels like "Chicken Breasts" "10 oz. Filet" and "Shoestring Cut Potatoes." I saw several cardboard cases marked with Smith's Seafood logo, as well as a variety of other purveyors.

In the back of the freezer, on the left, were several seafood cases and other boxes with "Cater" written in bold black marker. Various dates were written underneath the word "Cater." Beside the boxes marked "Cater" were boxes marked "Banquet," also with dates. The dates were the day the function would take place, all less than a week away.

My teeth started to chatter as I turned to look at the door. The emergency release mechanism was on the right side of the door, labeled with an orange fluorescent sticker. I read the directions, and they were straightforward. Rotate the pin to release tension, pull it completely out of the hole in the lock stem, and push the door open. Simple. Why hadn't Darryl used this?

I thought of Darryl, locked in here, beating on the door until his hands were numb and he was hoarse from screaming. It had been in April, and he had probably been wearing short-sleeves. At first, had he thought it was a joke when he could not get out? Had he seen the person who had done it? At what point had he realized that it wasn't a joke? *How long had he been in here?*

My breath started coming in short snorts and I felt a light sweat break out all over my body and quickly freeze on my arms and back. My heart was pounding, and I closed my eyes against the dizzying rush that swam through my head.

I shoved the door, half expecting it to be locked, and stumbled into the bright, warm hallway. I had not had an anxiety attack in almost five months. I leaned my back against the wall, and took deep calming breaths, forcing myself to the here and now, telling myself I wasn't back in that 7-11 in Palo Alto.

Finally I was able to open my eyes and lock the metal arm back over the freezer door with some semblance of calm, though my fingers were shaking badly.

I think I had been treating this as a game, a sort of brain teaser to be figured out.

All of a sudden it seemed horribly real.

CHAPTER TEN

Early Mornings and the Fourth of July

The worst part of my job was that several times a week, I had to get up at the crack of dawn and go to work. And when I had just fallen asleep as the dark velvet of the sky was being touched with the glowing rays of hidden morning sunlight, it made for a hard day.

But once I was up, and at work (and after at least two cups of strong coffee), I was actually glad I was awake to see the crimson opal of the sun slide its way over the slippery black waters into the delicately paling sky. I was relieving my a.m. supervisor this morning, trying to ignore the aching, tired clamp on the back of my head.

A.m. is completely different from p.m. In p.m. the emphasis is on service, and food presentation and the quality of food. In the morning, the emphasis is on speed. Plain and simple. We usually served more than twice as many people in the morning as at night, but the night revenue was usually higher because of the much higher check averages. If I could, I would abolish breakfast before ten o'clock off the face of the earth.

I am not a morning person, could you guess?

I went into the kitchen and talked with the two large women breakfast cooks, who joked and laughed as the orders flooded in.

"Oh shoot," said Leah, slapping a pancake over, her big bosom shaking with laughter. "Look what I did. Jerry is goin' to have to spank me."

"Oh girl," said Saundra, peering over at Leah. "You done dropped the eggs."

Leah, who was known for pulling up her shirt and flashing her impressive breasts at the new waits, roared with laughter and looked up at me. "Hey Callie, you going to fire me, I just dropped half dozen eggs on the floor."

"Leah, honey, you're fired. Just finish out the next ten years, okay?"

The cooks shook with hysterical laughter, and I decided I was missing something. "Callie, would you write it on the waste report for me," Leah asked. "I'm kinda busy here."

"Sure," I said, and went into the back hallway where a bulletin board was filled with clipboards labeled for the days of the week, and information on upcoming banquets, cater and restaurant functions was clipped to the appropriate day. An eighth clipboard was labeled "Waste," and I filled out the columns, the date, the item and quantity, reason for wastage and my initials. It was only the beginning of the month, and I was surprised at how long the report already was. Listed were such things as " Six dinner rolls– moldy" or "Two pieces Bumbleberry Pie– squished." Those were Luigi's initials. "Hotel pan of chix–bad" and "Crabmeat–spoiled." For the first week of the month, there were quite a few entries.

Shaking my head, I went back out into the restaurant.

I smiled, and rang up checks, and helped the hostess seat people. I poured coffee, made hot tea (anybody who drinks hot tea in a busy restaurant should be taken out in an empty field and shot), bussed tables, made toast, carried food, soothed disgruntled customers, and generally did anything that needed to be done.

By the time breakfast was over and I had counted the money, did the checkout and took all the paperwork downstairs and put it in the accountant's box, I was pooped.

And it was only 11:30. Ugh.

Jerry was supervising the unloading of an order as I came through the back hall on my way to the F&B office.

"How was the show?" Jerry yelled down the hall.

I shrugged. "Interesting. How did you get this wonderful chore?" I asked, looking around at the boxes stacked against the walls.

Jerry looked down at his checklist and directed the delivery man to the first walk-in. "Just happened to be here. That's how it works. It's a pain in the butt, though." He checked his clipboard again, and leaned down and wrote "Banquet- 7/9" on one of the boxes of chicken.

I went into my office and collapsed into my chair. I glanced at my watch and picked up the phone. I had been waiting for a decent hour to call Darryl again and now seemed as good a time as any. I had an idea about at least one of Darryl's cryptic notations, and if he wouldn't answer my straightforward questions, I would try a little subterfuge.

Darryl answered the phone himself.

"I don't want to talk to you," he said immediately when I identified myself. "I'm real busy, and I've got to go."

"Real quick, I've just got one question. When did you go see the Miami Dolphin's game?"

There was a long silence. "September, four years ago," he said finally, very soft.

And he hung up.

I replaced the phone in the receiver. Darryl had been in Miami in September, four years ago. Janet's words about Frank ran through my mind: *He lived in Florida for a couple of years. To tell you the truth, I think he had a little trouble down there right before he moved up here about four years ago.*

What had happened? How was Darryl involved? I could only think of one way to find out. I picked up the phone and dialed the familiar ten-digit number.

"Debbie? How are you? I have a favor to ask you..."

Jerry came in to the office just as I was hanging up the phone, and sat down at the computer station.

"The specials for tonight are on your desk," he said. "Tell me what you think." He flashed a boyish smile at me. Jerry had been treating me differently ever since the other night when we had exchanged confidences at the bar. He was more focused with me, less apt to let his eyes wander while I was speaking.

I read over the special sheet, noting a few grammatical corrections and looked back at Jerry. "Sounds scrumptious," I said. "I'll post them around the hotel."

Jerry nodded without taking his eyes off the computer screen. I rifled through the papers on my desk, function sheets for upcoming banquets and caters, memos from sales, hotel forecasts from the front desk, and rumpled scraps of paper from various waits, requesting days off. I always made the schedule on Wednesday, and there was always a pile of these requests on my desk Tuesday.

I sorted through the stack, and Mac stuck his head through the door. He was barefoot, and I could smell the aroma of eau-de-unwashed-young-male from where I sat.

"Hey Jerry, you done the schedule yet?"

Jerry dragged his eyes off the screen and looked at Mac, smiling. Jerry treated Mac as if he were his little brother, which meant that some times he was supportive and approving and other times he was impatient with Mac's perceived ineptitude. I wasn't sure what Mac thought of Jerry.

"Not yet," Jerry said coolly. He sat back in the chair, and put a stocky arm on the back of the chair. Today, his long hair was protruding out of the back of a pink "Holiday House" hat like a horse's tail.

"Cool," Mac said, coming in and perching on the edge of the desk. "Can you give me Tuesday through Saturday off next week? I know it' short notice, but a friend of mine just invited me to go to a surfing competition in Ft. Lauderdale."

Jerry turned back to the computer, and Mac apparently took that as assent.

"Are you coming up on the roof for the fireworks?" Mac asked me.

Janet came into the office, winding her hair in a bun at the base of her neck. "Are ya'll doing that again? Better not let Lilly hear you."

"Why not? It's the best view on the beach," Mac said, and Janet shrugged.

"The roof?" I asked, as Jerry said, "Do you have enough money to go to Ft. Lauderdale?" sounding all the world like Mac's dad.

Mac answered me first. "Yeah, right around nine we go up on the roof and watch the fireworks. Come on up." He turned to Jerry. "I'm pretty sure I got enough money. It'll work itself out."

I saw Noel go by in the hall, his white hair in tufts around his head, his chef coat blotched with unidentifiable stains. I waved at him, trying to ignore Jerry and Mac's conversation.

"Jesus Christ, you just went away for three weeks in March," Jerry said. "But go, go. I'll work doubles, or something."

"Thanks man," Mac said, either oblivious to Jerry's martyred air, or ignoring it. "Cool." He disappeared down the hall and the door slammed behind him.

Jerry shook his head. "He's so irresponsible. I just busted him again for taking the hotel cater van to the store to get cigarettes because his Suzuki's tags are dead. I had been on my own for years by the time I was his age. I worked so hard to get what I wanted. And he could care less. Chef or I cover him if he gets in too big of a hole, and he thinks we'll do it the rest of his life." He looked at me, and I saw exasperation and concern in his eyes.

"He'll figure it out eventually," I said gently. "They usually do."

"I hope so," he said and turned back to the computer.

I had planned to go home and take a nap in the middle of the day before I had to come back for the dinner rush. As it was, I barely had time to rush home and take the dog for a walk before I had to be back.

When I let myself into the back hallway, I saw Mac talking to a scruffy little man by the back loading dock.

"So you need anything?" the man said, with an accent that I couldn't place. He was wearing a black wool cap, despite the heat, and white boots pulled up around his knees over grayish sweat pants and a plaid shirt. His face was grizzled with brownish fuzz, and his chin seemed too big for his face, making him look pugnacious.

"Nah, man, you know better than to come here. We'll call you," said Mac. He had his back to me, and the little man had not noticed me.

"Let me talk to the big boss. It's prime stuff. Give me a box, I'll fill it up. No problem. Tell me when, I'll meet you at the house." The little man shifted, and I stepped back so the Coke machine blocked me. What the hell was going on?

"I said no," Mac said forcefully. "Go on, get out of here. We told you not to ever come here."

"Man, I just caught a twenty-pounder, you got to see her. The scallops are plump and luscious just like a new mother's tit, and I got flounder up the yin-yang."

"Nah, man," Mac said, and walked back toward the freezer. After a moment of silence, I peeked around the corner and saw the man getting into a rusty black pickup truck.

I stepped back behind the Coke machine and wondered what to do. What first had sounded like a drug deal had turned into a black-market seafood deal. Which "big boss" was buying black-market seafood and why?

It was illegal for fishermen to sell their catch without a license, and it was just as illegal for a restaurant owner to buy
right off the boats without a license. But license or no, black-
market selling went on. The food was cheaper, if not necessarily
better. But why would anybody in the Holiday House want to
buy black-market seafood?

The door to the hotel offices opened behind me and I
quickly stepped out from behind the Coke machine and walked
casually to the elevator.

Mac stuck his head from the walk-in hall and gave me a
wary look and a smile. I waved, but he still looked suspicious.

As I stepped out of the elevator on the fourth floor, Chef
was opening the doors with a key from his own ring.

He saw me and grinned, holding up the key, not at all re-
pentant. "Only takes five minutes to get a key copied," he said.

I was pissed. I strode off the elevator and over to face him,
hands on hips.

"You think it's funny?" I said quietly, wanting to smack the
smirk off his face. He held the keys loosely between us, as if they
were a prize he wanted to dangle in front of me.

"Callie, it's absolutely ridiculous-"

"Every month for the last six months, somebody has been
coming in here," I gestured with my hand to the banquet area,
"and stealing things. I do not think it is funny." I emphasized the
last words so hard that I almost spit them out of my mouth like
they were bullets to smash into his chest. "I do not think it is
funny, *at all.*"

I grew up with an older brother and sister. My sister was
always in her own world and didn't have much to do with my
brother and me. But my brother and I were too much alike, and
I was too much the baby of the family for us to get along very
well. For years, he tormented me, locking me in the bathroom
for hours on end, throwing me out of trees, hitting me under
the kitchen table. I did not think I could ever forgive him or like
him.

But we grew up. And I learned that the more I screeched
and screamed the more he taunted me. The more he knew he
was getting to me, the more he would tease me. So I became
cold as ice. Nothing he said or did would faze me. I refused to
run crying to Mom, or scream in frustration. I spoke quietly, or I
ignored him. Finally we got along, and became best friends.
And I learned a valuable lesson on controlling my anger.

I was using that skill to the limit at this moment, because I wanted to yell in frustration, call Chef every name in the book, screech at him until my lungs hurt.

Instead I stood in front of him, refusing to be intimidated by his size, and tapped my foot. In rhythm to the tap, tap, tap, I said, "I am trying to do my job." Tap, tap, tap. "I'm doing it the best way I know how, and you are undermining my efforts. I do not appreciate it." Tap, tap, tap.

Chef looked, well, frankly he looked flabbergasted. He stared down at me, his eyes slightly blurred, the expression on his face so comical I had the sudden urge to laugh.

I held out my hand, palm up, and waited.

Tap, tap, tap.

After a minute, he took the shiny new key off of his key ring and handed it over. I turned around, and went through the fire door into the stairwell.

Only then did I begin to shake.

The Fourth of July was turning into an unmitigated nightmare. We were even busier than expected, and they all wanted to be served yesterday so they could go out on the deck and get a good spot to watch the fireworks. Screaming kids, cranky half-drunk parents, and scheming teenagers, trying to get in and out without paying.

I had over-staffed, from sheer nervousness. The kitchen had not.

The food was taking forever to come out of the kitchen. When people had waited some forty minutes to get seated and then their food was taking another forty minutes to arrive, they were not happy campers. And they were not quiet in their displeasure.

I got through it as best I could, discounting the checks of disgruntled guests or giving them free salads or deserts, but it was a restaurant manager's nightmare. At the beginning of the back-up, I had gone in the back to see what was happening.

Amid Lee the dishwasher yelling "'Can honor set a leg? No. Or an arm? No. Or take away the grief of a wound? No. What is honor? A word!'" and the blaring of the radio and yelling of the cooks, I was told that one of the line cooks had called in sick. Chef, Jerry, Mac and of all people, Noel, were working the line. Noel very rarely set foot behind the restaurant line.

It was a case of too many chiefs and no Indians. As good of an executive chef as he was, Chef was slow and easily frustrated when it came to actual cooking. Jerry was too caught up in his plate presentation and Noel wasn't used to cooking individual plates. The only one capable of getting the plates out in a hurry was Mac, and he had too many people telling him what to do to do what he had to do.

So I told them what orders needed to be done right away, and I escaped the hellhole.

By nine o'clock, the people were streaming out of the restaurant to jostle for a good spot to watch the fireworks, and I told Kate that I would be back in about thirty minutes. It was all over but the crying.

I went through the kitchen, which was deserted, dirty pots and pans everywhere. I passed through the kitchen to the utility closet off the back hallway. The door, which was usually locked, was open, and I went inside the closet, packed with electrical wiring and other gadgets. A dark tunnel and a ladder led up to the roof.

I easily climbed the ladder and found that a door, much like a hatch, had already been opened and was lying on its side. I swung myself onto the roof, and walked quietly across the thick tarpaper amid the tall air conditioner units. There was only a sliver of a moon, and the sky seemed to be actually glowing like a black light. Light splattered over the roof and I saw crimson and gold light climbing high into the sky immediately to the left. Further away I saw a mushroom cloud of fiery green and red.

I could hear the muttering of people, and I made my way to the group standing on the edge of the roof, separated from a five-story drop by a low wall. In the light and cannon thunder of the next set of fireworks, I saw Jerry and Chef and Mac, but mostly the crowd of people was faceless, a chattering mob hidden by the velvet night. Somebody had managed to lug a cooler up the ladder, and Chef was distributing ice-cold Coronas from it. He handed one to me silently. He had been like that with me all night, not ignoring me, but just avoiding me. I didn't mind that one bit.

"You can even see Manteo if you look behind us," Jerry said to me, standing with me at the edge of the drop. I turned around and saw a distant flower of light, shimmering like fairy dust.

"This has got to be the best seat on the beach, where you can see three shows at once."

"The one closest to us is Nags Head Pier, and the one further north is Avalon. They started earlier, so they should be finishing up soon." As he spoke, a barrage of light cascaded into the sky, and even from this far away we could hear the muffled thump as they exploded.

When I turned around, Jerry had disappeared. I had been pushed back toward the back of the crowd and was having trouble seeing over the tall people in front of me. I sipped on my Corona, and made my careful way over the roof to a spot on the edge, a little away from the rest of the crowd. There was an air conditioner at my back, and it was humming loudly in the still night air. I saw movement off to my left, further down the roof away from the crowd, but when I turned to look I saw nothing.

Far to the left, Avalon Pier was just finishing up its finale, and Nags Head Pier was taking a few moments to prepare for the next barrage. To my right, I heard Mac say, "Oh shit, I almost dropped my Corona on someone's head." I smelled cigarette smoke, and wondered idly if I could bum one off somebody.

At that moment, when the only light peeked from the thin crack of the moon, I felt a hand on my back and found myself propelled toward the edge.

CHAPTER ELEVEN

Fireworks

"Oh God," I said, leaning desperately away from the edge against the pressure on my back. Fireworks exploded above me and I yelled as with one last push, the pressure on my back was gone. I was propelled forward, my arms windmilling, and my shins slammed up against the short wall. Below me, I could see soft grass-covered dunes, and the hard wood of the deck–which would I land on?

"Callie!" I heard somebody yell, and I was grabbed by the arm and pulled to safely.

I was breathing so hard I couldn't talk, and I dropped to the sticky tarpaper of the roof.

"What in the hell are you trying to do? Kill yourself?" Chef said, dropping on one knee beside me. "Are you all right?" This because my breath was now wheezing in and out of my lungs. "Callie?" He put an arm around my shoulders, and at this simple kindness I leaned against his shoulder and tried to regain my breath. Above us, lights flashed like an insane kaleidoscope.

"What's going on?" I heard Jerry ask, and I heard footsteps behind me. I instinctively braced myself, wanting to be prepared if this was some elaborate hoax and somebody was going to kick me from behind toward the edge.

"Somebody tried to push me off the roof," I said, my voice low under the thunder of the fireworks. I looked up at Chef, and in the cascading light I saw nothing but concern. Jerry was kneeling beside me too, and when I turned to look at him, I saw confusion, but no malice. Could one of these two possibly have tried to push me off the roof? If so, they were damn good actors, because I could find no trace of it in their voices.

"Somebody tried to push you off the roof?" Jerry asked incredulously. He rocked back on his heels, and when I looked at him, red and blue light shone eerily off of his face and cheering and yells from below us resounded through the air.

"I looked over and saw her teetering right at the edge," Chef said. His voice was subdued, and he still had an arm around my shoulder.

"Why would someone try to push you off the edge?" Jerry asked, sounding genuinely bewildered. "It doesn't make sense. I bet someone accidentally brushed against your back. You were standing too close to the edge."

I thought about that hand on my back, inexorably pushing me closer to the edge. I had leaned back against the pressure, and the hand had given me one good push toward the edge and then disappeared. The person had not spoken, I had not seen who it was. Chef, who had apparently seen me about to go over the edge, had not seen my attacker in the dim light.

I struggled to my feet, and while above us the skies detonated into a flaming shower of light and sound, the two chefs helped me to the ladder down to the kitchen. I didn't suggest a search the roof, and neither did the chefs.

Somehow I doubted I would find anybody who wasn't supposed to be there.

I thanked the men for their help, and Jerry ruffled my hair affectionately.

"Maybe you should try staying away from high ledges," he suggested, with the air that I had imagined it all, and climbed back up the ladder to watch the finale.

"Are you sure you're all right?" Chef asked. He was still wearing his chef coat, but open to reveal a UCLA T-shirt underneath.

"Just shook up," I said, looking ruefully down at the dark smudges on my green linen dress.

"Look Callie, back and front of the house are always at odds," he said. "I've been going through a bad time, and I know it makes me snappish. But I want you to know there are no hard feelings."

I looked him in the eye and noticed that they were widely dilated even in the bright florescent light of the kitchen. He looked haggard, as if he had been staying up late too many nights, for too long. It was an apology, or as close to one as I would get from him.

"No hard feelings," I agreed and solemnly shook his hand.

On going out into the restaurant, I found the waits and Kate close to being finished, and the bar starting to fill up as people poured in off the deck.

"Do you need any help?" I asked Kate, but she waved me off.

"Go home, will you? You look like death warmed over," she said, flicking me a smile.

So I did.

I had trouble sleeping that night. I wasn't surprised.

Had I been mistaken? Had somebody really put a hand on my back and tried to force me over the edge? Or had it been an accident, a drunk coworker accidentally stumbling into me?

Had someone tried to kill me?

It had happened to me before, somebody had pointed a gun at me and pulled the trigger. I had the scar to prove it. But it was still very hard for me to believe that somebody had tried to kill me, had tried to push me off the roof.

After several hours staring at the flickering TV– no sound– I came to a couple of conclusions.

I had not imagined the incident. I had been standing apart from the group of people on the roof with nobody around me. Someone had deliberately pushed me toward the edge.

But whether they had planned for me to go over the edge or not, I think at the last minute the pusher had chickened out. For a few horrible seconds, as I was tottering on the edge, one push would have sent me over.

But the final push had not come.

It was possible that the whole thing was meant as a warning, or the person could have started out with the intention of killing me, and then had not been able to go through with it. But I had no doubt that somehow it was connected with Darryl Menden and that infernal memo.

I turned in my bed, the cotton sheets damp with sweat, despite the high-power fan that was pumping cool air over me. Kim was downstairs asleep, and all the doors and windows were securely locked. I had checked. Twice. I had even looked under the beds

I was safe here, lying in my bed. But still I could not sleep.

Six o'clock came entirely too early. Once again I was driving to work as the sun rose over the heaving, dark ocean. I had scheduled myself this morning because it was a good bet that the restaurant would get slammed for breakfast the morning after the Fourth of July. I won the bet.

But after breakfast I was able to leave the restaurant and go downstairs to my office. I was off the rest of the day, but found myself at sixes and sevens, not sure what I wanted to do. After doing some miscellaneous paperwork, I went home and made myself a spinach and ham pasta in a Dijon cream sauce for lunch. The dog stared at me with his pie-eyed gaze. Ice had apparently decided to tolerate the dog, if not become his bosom companion, and he contented himself with a few half-hearted snarls in the dog's direction.

The dog rubbed his ears against the carpet and resumed staring at me, despite the full bowl of dog food in the closet.

"None for you, dog," I said. "Don't beg." He promptly laid his head down on the carpet, though his mournful eyes watched my every movement.

"I'm not going to name you," I told him around a mouthful of angel hair pasta. "Then you would get the wrong idea and think I was going to keep you. Which I'm not. Someone will call about you soon."

Ice, sitting on a stool beside me, said "Yeow" in disgust and industriously began washing his back.

The dog wuffle-snorted, and put his chin on his paw.

"No sirree," I said. "I am not going to name you. I bet you're not even a very good guard dog."

Snort, wuffle, wuffle, he disagreed.

I finished my pasta and put the bowl in the sink and retrieved the cordless telephone. Reading from the number written in my leather-bound address book, I dialed Darryl Menden's house again. I figured he owed me an explanation. He was going to talk to me whether he wanted to or not.

The phone rang and rang, but no one picked up.

"Well guys," I said to my audience, who had pretty much lost interest in me when I stopped eating. "It looks like I'm going to Virginia."

It was the first time I had been off the Outer Banks since I had arrived two months ago. It was the first time I had been to Virginia in over two years. The drive was hot and boring, and I was tired of looking at fruit stands and fields by the time I made it to the Virginia border. I stopped and bought a map and pin-pointed the Menden's address. Even though I had grown up in Virginia Beach, it was a big city and I was not familiar with every little side street.

Driving and reading a map for me is like walking and chewing gum is for other people. After almost running over an old lady and a poodle, coming close to rear-ending a trash truck, and running three red/yellow lights, I found the street I was looking for.

I turned into one of those peaceful suburban pockets amid the hustle and bustle of Virginia Beach. Rambling brick ranchers stretched leisurely among emerald lawns and oak trees, which were kept alive by incessant sprinklers. As I drove deeper into the neighborhood, the houses became smaller and older, though still neat and clean. The house that matched the address that the bartender at Fishbones had given me was a small, square one-story, painted a faded dark green with white trim. The lawn was freshly mowed, but not as brilliantly green as most of the other lawns, probably from lack of sprinkling.

There were no cars in the driveway. I pulled onto the cracked, stained concrete, got out of the Jeep and walked up to the house. Heavy curtains framed the dark windows, and I could hear the sound of a blaring TV.

I rang the doorbell.

After several moments, I opened the storm door and rapped on the door. Loudly.

I heard shuffling, and a thumping noise.

"Hello?" I called, holding the storm door open and knocking again.

Thump, thump, thump. Then somebody fumbled with the door handle and the door opened. A stooped old woman clutching a cane stood peering at me. She had thick glasses over bright blue eyes, and a lined face that drooped approximately to her breast bone. She wore a thin flowered dress, and as she moved I could see flesh rolling and moving under her dress.

"Mrs. Menden?" I asked.

"Yeeesss," she said, and I recognized her voice from the telephone. As suddenly as a flash of white tail from a deer in the woods, her face creased into a smile as she twisted her head to peer up at me. Without speaking she put out a trembling hand to open the storm door, wordlessly inviting me inside.

I was uncomfortable, wondering if she thought I was someone else. Did she invite inside everyone who came to her door, the mailman, Jehovah witnesses, burglars? Was she senile?

Swallowing my uneasiness I followed her into the house. The first thing I noticed was the noise, the second, the heat. She had all the windows closed and no AC running on a hot summer day. I breathed in the air and felt the heat in my lungs.

She thumped along a faded runner into the living room on the right. Heavy, dusty pale blue drapes blocked out the sun, and the faded gold shag carpet almost disappeared under chairs and couches and tables, all crammed into the space with no apparent thought to how it looked.

The woman moved to a tan recliner and lowered herself down into its sagging depths. No wonder it had taken her so long to get to the door. It was a wonder she ever got out of the thing.

The recliner was obviously her throne. A faded bone colored shawl draped across the top of the chair and two arm pillows rested behind her as she sat down. A TV tray and end table on either side of the chair were cluttered with pill bottles, remote controls, paperbacks, an extra pair of glasses and a glass of what looked like watered-down tea. The TV was set on an afternoon soap and the volume was up so loud that the voices of the actors had become tinny and almost unintelligible.

"Mrs. Menden," I said, wiping the sweat off of my face.

She smiled again, and fumbled through the items on the TV tray until she found the remote. With two hands she brought it up toward the TV, almost as if she were aiming a gun, and five trembling seconds later she had managed to change the channel several times, turn the TV up, then down fractionally, and then she found the mute button.

I almost sighed in relief. My wound-up nerves were twanging in protest.

"Mrs. Menden, my name is Callie McKinley. I work at the Holiday House where your son used to work," I said loudly, guessing that she was Darryl's mother.

She shifted in her chair. She tried to speak and made a muffled gargling sound, cleared her throat, and said in a surprisingly deep voice, "Darryl's not here anymore. He and Linda left last night." Her voice shook and wavered like an earthquake rumbling underground through nooks and caverns.

"He left last night?" Dammit! My shirt was sticking to my back as if it were covered with wet glue, and I wiped the sweat off my top lip.

Mrs. Menden nodded. "I was so happy when he and his wife came to stay with me," she said, the words dipping and soaring.

"I guess that was last week?" I asked. She thought a minute and then nodded. That fit with what the bartender at Fishbones had said. "Did he say why he left the Outer Banks?"

She dipped her head to the side and regarded me like an inquisitive squirrel. "He said he needed peace and quiet."

"So he was planning to leave last night?" I asked. "Do you know where he went?"

"Oh no," she rumbled, reaching over her shoulder and pulling a shawl over herself. She huddled under its folds as if she were freezing. "He left real sudden-like. He said he would call me when he got settled. He's fallen on hard times, my boyo." She nodded her head, and then kept nodding as if she couldn't stop.

"Why did he leave?"

"He got a call yesterday afternoon. He was real upset and then he and Linda just packed up and left. Left all of Linda's crochet needles behind, she'll miss them."

"Did he have more than one phone call yesterday?" I knew I had called Darryl yesterday morning. Had my question about Miami scared him enough to make him leave town?

Mrs. Menden stared at the TV a moment, and then nodded. "It was the second call, in the afternoon, that made him decide to leave." She shrugged, the flesh jiggling and wiggling under her dress. "He said it was a job offer that he had been waiting for."

"But you think he was scared after that second phone call?"

"I'm old, not senile," she said simply.

Had somebody found out I had called Darryl asking questions? Had he been bullied into leaving town because of me?

And could it be possible that the same person had tried to push me off the roof of the Holiday House Hotel?

CHAPTER TWELVE

Mind is Goin' Out of Business

Traffic on Virginia Beach Boulevard was stop and go.

Someone must have figured out that I had called Darryl. I couldn't think of any other reason that a phone call to Darryl would scare him enough to leave his mother's house; and that the same person would attempt to push me off the roof the same night. What had Darryl known that someone hadn't wanted me to know? How had the person known that I had called Darryl?

The first time, I had called Darryl from my house, and I wasn't paranoid enough to think someone had my phones tapped, so they couldn't have figured it out that way. Yesterday, I had called from the F&B office, but no one had been around.

Had the bartender at Fishbones called somebody as soon as I left, reporting that I had been asking about Darryl? Then why would she give me his address? I never would have found him otherwise. Had Darryl himself reported that I had called? I dismissed that right off. The impression I had of Darryl was that he was trying to get as far away from the people of Holiday House Hotel as possible.

The only possibility left was that I had given myself away somehow, and the person had called Darryl, found out for sure I had called and told him to leave town. But try as I might, I could not remember telling anybody that I had called Darryl.

But I had been asking everybody questions about Darryl. It wasn't hard to guess that I might try to contact him and ask him the questions I'd been asking everybody else.

I had questioned Mrs. Menden about the person who had called, but she said Darryl had been on edge since the day before when I had called the first time, and had been snatching the phone off the hook every time it rang, so she hadn't heard the voice.

I shook my head and made a sudden right as I saw a road sign ahead.

Something that I did not want to think about was this: Who was responsible for all of this and why? Was the person stealing supplies from the hotel, and trying to cover up for it? A few steak knives and water glasses just didn't seem to be a good enough reason for attempted murder. What about the black-market seafood? How did that fit in? I shook my head in frustration.

Try it from another angle. Lily wanted me to spy on the chefs for her, so she suspected one of them. Of course, Lily could be throwing me off, and actually she was responsible for the strange things going on in the hotel. Or it could be Janet, or Mac. Until I knew what the scam was, it would be damn near impossible to figure out who would have a motive for attempted murder.

Another angle. Who had been on the roof the night before? It had been dark, and I wasn't sure who was hidden in the depths of the crowd. But I knew Jerry and Chef had been there, as well as Mac, who I had seen talking to Chef over by the Corona cooler. Something else about Mac, what was I forgetting? Chef had been the one to pull me back from the edge. Had he been the one to push me as well?

Who else knew I would be on the roof? The afternoon of the fourth, we had talked about going up on the roof. Janet and Mac had been there, and Jerry. I knew Jerry and Mac were on the roof that night. Had Janet been there? Anybody could have been hiding behind the air conditioner units and I never would have seen him or her. And it was possible that the push was not premeditated at all. The person could have seen the opportunity as I stood too close to the edge and taken it.

So I was left with nothing. No idea who the attempted murderer was, or what the motive was.

I saw the sign, "Peaceful Times Nursing Home" and

slammed on the brakes to make the turn into the parking lot. A sprawling one-story brick building spread several wings over a bright green lawn with graceful weeping willows and sturdy oaks partially blocking out the sight and sound of cars speeding along on either side of the nursing home.

I parked the Jeep, and ran a brush through my hair before hopping out and heading toward the entrance ,which was just an overhang covering a circular drive and two glass doors. I went inside the doors and found myself in a surprisingly well-furnished lobby. A fountain tinkled softly in the middle of the room, tile was arranged in a circular mosaic spreading outward from the fountain, and the furniture was spindly Victorian knock-offs, not in the least institutional.

I went up to the window, set unobtrusively back and to the side of the front door and spoke to the young girl in the dark blue suit within.

"I'm here to see Samuel Delaney," I told the girl, and she silently punched the letters into the computer.

"Name?" she asked, gazing up at me. I noticed that her eyebrows had been plucked to almost a minuscule arched line. It made her forehead look huge, and she suddenly reminded me of one of the aliens from Star Trek.

"Laurie," I said, taking a deep breath. "Laurie McKinley."

No flashbulbs popped on over her head, no alarm bells went off behind her smile. "Relation to patient?" she asked calmly.

"I'm his granddaughter," I said.

She glanced at her screen to confirm my identity, and I was relieved that my mother had thought to put my name down as a potential visitor. "The Alzheimer's Unit is in the Grant Wing, room G thirty-one," she said with a professional smile.

I smiled back and began to think I was getting my armor of anonymity back. Perhaps I would never again have to go through the hassle of recognition, and being accosted in the street, in the grocery store, in my car. Many people had been almost frightening in their familiarity with me, acting as if they knew me, angry if I tried to escape politely. I had got to where I didn't want to go out.

"Sign in, Ms. McKinley," the receptionist called after me, and I turned to see where she was pointing. Near the front door was a podium with a map of the nursing home and a bright red star indicating "You are here." Beside the map was a sign-in book. I scribbled my name, and studied the map. As I turned away, I almost ran into a little, old woman standing behind me. She was dressed in a white and blue sweat suit and clean white sneakers, and she looked like she should be on the tennis courts, not in a nursing home gazing at my face.

I smiled politely, and moved past her down the hall that led to the Grant Wing.

"You *are* Laurie McKinley," the little woman cried, and I turned around to see that she was studying the sign-in book. "I told Yvette, but she wouldn't listen." She came bustling up to me and grasped my arm with surprisingly strong fingers.

"What?" I said, but my heart sunk to roughly the tips of my sandals.

"Laurie McKinley!" she said, her eyes probing my face. "You look different, but I just saw you in my *People* magazine. You and the little boy–"

"No, ma'am, " I said, gently disengaging her fingers. "I'm afraid you are mistaken. I'm not Laurie McKinley, I'm Callie."

"But I thought–" Her eyes were troubled, and I realized that she had trouble seeing, which was why she was looking at me so intently. She ran light fingers over my face. "You're right," she said softly, "You're not her." I touched her hand lightly, and she dropped it away from my face. I turned away and went along the hall, but not before I heard her say under her breath, "You're not her."

I passed along medicinal corridors lined with pleasant cheery rooms, common rooms with blaring TVs and older people staring intently at nothing. Nurses in rustling white dresses and sensible white shoes bustled here and there among the halls, and paid me no attention.

Eventually I came to locked double doors, and I pushed the small red button on the side of the wall. A few moments later, the doors swung open. A skinny old woman was waiting, and she tried to scuttle out the open doors. A nurse caught her gently by the arm and pulled her away from the door.

"No Angie, it's not time to leave yet," the nurse said. "Soon, we'll go for a walk and find your dog."

"Scottie," Angie wailed, and burst into tears.

"Hi," the nurse said to me, patting Angie's back. "Can I help you?"

"I'm looking for Samuel Delaney's room," I said.

"Oh, Sam's not in there. They're having ballroom dancing in the common room. He wouldn't miss it for the world," the nurse said, with affection for my grandfather in her voice. "Just along that corridor," she said, pointing down the rose-colored hall with its functional white linoleum floor.

I went down the hall and found a small group of older adults clapping their hands and swaying unsteadily to the music of Bing Crosby.

My grandfather, however, was on the dance floor, dipping and swaying a pretty woman in street clothes as she laughed, pink-faced.

I stood back and watched as my grandfather expertly moved around the floor, in a plaid shirt, flannel pants and baseball hat perched precariously over a wide smile.

My grandfather had been a substitute father to me, patient and understanding, irascible and ornery by turns, he had always loved me unconditionally. And now he had forgotten who I was, who he was, as the ravages of Alzheimer's swept through his brain. My mom and aunt had struggled for two years to keep him at home, but he had finally become too much for them to handle. They had put him in the nursing home, and from what I could see, he was happier than he had been in years.

After about fifteen minutes, the patients in dressing gowns and pajamas slowly began to drift away to their rooms, until it was only my grandfather and the pretty young woman left on the floor.

"Okay Sam," the woman said laughing, breaking off from him and turning the music off. "Enough for today. You wear me out!" She began packing up her CD player and CDs and I went over to my grandfather.

"Hi Sam," I said softly. He turned around and flashed me a wide grin showing his perfect white dentures, and held out his arms for a dance. I twirled around with him for a turn or two and then led him by the hand to a nearby couch.

"Do you remember me, Sam?" I asked.

"Oh yeah, yeah," he said, his eyes sliding quickly off of me. "How you been?"

He didn't remember me, not that I was surprised. "I'm doing good, Sam," I said. "How about you?"

"Well, the mind's goin' out of business," he said, tapping the side of his head with a knarled finger, "but I'm going back to Gloucester soon. Going over the top." He glanced at me slyly, and I groaned.

"No Sam, you can't leave," I said and then changed my

mind. What could it hurt? "Yep, going to Gloucester soon," I agreed, and he laughed merrily with me.

"Have you seen that other little girl?" he said. "And the big one?"

I stifled a laugh. I had heard from my mother that Sam had taken to calling her "the big one" and my aunt "the little girl," much to my mother's dismay and my aunt's delight. Not that they were very far apart in weight or age, but even though they were over fifty, sisterly rivalry still ran deep.

"No," I said, but he was already taking me by the hand and pulling me down the hall, mumbling about Gloucester and going over the top. My mother had told me that Sam had made a break for freedom with three other patients six months ago, and the nurses had found them wandering around the grounds, heads together as they tried to figure out how to cross the street.

Sam led me to a room, not G31, and started rummaging through the closets. He went into the bathroom. He found a man's shirt hanging in the bathroom, and put it on over his flannel shirt. Gesturing for me to follow him, we left the room. A few steps down the hall was a big sign on the door reading "Samuel Delaney's Room" and a poster of sun-lit marshes and a river, to remind him of his beloved Gloucester. He stopped, and traced his fingers over the picture and turned to me with a bright smile. "Going home soon," he said and my heart almost broke.

It had been little things first; he would forget our names, or names of objects. Then he started letting his normally neat house go to seed, and finally he got to where he wasn't bathing, and wasn't eating. He was hiding bags of clothes in his closet and talking to them. He was filling his truck up with gas and driving off without paying, or going into a store and calmly eating a tub of ice cream while sitting on the floor. Thankfully, he lived in a very small town and everybody knew and forgave Mr. Delaney.

We had wanted him to stay in Gloucester as long as he could but finally he had deteriorated too far. I had been in California, and was unable to help my mom and my aunt as they struggled to take care of him for those two long years. Finally, close to a mental breakdown, they had surrendered him to a nursing home. Where, strangely enough, he thrived. He liked pretty young women, and he spent most of his day hanging around the nurse's station, my mom had told me, charming the nurses. My mom and aunt took him out every weekend, and he seemed content.

He opened the door and went into his room. Several pairs of pants and shirts lay on the bed, and he immediately went over and pulled on another pair of pants. He posed for me, hand on hip, like a runway model and grinned.

"Oh Sam," I said softly.

"Missy wanted to bake me a pie," he said. Missy was his sister, long dead. He rummaged through his drawers, and found another hat, which he exchanged with the one on his head. He continued to mumble, and I heard him mention my mom and aunt's names as well as mine.

"Laurie!" I said, pouncing on my name. "Yes! I'm Laurie!"

He turned to look at me, his thin face unlined but splotched with age spots, and chewed his lip. "Oh Laurie, my little girl," he said, but he wasn't talking to me. "Such a pretty little thing, all elbows and pigtails. She used to sit on my lap. We used to sing together. We sang–" He wrinkled up his forehead as he tried to remember my favorite song as a child.

"*Della and the Dealer*," I said softly.

"She loved to sing," he said. "I haven't seen her in a while, my sweet little girl." In a low wavering voice, he started singing: "*Della and the dealer and a dog named Jake, and a cat named Kalamazoo...*" He trailed off, looking bewildered as the familiar words failed him.

I finished the refrain: "*Left Tucson in a pickup truck, goin' to make some dreams come true.*"

"My little Laurie," Sam said affectionately, with a wide smile. "We used to call her Callie, after the cat named Kalamazoo, did I ever tell you that?"

Tears came to my eyes and I said, hopelessly, "I'm Laurie, Sam."

"He doesn't know who any of us are anymore," I heard a familiar voice say. I looked up and saw my mother, dressed in a smart pumpkin-colored dress with gold jewelry and dark hair the exact color and texture of mine pulled back in a bun at the nape of her neck.

But whether Sam knew who she was or not, he evidently recognized her, because he went to her and urged her into the room, and took her hand and kissed it.

"Oh Dad," Mom said, and sat composedly in a chair. She looked at me, and I gazed back at her. It was the first time I had seen her in over two years, the first time I had seen anybody in my family, and we used to be so close. My mother and aunt, brother and sister and Sam, those were all the family I had. But things had changed, my life turned upside down.

"I've missed you," she said, my very undemonstrative mother, and a tear slid down her cheek, which she ignored.

"Me too," I said huskily.

"So," she said, smiling up at Sam who was swinging her hand back and forth. "You came to see him. Good. He's talks about you all the time."

"But he doesn't know who I am," I said.

"No, but he knows who we were," she said. "It's kind of nice, because he remembers us all when we were young. He talks about stuff that we've forgotten." She shifted in her chair, and put her leather pocketbook on the floor.

"Henley asks about you," she said finally. "I tell him the truth, that I'm lucky to hear from you every two or three months, that you haven't been the same since your accident. He wants me to tell you he loves you."

I nodded, my face blank. Henley was my beloved brother, who had shared the adopted father role with my grandfather; I had not spoken to him for over a year.

"How is he?" I managed to ask.

"Fine. He's studying for his masters."

I nodded, unable to speak.

"How are you? How's the..." She trailed off, staring at me hopelessly, unable to ask me about my wound, which had required two operations.

"I've been good," I said. "I got a post card from the little boy, Andy Gray. He has to go in for another operation, but I talked to his dad, and he said he should be fine."

"You talked to Henry Gray?" Her eyes were big, as if I had just revealed that I had spoken to the President yesterday over lunch. But to many, Henry Gray was more popular than the President of the United Sates. After all, did the President regularly save the world on movie screens across the country every couple of months?

"Yes," I said nodding wearily. "I talked to Henry Gray. Andy needs this operation, but in a year or so he should be close to normal."

She was silent, watching me with large green eyes that were a mirror to my own. I didn't need to see the future to know what I would look like in twenty-five years. All I had to do was look at my mother; age had blurred her fine fragile cheekbones, and stroked silver-touched fingers through her dark silky hair; had added weight to her slender frame and a droop to her determined chin. But we were undeniably mother and daughter.

"Laurie," she said, and I closed my eyes at the pain in her face. "Why did you close us out, after the accident, after your husband, why did you close all of us out?"

I was silent, unable to answer. I wasn't sure exactly why I had responded to tragedy the way I had, closing out my family and friends, retreating inward, changing my appearance and trying to forget that I was Laurie McKinley. But that was the way I had dealt with it, just like someone else might scream and shout, and another go quietly mad. Everybody had their own way of dealing with pain and grief.

"I don't know," I said.

"You're running away as fast as you can from everyone who loves you," she said softly.

Running? If only I could have run or moved that fateful night. Instead I had been struck as immobile as a deer in headlights.

"Are you still singing?"

I smiled, blinking back the tears, because singing had been one of the greatest joys in my old life. But how could I sing in public when anyone might see me and realize who I was?

"No, no yet. But I'm getting there, Momma. I'm getting there."

CHAPTER THIRTEEN

Fixes and Birthdays

It was amazing how good it felt to drive over the Wright Memorial Bridge, one of the bridges connecting the Outer Banks to the mainland, and knowing I was once more at the beach.

I drove down the Bypass, past the Wright Brothers National Memorial, a huge granite memorial on top of a grass-covered hill, where on December 17, 1903 at 10:35 a.m., history had been changed forever when Orville Wright achieved flight on Kill Devil Hill, watched by only a handful of astonished locals.

It was getting close to dark, and I switched my headlights on as the sky faded from pale blue toward darkness. I was tired, but I was wound up, and I knew I could not sleep. I pointed the Jeep toward Sharkey's. On the radio, the DJ was talking about Hurricane Carrie, a Category Two hurricane, churning its way across the Atlantic. At the moment the hurricane was weaving an erratic path, but St. Thomas and the other Virgin Islands had been put on a Hurricane Watch.

A new Sarah McLachlan song came on, and I turned the volume way up, and sang at the top of my lungs, oblivious to the curious and amused looks directed my way.

It was early, and there weren't many people on the bar side of Sharkey's. Kyle Tyler was sitting at the end of the bar next to

Susan, and I hesitated before going down to sit with them. Melissa brought me a drink, and I ordered a pound of crab legs with a salad for supper.

"So how was your day?" Kyle said. Today he was wearing jeans and a T-shirt with Daffy Duck across the front, and he smelled comfortably of food and bleach. I tried to ignore the tingle of heat that burned through me as he came over to stand close behind me.

"Okay. I went to Virginia to visit some relatives," I said coolly, looking over my shoulder at him.

"Where in Virginia?" Susan asked.

"Oh, just Virginia Beach," I answered. "So Kyle, who did Hitler marry the day before he killed himself?"

"Eva Braun," he said. "On April twenty-ninth. You're really slipping."

"That's a damn strange game you've concocted," Susan complained. "Half the time I don't know what you're talking about."

"Well, you should know this one, Susan," Kyle said. "What was the date of Pearl Harbor?"

"It was in December," she said slowly. "In nineteen forty-one. How's that?"

"December seventh," I said, looking a challenge at Kyle.

Susan shook her head at us and turned to the person on the other side of her. I took a sip of my drink.

"I heard you almost had a nasty accident," Kyle said quietly. "Are you all right?"

I was surprised at the warmth in his voice. I started to ask how he could have heard, but it was useless. The Beach Grapevine had been working overtime.

"Yes," I said. "I'm fine. It was just an– accident."

Kyle gave me a funny look and sipped at his gingerale. I had never seen Kyle drink alcohol, and I wondered if he ever did, or if there was a reason why he didn't. It seemed unusual for someone who ran a bar not to drink.

"I've heard things..." he began, and then shook his head.

"What?" I asked, trying not to let my curiosity show.

"Have you ever been married, Callie?" he asked suddenly, his voice casual and faintly mocking.

I almost choked on my drink. I turned to look at him, and suddenly I found the situation funny. "Yes, I've been married," I said. "In fact, I *am* married, though I haven't seen my husband in over a year."

Kyle looked at me, but if he felt any shock, he hid it well. If there was anything that I liked about Kyle, it was the feeling that I could tell him anything and he wouldn't be shocked. He would just shrug and ask me if I knew the date of D-Day. "I thought it was something like that. Your husband must be a real jerk."

"Actually," I said, "You'd probably like him."

"Hmmm," Kyle said and kept his thoughts to himself. A boy in the kitchen gestured for Kyle and he smiled wryly. "Duty calls."

He leaned close to my ear and for some reason I didn't pull away. I repressed the delicious chills as he said softly, "Be careful in that hotel. I don't think things are what they seem."

My face was flushed when I turned around, and Susan was staring at me speculatively.

"Handsome devil, isn't he?" she said.

Just then my crab legs arrived, and I was able to get away with just a shrug.

Some twenty minutes later I had sucked the last bit of butter off my fingers, cracked the last little bit of meat out of the shell and scooped up the last of my lettuce. I had been hungrier than I thought.

A few minutes later, Chef made his entrance, kissing every girl sitting at the bar as he made his way to Susan and me. He kissed Susan's cheek, leaving her pink-faced and smiling, and tousled my hair.

"Round of drinks on me," he told Melissa. She looked skeptical, but when he repeated his request she shrugged. She started making drinks and pulling beers for the twenty or so people sitting at the bar.

"You're in a good mood," Susan said, looking up at Chef through her thick glasses.

Chef shrugged. "Might as well be," he said, sliding onto the stool beside mine. "You come here often?" he asked the tanned tourist sitting beside him. "Have you seen the balloon yet? What balloon? You know, the one they fly over here from the mainland and drop supplies to us. How else do you think we get supplies all the way out here? It's out there now, big, blue, yellow and green, right outside."

He kept talking, and the tourist, whether he believed him, or just wanted to get away from him, walked outside and took a look up at the sky.

"Wonderfully gullible," Chef commented with satisfaction. He had already finished his drink, and banged loudly on the bar to get Melissa's attention. "One chicken strip for everybody at the bar," he told her. She looked at him, used to his strange requests.

"One," Chef said, holding up a finger. "Chicken strip for everyone," he said, waving his hand around the restaurant. Melissa sighed and went to put an order for three or four baskets of chicken strips.

"You seem to have money to spend today," I commented.

He shrugged. "Jobs on the Outer Banks don't pay as much as I'm used to, but not having enough money never stopped me from having fun. Tabs are wonderful things. I should know."

"Until they stop serving you and want you to pay," I commented.

"Oh, live a little, Callie. You ought to try it. Walk out without paying. It's a glorious feeling."

I shook my head.

"By the way, I heard you were interested in food costs. Don't rock the boat, okay?"

I was speechless, and he turned away to talk to yet another hapless tourist. Who had told him I had been asking questions about food costs? And why was he warning me?

"Chef," I said, tugging on his arm. "Real quick. What's the deal with food costs?"

He turned to me and looked at me with bleary eyes and I realized that he was pretty messed up. "It's been running right around thirty-nine percent. We've gone over forty a couple of months, but the year's average is still under forty. That number will get us our bonuses. Yes, it is frustrating that number is not lower. I would be happier if it was, but for whatever reason, it isn't. So we watch for stealing and wastage, we give away no food, and we hope for the best." He was enunciating very clearly, and slowly, as if his tongue was a razor blade and he was having to handle it very carefully.

"And you raise pricing and have a wastage report a mile long," I noted, not mentioning that it was his job to know why the food costs were rising, and he obviously hadn't taken the time to figure out why.

"Just as astute," Chef said. "Look, it's no big deal. The purveyors have raised their prices and the waits are taking home boxes of cappuccino moussecake. It happens. We're going to get our bonuses, just forget about it, okay? Don't rock the boat."

He got up, and swayed his way down the bar, just as Melissa delivered one chicken tender on a napkin to everyone at the bar.

I had just begun my second drink when Janet, Noel and Noel's beautiful wife Lisa arrived. They were there for dinner, and waved at us before they took their seat on the restaurant side. Chef immediately went over to their table and sat down, uninvited. Lisa, wearing long black hair and brown lustrous eyes, laughed gently at Chef's antics, who was either telling a story about reeling in a big fish or had temporarily lost control of his arms.

I had met Lisa on two other occasions, and her gentleness and her kindness had impressed me. From what I understood, she ran an informal home for abandoned animals, and had been known to take a foster child or two into her home. She was half-Chinese, and very beautiful, and at least twenty years younger than Noel. I would have loved to hear the story of their romance, because, judging from the loving expressions that they exchanged, their love was abiding and deep.

"I'm surprised Janet didn't bring her secret lover," Susan said. "I guess that answers the question of whether or not she's gay." She lit up one of her Virginia Slims, and peered over the lighter at me, eyes twinkling and inviting me to gossip.

"Secret lover, huh?" I said. "Would he happen to be the owner of a well-known seafood distributor, say, Smith's Seafood?"

"Ahh, you're playing *my* type of game now," she purred. "That's exactly who I mean. That Frank Smith is a handsome man; he comes in here whenever he's in town. But *not* with our Miss Janet."

We both turned and looked over at where Janet sat. Noel saw me, and gestured me over. I picked up my drink and went over to sit beside Chef.

"Guess whose birthday it is," Noel said to me. I was happy to see that his wife had not let him leave the house in his dirty chef's coat. His hair was freshly washed and combed and he wore an oxford button-down shirt and tan trousers and he almost looked like the accountant he used to be.

"Whose?" I asked.

Noel indicated Janet with his cigarette, and I turned to congratulate her. Janet was in a good mood tonight, and when I ordered her a Woo-woo shooter, she threw back her blond hair and gulped it down in one swallow.

"Wooo-ey," she said, laughing.

"It'll be our fifteenth anniversary next month," Noel said to me out of the side of his mouth.

"How wonderful!" I said, and turned to congratulate Lisa, who was talking to Janet.

"Shhh," Noel said quickly. "I'm throwing a surprise party, so don't say anything, okay? Do you think she'll like it?"

"I'm sure she will," I assured him. "She's lucky to have you."

"No," Noel said feverishly. "I'm lucky to have her. My ex-wife was such a witch, she really was. I don't know what I'd do without Lisa."

"Fortunately, I don't think you'll ever have to find out," I said, smiling.

"She's so much younger..." Noel said. "I want to give her the world, but usually all I end up giving her is stuffed salmon and Baked Alaska. Pretty lousy, huh?"

"No," I said sincerely. "I think that's perfect."

Lisa turned at that point and asked me how I was doing, and I told her about the dog I had found. When I told her how skinny the dog was and that he was still limping, her slender face tightened with anger. "People can be so cruel," she said, tears filling her eyes. "It was nice of you to take him in. Have you been able to find his owner?"

I told her about putting the ad in the paper, and she nodded her head in encouragement. "Sounds good," she said. "Just call me if you have trouble finding him a home. I might be able to help. Though Noel says our house is starting to resemble a zoo, I know he wouldn't be able to say no to one more." She reached across the table and took her husband's big hand in her two small hands, and the look he gave her was so filled with love and adoration that I had to look away.

Lisa turned back to me. "Noel's really very patient with me. I just can't seem to turn away animals. It was like this in Maryland, as well, but we lived in a condo, and it was harder to have as many animals."

"You and Noel always look so happy together," I said, trying to ignore Chef whose voice was getting louder, his hand gestures wider.

"We're going to celebrate our fifteenth anniversary next month," she said proudly. She was still holding Noel's hand, her fingers entwined in his. "He throws a surprise party for me every year on our anniversary," she confided to me, her eyes twinkling. "He started it when we'd only been married a couple of years, back in Maryland. I still act surprised, every year. He says we'll celebrate in the Caribbean when he retires, but I would be just as happy staying here."

"You must miss Maryland, after living there so long."

"Not really," she said, glancing at her husband, but he wasn't paying attention to our conversation. "We have a lot of bad memories there. I'm so proud of what Noel has been able to accomplish here in such a short time. Banquet chef, and he hadn't stepped foot in a kitchen for twenty-five years!"

"That'll teach those bastards in Mary-land," Noel roared, hearing her last words.

Lisa just smiled.

I was still on my second drink when I made my way back to my stool at the bar. I waved hello to Jarred Kent, who was setting up his Karaoke equipment.

"You going to sing?" he called to me over the noise of the crowd.

"What do you think?" I called back.

"One of these days..."

I reached Susan and sat down. Chef was busily talking on the telephone, covering the mouthpiece as if he were afraid someone would hear him.

"Probably calling for his fix," Susan said disapprovingly.

I looked over at Chef and saw his bloodshot eyes and trembling hands. "My God, is he addicted to something?" I asked in astonishment.

Susan looked at me with wide eyes. "Well of course he is. Everyone knows that," she said, a tad bit reproachfully. I had fallen behind in our gossip game.

"What...what is he on?" I asked weakly.

"I don't know, heroin, cocaine, whatever. Probably cocaine, it seems to be all over the beach these days. The kitchen manager at the White Gull got busted for distributing it just the other day."

I nodded, because I *had* heard that. I was shocked, and a little bit disappointed. I had just started to like Chef, and he was an addict. I don't know why it bothered me so much, but it did.

"It's always been amazing to me," Susan was saying, and I looked at her blankly.

"What has?"

"That Chef and Noel get along as well as they do. Noel should have gotten Chef's job, you know. But Jerry finagled his friend Chef into the position and Tom Peterson is just enough of an idiot to fall for it."

I looked over at Noel, who was laughing and joking with his gorgeous wife and Janet.

"I guess he's just one of those lucky people who doesn't feel bitterness," Susan said. "I don't know him too well, though I hear his wife's a doll."

I said nothing, though I knew that Noel was capable of feeling great bitterness toward the corporation in Maryland who had screwed him out of his retirement. Perhaps he had not felt qualified to take over the executive chef's position. He probably wasn't, for that matter.

It was getting late, and I had paid my tab when Mac showed up to pick up Chef. They left, and I noticed that Chef didn't bother to pay his tab.

"Well, I guess he got his fix," Susan murmured, as I gathered up my purse and car keys.

"What do you mean?" I asked.

"Why, Mac, of course," she said. "Mac supplies Chef with his drugs."

CHAPTER FOURTEEN

Jinx and Bobby

I had the nightmare again that night. It was the same as always, because it was a real night I dreamed about, a night that I could never forget.

I had stopped by the 7-11 to buy a pair of panty hose. I was on my way to a Christmas party at the restaurant where I worked, and as I was getting in my Jeep, my hose had snagged on a pencil I had dropped carelessly on the seat the day before.

It was seven o'clock on a warm and balmy California night, and I thought about Dave, who had left me a note telling me he wouldn't be attending the party, after he promised last night he would. I pulled into the 7-11 that I often stopped at on my way home from work for milk and bread. I had bought the Jeep only the previous fall, and it still needed a lot of tender loving care.

As I came into the store, I smelled the unmistakable aroma of chili and cheese burritos. In the back of the store, a flashy young man in a designer silk shirt and stylish crew cut was studying the microwave. The woman cashier beamed at me, flashing a loaded silver smile. A little boy and his mother were in the store, the woman wearing dark black sunglasses.

"We need *two* bags of Puppy Chow," the little boy insisted. "Spots is growing fast."

I smiled and went down the aisle with toothpaste and aspirin and deodorants, and found the pantyhose eggs. I fumbled through the eggs, searching for my size and color.

I didn't see them enter.

Later, during the trial, I saw the store video of that night. I saw the two young men enter the store, one sallow-skinned and dirty with blond dreadlocks, pulling at his companion's arm, whispering urgently to him. Even though we can't hear what he's saying, I can imagine. "Come on man, it's not cool, there's too many people, *it's not cool.*"

But Bobby Little, in a black leather jacket and bald head, was too strung out to care about anything but getting money to soothe his aching need. He pulled out a gun and pointed it at the Mexican clerk and said thickly, "Money." His hand was shaking so bad it was a toss-up whether he was aiming at the clerk or the slurpee machine beside her.

"It's not cool, man," said Jinx, the sallow-skinned young man, who I found out later was only nineteen. He had pulled out what looked like a small machine gun, and was training it at the store at large. He had his back to the glass doors, and he kept glancing over his shoulder.

"Money!" Bobby screamed, and he frightened the woman clerk so bad that she slammed the cash register door shut. Bobby leaned over the counter and stuck the barrel of the gun in the woman's throat. "Do that again," he said quietly. "Your head will be all over the next aisle."

When Bobby had pulled the gun on the clerk, I was coming toward the counter to pay for my two pairs of panty hose– you can never have too many pairs of panty hose. The flashy young man had just taken a bite of his burrito. Andy Gray was directly across from me, rifling through the donut section while he juggled his bag of Puppy Chow. His mother was in the back of the store, dithering over one percent or two percent milk.

When Bobby pulled his gun, Andy Gray and I were less than ten feet from him.

"Bobby man, a cop just pulled up. Bobby, it's all going to shit!" Jinx moaned.

At this point Andy Gray lost his nerve. He had stood quietly through the screaming and the gun waving, but now he said softly, "Mommy."

"What?" Bobby screamed, turning toward the little boy. "*What did you say, you little faggot?*" He had completely forgotten about the cashier and the money drawer.

"Bobby, man," Jinx said, nervously spitting dip spit on the

floor and moving to stand behind a column. Now blue and red lights washed through the glass plate windows.

"I heard what you said," Bobby said, and I wasn't sure if he was talking to Jinx or Andy Gray. He raised both hands to steady the gun and pointed it at Andy Gray's head.

Without thought, I took one step forward and shoved the little boy down on the floor behind me. I think I had intended to fall down on the floor with him, or maybe I had meant to jump to safety on the other side of the counter. I don't know. Instead I stood and watched as Bobby Little pulled the trigger.

"Don't shoot the chick, man," said Jinx. To my mind it almost seemed casual, but in the tape, he is screaming.

The bullet sailed toward me, as I stood there motionless, frozen. And then it was past and behind me the glass door of a refrigerator holding cans and bottles of soda drinks exploded. Brown foaming liquid began spreading across the floor, and I found out later that the flashy young man who had dropped to the floor on seeing the gun had lain there as several gallons of pop soaked his designer silk shirt.

"All righty," said Bobby Little to me, and I saw dancing in his eyes mad glee and childish excitement. I stood there motionless, unable to move. He took three steps over to me and hit me in the face hard enough to break my cheekbone. I fell on the floor on top of Andy.

Then he pumped two bullets into us.

One lodged in my side and stayed there. The other grazed my arm and buried itself into Andy Gray's lung.

Bobby would have continued shooting. I know, because I saw it in his eyes.

But several police officers burst into the store and shot Bobby at almost point blank range. He fell on the floor, his face inches from mine. I watched as blood bubbled out of his mouth, and he choked horribly before his features went slack and he was dead.

I closed my eyes.

I opened my eyes. I lay in my bed in South Nags Head nineteen months and three thousand miles away from the incident. I got out of bed and turned on the light. In my briefcase was *People* magazine, which I had picked up in Virginia. I hadn't looked at it.

I flipped though the magazine and found the article about Henry Gray's new movie. There was a full page picture of

Henry, sitting in his kitchen and looking pensively out the window while stroking one hand down the back of his lanky greyhound. On the facing picture was a smaller picture of me and Andy Gray.

I stared at the picture. My hair was down around my shoulders, my face fuller, the name under the picture different. I wore glasses now, though my vision was twenty-twenty.

It didn't look like me.

Andy Gray was the son of Henry Gray, the mega-star of countless karate movies. Of course you've heard of him. I had, but I had no idea that the little boy in the store was his son. The picture in the magazine was a formal photo shoot that Andy and I had done at Henry Gray's insistence a couple of months after the shooting. My face is healed, but I have a haunted look on my face, as if I had spent too much time looking over my shoulder. The question is whether I was looking for madmen with guns or reporters. Andy Gray sits cuddled in the crook of my arm, small for his six years, with bronzed skin and shiny black hair. In the picture he is wearing the portable respirator. He could have taken the picture without it, it was mainly for emergencies, but the photographer had wanted him to wear it.

It had been one of those flukes that happen in the media sometimes: an ordinary person is pushed briefly into the brutal spotlight of the very famous. OJ's Kato Kaelin, Monica Lewinsky and JonBennet's parents have also known that life-changing, soul-withering sudden attention.

It was partly because it was close to Christmas, and the story of the ordinary restaurant manager from Palo Alto saving the son of Henry Gray was a feel-good story. The fact that Henry Gray and his wife Donna were going through a particularly nasty, public divorce at the time didn't help matters.

For whatever reason, the day after that December night when I shielded a little boy's body with my own, I woke to national media attention. The woman who was credited with throwing her body in front of a bullet to save Henry Gray's son was front page news, and everyone wanted to know everything about me.

I don't understand how movie stars and other public figures survive the constant spotlight. It almost killed me. It wouldn't have been so bad, I don't think, if Henry Gray and his wife were not going through their divorce. But one of the gossip magazines started the rumor that Henry Gray and I were having an affair, and that I had been stalking his wife, which was the reason I had been in the 7-11 at the time of the shooting. And that was the end of my privacy for a long time.

The publicity had ruined my life. My entire life, my marital problems, my job, and my singing had been laid bare for public view.

Six months later, the media had forgotten me, but by that time, my husband had cheated on me, and I was in the throes of a very quiet nervous break down.

Soon after, I packed up my Jeep and left the state. Goin' to make some dreams come true.

I flipped through the pages of the magazine and found that I could read about it without too much pain. I had told my mother the truth. I was getting over it.

As I put down the magazine, my thoughts returned to the incident on the roof, where once again I had faced my own mortality. And the memory that had been bugging me clicked into place. I might not know who had tried to push me off the roof, but I did know something: I knew who *hadn't* tried to push me off the roof.

As I was walking down the back hallway that afternoon, I saw Mac in front of me, swaggering along in a cut-off T-shirt that showed his tattooed arms, jeans hanging around his waist and jangling with change and keys.

"Hey Mac," I said, and he turned around to give me a huge grin.

He waited for me as I walked up to face him. "Tell me," I said, "what in the world do you do with all that stuff you take from here?"

His face went blank. "What?" he asked carefully.

"You know, the steak knives, the glasses, the plates. What do you do with them?"

"Just shut up, Callie," Mac said, and I saw anger flicker in his eyes. "You don't know what you're talking about."

"Oh but I do," I said, and reached into his pocket and grabbed his keys. Thankfully his pockets were big and baggy. I pulled them out, and breathed a sigh of relief when I saw the shining, newly-made food and beverage key.

"What are you doing with this?" I asked. "Chef make you one too?"

"So I've got a key," said Mac. "So what?"

"It's not just that," I said sweetly. "I saw you run away the other night when you stole the steak knives. Oh, I wasn't sure who it was, but you and Jerry were in the lobby, waiting for a cab that took forever to get there. What did you do? Tell Jerry you were going to the bathroom and run upstairs to the storage room? I guess I really don't understand why you would steal all that stuff, but I never said I understood the criminal mind."

"You've got no proof," Mac snarled.

"Well, I do know that you took a vacation in March, and that the stealing stopped for that one month. That's kind of a coincidence, don't you think? And I bet if I called the police, they could figure out where you've been selling the stuff. Kind of nasty, and you're still on probation, aren't you?"

I felt high, as if I had injected something into my system that made me feel euphoric and crazy. Looking at the magazine had left me feeling invulnerable.

Yes, I was crazy.

"So what do you want?" Mac asked, glancing around to see if anybody was nearby.

I pulled him by the arm into the small hallway with the walk-ins. I pointed at the freezer. "Darryl Menden," I said.

Mac looked surprised, and then something like fright slid over his face. "You don't want to be asking these questions, Callie," he said quietly.

"What do I have to lose? Somebody already tried to push me off the roof. I know it wasn't you, because I remembered last night that I heard your voice to the right of me, talking about dropping a Corona bottle on someone's head, right before somebody pushed me from behind. So it couldn't have been you. But I don't have anything to lose, Mac, somebody tried to kill me and I'm not standing still." *This time.*

Mac stared at me, and the ring in his nose flickered with the light of a faulty fluorescent light above us.

"So tell me about Darryl Menden and the freezer," I said.

"We put him in there," Mac said finally, "until he would agree to leave. Eventually he did."

"Yeah," I said, "after he had gotten frostbite in his fingers. What, did you forget you put him in there?"

Mac just stared at me. "You don't know what you're getting into," he said. "You really don't."

"How did you convince him not to tell anybody about the freezer?"

"Darryl was convinced that we were not kidding. He's got a beautiful wife," Mac said.

"Oh you threatened his wife?" I was disgusted. "Big man, to threaten a man's wife. What about the fisherman I saw you talking to? Who is buying black-market seafood, and why?"

He was silent. Then, "I thought you might have heard something. That little bastard is not supposed to come here."

"Why, Mac?" I pressed. "I'm sure the police would be interested in—"

"To replace some stuff, okay? Sometimes we get some cheap stuff to use."

"Is that what happened New Year's Eve?"

Mac said nothing, but I could see the truth in his face.

"Okay, so why do you need the black-market stuff, and who's buying it? You?"

"No, not me," Mac snapped. "I'm just a line cook. I do what I'm told. And I'm not going to tell you another thing. Look, Callie," he took a step toward me and looked down at me. Incredibly, he was smiling. "I like you. You're a cool lady, even if you are a big boss. But you got to understand, this is a hell of a lot bigger than you think. It's dangerous."

"So why do you do it?"

"It's easy money, okay? And I need money."

"What do you do to earn this easy money? Lock people in the freezer? Steal boxes of knives? Buy black-market seafood? What's going on, Mac? Who's paying you? Frank Smith?"

"No, not Frank. Just leave it alone, okay? I didn't know about the roof, no one said a word about you almost going off the roof. I don't like that at all, and I'll make sure it doesn't happen again." He was full of bravado, but I could sense underlying unease. "Okay, are you happy? I'll make sure you're safe, you just need to leave it all alone. Don't worry, the food costs will come in under the cap, and you will get your bonus."

He turned and walked off, leaving me feeling as if I had completely lost control of the situation. I opened my mouth to stop him, but then thought better of it. I was struck by the fear in his eyes, and the statement, *This is a hell of a lot bigger than you think.*

Even stranger was Mac's last statement about the food costs and bonuses. The last person I would have expected to know anything about food costs and manager bonuses would be this colorful, often lazy, line cook. He wasn't a manager, he had no reason to be concerned with the bonuses. So why was he so familiar with them?

Jerry came around the corner of the hall with keys in his

hand. He stopped when he saw me. "Jesus, Callie, you look pretty bad. Are you feeling all right?"

I realized I was standing in the short hallway, staring at the freezer as the fluorescent light flickered above me. I also realized that Jerry and I were alone down here, and that I was frightened. I had lost trust in everybody around me.

"What's wrong, Callie?" Jerry asked as I backed away from him until my back was against the wall. The concern in his voice had twisted into something uglier, and I realized that, like a dog, he had scented my fear. He advanced on me until I had backed into the wall.

"I've been meaning to talk to you," he said, and I forced myself to gaze up at him without blinking. Not for the first time in my life, I hated that I was short.

"About Chris," Jerry continued. "I think it is imperative that the waits undertake a thorough training course — perhaps two weeks — before they start working, and are educated in the finer points of food and wine. We can't afford to have one of them making the stupid mistakes Chris has been making. He doesn't understand the work and effort that it takes to create an outstanding dish — all aspects, the taste, the texture, the presentation. All of it's important. The front of the house just isn't educated enough to understand our difficulties. I might not make a whole lot of money here, but I still take pride in my job," he said, and I relaxed a fraction. This was a familiar argument.

"*None* of us make a whole lot of money on this beach!" I said angrily. "But you chose to live here, and so did I." I lit into him, angry that I had felt that instant of fear, and that he had exploited it. "First of all, the waits don't have to go to school to become certified servers, so of course they are not as educated about food and beverage as you are. Second, most of them are not in this as a career, so there is no reason for them to be as dedicated as you are. Third, in case you haven't noticed, we have been going through waits like toilet tissue, no thanks to the way you and Chef treat them. If you think I have time to train each wait for two weeks before I even know if they're going to stay for the week, you're insane!" My voice had risen, and I advanced on Jerry until now it was he who was backing up. I was angrier that the situation warranted, I knew, but my anger felt good.

"Callie," he protested, and the dominating posture had gone out of his face and body.

"Look," I said. "I understand that you are a highly-trained chef who has been classically trained and worked in wonderful, highly-expensive restaurants. That's great. But *you've* got to understand that the waits are not perfect, and most of them have no desire to be professional servers. This is not to say that I will not work with them as much as I can to make them good servers. I have and I will. Are we clear?"

Jerry was staring at me perplexed, as if he could not understand my aggression. "Okay, Callie," he said easily. "As long as you agree to work with them more. I saw Luigi wiping off one of my plate designs before he left the kitchen."

Ah, and now we got to the root of the problem. *This* is what had been bothering Jerry.

"I'll talk to him," I promised, and turned to walk from the hall.

"Did you hear the hurricane's heading this way?" Jerry asked.

CHAPTER FIFTEEN

The Hurricane Cometh

"You better go to the liquor store while you can," Chef said when I came into the office the next afternoon.

"I went by the grocery store and picked up some water, batteries and canned foods," I said. "I figured I was well and truly prepared for the emergency."

"Nope," Chef said. "The liquor store's imperative. If they evacuate, they'll probably declare a state of emergency and close down the liquor stores and the bars. Do it every damn time. And what's a hurricane party without liquor?"

"Ah," I said, looking out the window at the parking lot. It was a hot and sunny day, but driving to work today I could feel the tension in the air. Tourists with out of state plates drove along the Beach Road, craning their necks to look at the ocean and sky. But the ocean was as quiet as baby's breath, humming softly as it splashed gently ashore. The sky was cloudless and a bright summery blue. The weather was absolutely perfect for a summer vacation on the Outer Banks.

Except for the hurricane steaming up the East Coast.

"The last projection I saw, they've got it aimed at the middle of South Carolina," Jerry said as he came in the office. "Ray said people have been canceling reservations for this weekend, and a bunch of people have already checked out. Those are the ones who know how bad the lines to get out of town are."

"I can't believe there's no shelter actually on the Outer Banks," I said. "Where do we go?"

"We come here," Chef said. "Everybody does."

I still was hesitating about staying in a hotel on the ocean with a Category Four hurricane heading up the coast. "I don't know," I said.

"You don't have a choice," Jerry said a little bit maliciously. "The restaurant has to stay open."

"For who?" I asked incredulously. "The tourists are required to leave, right? So who are we staying open for, the staff?"

"Nope," Chef said. "The media. They flock down here as fast as the tourists are flocking out. It's great news, you see, to cover the hurricane as it hits."

"Ugh," I said. "Well, it looks like it's going to hit South Carolina, so we won't have anything to worry about."

"We'll see," Chef said darkly.

I had had plenty to think about the night before, while I took the dog for a walk along the increasingly restless ocean and played swing the Venetian blind string for Ice.

I had already decided that Mac hadn't been the one to push me off the roof. The memory was very clear: I had heard his voice at least ten feet to the right of me when I felt the hand in my back. Chef and Jerry had been on the roof for sure, and I wasn't sure who else. So all I knew was that Mac wasn't the one to actually try to push me off the roof.

However, he knew who it was, and he wasn't telling me. He had said that he hadn't known that the person had tried to push me off the roof, and that he would make sure that it wouldn't happen again. But he hadn't sounded too sure of what he promised.

In a roundabout way, Mac had admitted to stealing from the hotel. He had confessed that somebody was buying black-market seafood to "replace stuff." Replace what and why? And finally, he had indirectly confirmed my suspicion that black-market seafood had caused the New Year's Eve disaster, when several people became sick from tainted seafood.

I still felt in the dark about why everything was happening. It had something to do with food costs and black-market sea-food. I thought about Darryl's notes on the manila folders.

I was in danger because I had been poking around, asking questions. Darryl Menden had been locked in the freezer until he agreed to go, peacefully. Mac had helped in that. Now someone had almost pushed me off the roof. It seemed that the person was getting more desperate. Why?

That night was slower than a normal Friday in July. Everybody's eyes were glued to the weather station on the TVs, the volume turned up so everybody could hear. The great curling mob of clouds inched its way closer to the North Carolina coast.

"I think we should leave tonight," said a woman to her husband. "We can beat the rush. I heard that we might have to wait in line for eight or more hours if they order an evacuation."

"But I'm going fishing on the charter boat tomorrow!"

An older woman came up to me and pulled me firmly by the arm to her table, where her husband in a wheel chair waited, looking disgruntled. "Tell him it's safe to stay," she ordered me. "The hurricane isn't going to hit here. This is our first vacation in over five years, and I don't want to go!"

Everywhere guests were concerned, upset and angry. Oh yes, and there were always those fine people who took their frustration out on the people around them.

"I think it is absolutely despicable," the woman announced as she marched into the restaurant. She wore a bright green tank top and glowing orange shorts with sunglasses perched atop her curly brown hair. "Absolutely despicable."

"And how are you doing tonight?" I said, as a group of brightly-dressed people followed her in.

"I'm never staying in this hotel again," she told me.

"I'm sorry you're unhappy," I said. "How many for dinner?"

"Five. Smoking. Window seat, and don't put us by any children, there were too many of them in the pool. There ought to be a law. Your front desk man just informed me that if a mandatory evacuation is ordered that everyone must leave the hotel. That is despicable!" She liked the way the word rolled off her tongue. "I've paid for the week!"

"I'm sure they will give you your money back," I said, gathering the menus, and ignoring Jen the hostess who was staring at the woman in fascination.

"Of course they will!" she snapped. "That's not the point. The point is I had planned on staying here, paid my money, and they are going to try to force me to leave. It's unconstitutional. They'll have to drag me out of here kicking and screaming."

"Ma'am, there's a Category Four hurricane heading this direction with winds blowing one hundred and forty miles per hour. The hotel can't be responsible for people in the hotel."

"I paid my money!" she almost yelled. "They'll have to drag me out of here kicking and screaming!"

"Hopefully it won't come to that," I said. "If you will follow me?"

She glanced disdainfully around the half-full restaurant. "It's just too crowded," she announced. "We're going elsewhere."

I went into the kitchen where Jerry and a line cook, not Mac, were working.

"Where's Mac?" I asked casually.

"He called in," Jerry said, biting his lip as he drew a perfect daisy in yellow sour cream on the edge of the plate.

Darn. I had wanted to have another little chat with Mac.

I went to the back of the kitchen to pull a box of bread from one of the reach-ins and saw one of the prep guys carefully peeling and de-veining a pile of shrimp on the back prep table.

"Jesus Christ!" he said in disgust. "Why in the hell can't they order peeled and de-veined shrimp for Bingo Shrimp Night? Every month I go through this. Anyway, if this hurricane hits they'll cancel it anyway, so why am I doing all this?"

I shook my head in sympathy, my glance falling on the Smith's Seafood box on the table. It was 31/35 shrimp, which meant that there was thirty-one to thirty-five shrimp in each pound. This also meant that the shrimp was pretty small, and I sympathized with the prep guy who would be peeling and de-veining a whole lot of shrimp for tomorrow's function.

I grabbed the box of bread and then looked back at the box of shrimp. 31/35... Was that what the 16/20 referred to on the back of manila folder? Shrimp? It was what I had thought of when I had seen the numbers, but I still didn't know why Darryl would be writing it on the back of the folder.

Before I left for home, the projected path of the hurricane had moved further north, closer to the Outer Banks. We were now under a hurricane watch, which meant it was possible that a hurricane would hit in the next twenty-four to thirty-six hours.

"Why do they always wave their hand at the Outer Banks when they're talking about where the darn thing is going?" Margie complained. "Even when the forecast said it's still supposed to hit further south."

"It'll hit Wilmington like it has for the last coupla years," Matt the bartender had said, speedily moving around the bar as the jazzy music accompanying the Weather Channel's "Local Forecast" blared from the TV.

Kim was there when I got home, frantically talking on the telephone. Boxes and suitcases were strewn around the living room.

"I'm leaving," she announced when she put the phone down. "I'm getting out of here before they evacuate us. I've been wanting to go see my friend Scott in Richmond anyway. Work can just deal with it."

And within fifteen minutes she was gone.

I took the dog for a walk, clutching my heavy flashlight and glancing over my shoulder. Across the street from me, a group of teenagers had rented the house for the week, and they were whooping it up. I sighed, and turned back to my house.

I didn't know what to think about the hurricane. I had lived in Virginia, close enough to the ocean and the Chesapeake Bay to have some experience with hurricanes. I had lived in the Florida Keys for the year. I was familiar with hurricanes, though I had never actually been through one.

But the reaction I had seen in people around me was unlike anything I had ever seen. It was a mixture of fear and almost frantic excitement. They dreaded a hurricane coming, but they secretly longed for the excitement of something different. I didn't know how seriously to take it all.

I checked the locks on all the windows and doors and went upstairs to my office. The dog was lying on the couch. I still hadn't received a call about him.

"Don't be getting too comfortable," I warned him. "You'll be going soon."

Ice meowed his agreement and jumped up on the desk. Downstairs, the weather channel was on with no sound.

I pulled out the Easter folder that Darryl had written the numbers and letters on:

SS
430-j
4899-j
6591-a
7542-s
8289-o
7845-n
9102-d
8611-j
9680-f
10421-m

I stared at them for several minutes, but could not make any sense of them beyond the fact that Darryl had been listing months and numbers. Did "SS" mean Smith's Seafood? I turned to the memos and inventories and looked through them. I just didn't see anything unusual. I read through Darryl's memos, keeping in mind that these were Darryl's reports on the chefs to Lily. As far as I could tell, it was all extremely petty.

November 30- *Jerry threw a hamburger at a wait because she asked him to cook it up to the proper temperature.* December 5- *Mac insisted on showing me a ring he had pierced in a very private place.* February 19- *Chef was quite rude to me when I attempted to explain to him the theory behind food costs.* March 15- *Noel yelled at me because I accidentally got a box of shrimp out of a seafood case marked Cater instead of out of a regular seafood case.*

I sighed. No wonder everybody was so fed-up with Darryl. I didn't blame them. The man had been a pain in the butt, though I knew the chefs could give out as good as they got.

I rummaged through my briefcase until I found the copy of the April 6th memo. I re-read it: Darryl had complained about high pricing and high food costs. He was worried about losing his manager bonuses. He said, "I do not mean to be an alarmist, but I feel that there may be a very serious underlying problem causing these symptoms. I am looking into it and will be seeking a meeting with you by the end of the week to inform you of my findings." But at the end of the week, he had left the Holiday House for good. Was that because he had been locked in the freezer for poking his nose where it didn't belong?

I flipped through the rest of the notes in the Easter folder. There were menus going back three years. On a piece of notebook paper, dated this year, Darryl had jotted notes to himself.

Get cappuccino machine up and running

Order carnations

Check supply of linen

Menu price change for BAC Easter Brunch- why not order from Sysco? Cheaper.

BAC. I puzzled over that a minute and then remembered that Darryl had been overseeing a function for Janet right before he had left. Born Again Christians. BAC. Lily had said Darryl had been upset about the increase in the price of the menu and had been bugging the chefs about Smith's Seafood being more expensive. So what? It was common to order a better quality product for a little bit more money. But how had he *known* the seafood from Smith's was more expensive? That implied he had been looking at food invoices.

And then the chefs started complaining he was snooping through their files.

Why had Darryl been looking at food invoices? And did that have something to do with the string of numbers he had written on the back of the Easter folder?

I remembered something and pulled out the empty folder with "Frank-Miami???" and "16/20" written on the back. I had already decided that 16/20 referred to shrimp, but that's not what was bothering me. I turned the folder over and saw "Smith's Seafood Invoices" written on the folder's tab. In Darryl's handwriting. Why had Darryl been looking at Smith's Seafood invoices? It was uncommon for a restaurant manager to keep copies of food invoices. And where had the invoices gone? Had Darryl taken them when he left, but not the picture of his wife?

I sat back, and regrouped.

From my talk with Chef, I knew that the chefs were concerned about the thirty-nine percent food costs, and had taken steps to correct it. Chef had said that the purveyors had raised prices or the waits were stealing. He had as much as admitted that he did not know the exact cause of the high food costs, and that raising menu prices was his method to bring the food costs back in line, whatever the cause.

Did he really not know why the food costs had risen so close to that forty percent cap that would cost the managers their bonuses? Or was he being less than honest with me?

What did the missing invoices from Smith's have to do with food costs? What had been going through Darryl's head?

I looked around my quiet loft office as the house shook a bit in the breeze. I could see the side door from where I sat, and the windows on either side of the fireplace. The dog yelped softly in his sleep and tattooed his paws against the carpet. Ice looked down at him and yawned, his small canines gleaming in the light of my lamp. The Weather Channel pumped out a constant stream of updates, and reels of film from past hurricanes.

Again I felt the house jiggle, which is about the only way I can describe it. If you've never lived in a house on nine-foot stilts it's hard to explain how the slightest bit of wind sets the top floor to waving, and the slightest footstep seems to travel up the timbers to shake the entire house.

There was no wind outside.

I stood up quietly, and went into my bedroom where beside my bed lay the powerful pepper mace, which I had dug out of an old purse after someone had tried to push me off the roof. I walked silently back out into the loft and felt the house shake a little bit more. A shadow passed by the windows. From the outside, the house probably looked mostly dark. The light from the TV was the only light downstairs, and the only light upstairs was the small lamp on my desk.

Downstairs, the dog stirred, and then lifted his head.

He stared at the door. I stared at the door.

One moment passed in sinuous slow motion, and then the door knob moved. First right, then left. Click, click, click as the knob caught on the locking mechanism.

The dog sat up and moved to the front door, sniffing under the edges of the threshold. The knob moved again and the dog barked sharply.

It stopped abruptly. A moment later, I felt the house shake as the footsteps receded across the deck, louder this time, and more careless. At the sound of the footsteps, the dog barked louder, and I came down the stairs and jerked open the front door, a bolt of anger ripping through me that someone would invade my privacy.

On the deck, I looked each way down the road, but the person had disappeared. The dog was on the deck with me, peering out at the night, his tail straight back as he concentrated on the information coming into his nose.

A few moments later, down the street, a car started, pulled sedately onto the road and turned right onto Route 12. It was a dark-colored four-wheel drive; it looked like an Explorer. I didn't know anybody who drove a dark-colored Explorer.

I went inside, locked the door securely, and went to bed.

When I woke, the TV was still on, as I had been unable to sleep without some type of light in the room. Ice lay on my head, and the dog lay on my feet. I tried to move and unanimously they protested in grunts and growls.

"Shush," I said, my attention caught on the TV. The channel was still set on the Weather Channel, and the screen was red. Emergency information was scrolling quickly up the screen.

The hurricane was coming and the Outer Banks were being evacuated.

CHAPTER SIXTEEN

Hurricane Party

"It's perfectly safe," Lily boomed at me over the telephone line.

"Then why are they evacuating?" I asked skeptically.

"A little rain, a little wind. Nor'easters are worse here than the hurricanes. You just wait until this winter. I'm not telling you that you have to stay, oh no, I couldn't be responsible for that. I'm just telling you that the restaurant will get busy as the media starts coming in."

"All right," I sighed. I hadn't really planned to leave, but I hadn't known exactly what Lily, as my General Manager, would say. Now I knew. Guilt trip.

"I'm going to close up the house and I'll be in. I need to talk to Ray and get a first floor room, because I'll be bringing the animals. How long do you think we'll be staying in the hotel?"

Lily laughed, as if I had said the funniest thing imaginable. "No one knows. That's the fun of it. Listen, Callie-girl, you never did get back to me after the other day. We need to talk. I'll see you later today."

"Sure," I said, trying not to show my unease. "No problem."

"Oh, by the way," Lily said. "Did you make it to the liquor store?"

* * *

Hurricane Carrie was headed directly for North Carolina, though still twenty-four hours away at her present speed of twelve miles per hour. But the hurricane had found the warm moist waters of the Gulf Stream and was picking up speed and steam.

Carrie was a tough cookie. It was rare to have such a powerful storm so early in the season. Her current wind speed was close to one forty mph, with gusts to one ninety, and the waves near the storm were forty feet and higher. Her counter-clock wise mass spread ominously across the weather map, and hurricane force winds stretched over a hundred miles in each direction from the center of the storm.

Ever since I had gotten off the phone with Lily, I had been fielding calls from frightened waits and bus boys, telling me they were getting out of town. I had already removed the deck furniture from the decks and stored it and the outside trashcan in the storage room downstairs. Using packing tape I had bought yesterday (when apparently, I should have been going to the liquor store) I taped huge X's across the windows.

Next door, I heard music and hammering, and stuck my head out the door to see my next door neighbor boarding up his windows.

I knew there were other things I should do to the house, but I was running out of time. I packed some clothes, important papers, cat and dog food and the cat's (clean) litterbox into the Jeep. The dog and cat were watching me in silence, waiting to see what crazy thing I would do next.

I looked around the quiet house. It lay still and somnolent under the haze of hot sunshine. I hoped it would still be here when I got back.

Taking Ice in my arms, I whistled the dog out of the house and locked the door behind us.

It took me an hour to get to work, usually a ten-minute drive. Cars lined the roads, escaping from the isolated islands from the south. As a matter of fact, Nags Head itself was not under an order of evacuation. Yet. The emergency plan called for the evacuation of Ocracoke first, then Hatteras, and then moving up toward the northern Outer Banks. Our turn would come later today, but most people were jumping the gun, packing up the vans and station wagons with the sun-burned children, the sandy dog, the beach towels and half-deflated rafts.

Stores and businesses were closed as the staff boarded up windows and removed outside furniture. Messages to Carrie were painted on the plywood which boarded up vulnerable windows: "Go away Carrie, we have no room for you" and "May Carrie be Spineless."

People stood on the side of the road, talking to the people in the cars who had to roll down their windows and turn off the air conditioner to prevent the cars from overheating.

I arrived at the hotel at 3:00, just as the piercing EBS signal came over the radio, sending a chill down my spine.

"This is not a test. Repeat, this is not a test."

I turned off the engine of the Jeep, and turned up the radio. All around me, people packing up their cars stopped to listen to the ominous message announcing the Hurricane Warning and ordering a mandatory evacuation of the northern Outer Banks. Across the parking lot, saws buzzed as plywood was fitted to plate glass windows. Horns honked as the line of cars inched down the Beach Road.

And still the monotonous voice droned on, broadcasting doom.

It was a sunny day, calm and clear, but clouds were creeping out of the southeast, and large smooth waves were rolling ashore. I went in the employee entrance, and saw Frank Smith come around the side of the hotel and get into a Buick.

The lobby was a madhouse as people waited in line to check out. Piles of luggage were stacked everywhere, and children darted through the crowd.

Many of the people were frightened, their eyes fixed on the television screen which, of course, was set on the Weather Channel, as there was no local television station. Emergency information scrolled like a ticker tape in red across the bottom of the screen. On the screen itself, meteorologist guru John Hope was sitting grimly at the weather desk, speaking about hurricanes of the past, and the damage a hurricane this size could do.

Some of the people were angry, and as usual, they saw the hotel staff as solely responsible for the weather. I saw the lady from last night in fluorescent pink speaking quietly and menacingly to Ray, and I almost wanted to stay and watch to see if she would be carried out kicking and screaming.

Lily came out of the back and saw me. She gestured me over and handed me an envelope marked "Callie." It was a room key to a room on the first floor.

"Get settled in and come talk to me," she ordered, and disappeared into the back to answer the shrilling telephone.

The first floor was designated the official "pet zone." There weren't many hotels that allowed pets, and we got a lot of business because those people wanting to bring their beloved pet to the beach couldn't get a room anywhere else. I was just glad I didn't have to sneak the animals in.

I moved all my boxes and the animals into the room, arranged the cat's litterbox in the bathroom under the sink, and used the suitcase rack as a barrier to keep the dog out of the bathroom– he had shown an alarming preference for "crunchy treats" from the cat's litterbox.

As I left, the cat had claimed the high ground, one of the double beds, and the dog lay under the table, gazing at me mournfully.

"Okay guys," I said. "Be good."

They stared at me reproachfully, not promising anything.

Jerry was already in Lily's office when I arrived. Jerry had his chin stuck out obstinately, and Lily stared at him malevolently. Today she was wearing shades of blue, and bright pink pumps.

"They're the *news media,*" Jerry was saying as I came in. "They might just mention the wonderful food we're putting out even in the midst of the hurricane."

"Okay Jerry," Lily said, "but remember we're working with a limited staff, mainly managers. Do you really think you can put out the full menu with just the managers staffing the restaurant?"

"Yes," Jerry said, his chin sticking out even further from under his baseball cap. "I do. I've even got some ideas for a few specials. A Hurricane Seafood Platter–"

Lily threw up her hands. "Do what you want, but I better not hear any complaints. Callie, I assume you know that you have no staff and that we will soon have a full contingent of journalists in the hotel with no where else to eat?"

I nodded. Kate, my p.m. supervisor, and one of the waits were the only restaurant staff staying through the hurricane.

"We'll do our best," I said. Outside the office window, I could see two news trucks setting up satellite dishes as the last of the tourists waited to pull out of the parking lot.

"I know this is your first experience with a hurricane on the Outer Banks, Callie. Hopefully it won't be too bad. This hotel has stood here for almost fifteen years; it's got a concrete frame and a thirty-foot dune between us and the ocean. We should be just fine, but of course all the guests will be leaving for their own safety. That reminds me–"

She slid a piece a paper over the desk to me and tossed a pen to me. I refrained from commenting that the phrases "we should be just fine" and "the guests will be leaving for their own safety" didn't seem to jibe.

I read over the sheet, a waiver of my rights for any legal recourse if something happened to me while staying in the hotel during the storm. I signed it, without comment.

"In the past and with lesser hurricanes, we've allowed those guests who wanted to stay through the hurricane to sign this waiver. But not with this one. Everybody's leaving for this one. So the only people who will be in the hotel will be staff and media."

Jerry was impatiently tapping on his chair arms with the tips of his fingers and Lily broke off to stare at him. He stopped.

"Everybody will be eating in the restaurant, as they won't be able to go anywhere else. They'll probably want to interview you, they usually do interview one or two of the staff. That's fine, just be as upbeat as possible."

I nodded, feeling my stomach clench with dread. What had I got myself into? I definitely did *not* want to be interviewed. I wanted to stay as far away from television cameras as possible.

"Okay," Lily said, sitting back in the chair and waving a hand at us in dismissal. "I've got a million and four things to do. Jerry, tell Chef and Noel to come in and see me when they get here, will you?"

I went up to the restaurant and started setting up for dinner. Kate and I were working tonight, and Kate hadn't arrived yet. I prepped tarter and cocktail sauce, salad dressings, mayonnaise and mustard, butter and sour cream, hauled ice and cut bread. Jerry was moving around the kitchen, chopping vegetables and singing off-key to the blasting radio.

I went downstairs to the freezer to retrieve bread and ice cream, something I would normally have gotten one of the dishwashers to do for me. But this gave me a chance to check something out.

I shivered as I entered the freezer, and glanced back apprehensively as the door swung shut. I would have propped it open to feel safer, but I didn't want anybody to see what I was about to do.

First, I hauled out the box of bread and tubs of vanilla and lime sherbet ice cream and stacked them on the cart I had brought.

Then I went back inside and looked at the shelves of frozen food. Cases of seafood were stacked neatly together. I examined the boxes, all marked with company names, and the type of seafood inside.

I began randomly peeling away the lids of the boxes marked with Smith's signature. Nothing out of the ordinary; blocks of ice encasing shrimp, bags of scallops, bags enclosing fish steaks.

I looked around the freezer. Three Smith's seafood cases were marked "Cater," and two Smith's seafood cases were marked "Banquet." All five had the date of the function at which they would be used.

The boxes were in the back of the freezer, up on the top shelf. I climbed up onto the first shelf, so I could reach the seafood cases and carefully peeled the tape off the top of one of the boxes marked "Cater." I lifted the flaps away and looked inside.

Five pound blocks of shrimp.

Sighing, I carefully resealed the box with the tape, though I was worried that it would be obvious that I had messed with it. Climbing down from the shelf, I looked back up at the box. I had turned the seafood case sideways as I tried to open it, and it looked out of place. As I climbed back up on the shelf, I noticed that the box had a small red dot on the side in magic marker on the bottom corner. I pushed it back in place and pulled the other two seafood cases out. Neither had the red dot. Hmmm. I jumped down, stuck my hands under my arms and hurried out of the freezer.

That first night wasn't very busy. The weather was still good, though rapidly clouding up, and many of the media people hadn't arrived yet. So Kate and I sat in the restaurant and watched the Weather Channel. In the back, Chef, Jerry and Noel manned the kitchen. I laughed when I went into the back and saw Noel washing dishes with a cigarette dangling from his mouth. He waved merrily to me.

"You know any Shakespeare, Noel?" I yelled.

"Roses are read, violets are blue..." he roared. "Are you ready for the hurricane? I had to leave my Suburban in the garage. I hope it's okay."

"I guess I'm about as ready as I'm gonna be," I said and went into the back hallway where Chef and Jerry were cleaning the dry storage pantry.

"How's your first hurricane?" Chef asked me, looking up when I poked my head in the door.

"Uneventful," I said. "I thought we were supposed to get a bunch of people?"

"It's only the first night," Jerry said cheerfully.

"How long do you think we'll be here?" I asked incredulously. "If the hurricane is supposed to hit tomorrow, we should be home by the next day, right?"

Chef laughed. "We're talking about a hurricane, Callie, they don't run on a timetable like the 5:52 train. She'll get here when she damn well pleases."

I shrugged and smiled. "I guess we don't have anything better to do than wait," I said.

"But we can certainly make good use of our time" Chef said, grinning at me roguishly. "Cocktails at ten in my room."

When I showed up at ten-thirty, the party in Chef's room was already in full swing. Lily grabbed me and pulled me into the room.

"Callie's here," she announced, as if no one else could see me. The chefs were sitting around the table with a couple of the maintenance guys, playing poker. Ray, the front desk manager, had a lei around his neck and clutched a frozen concoction. Several other people from the hotel crowded the room and spilled over onto the balcony.

Janet came in from the balcony and waved at me. I waved back, and Lily pulled me over to the dresser where she insisted that I make myself a drink. I made myself a very weak gin and tonic, as I had to be at work at six o'clock in the morning.

"The Pete called from Colorado," Lily said, "wanting to know if his hotel was going to float away. I told him, if it was we were all going with it!" She laughed uproariously, and I tried not to wince. Was I the only one who was thinking about the damage Hurricane Andrew had inflicted on southern Florida? Granted, Carrie wasn't as big as Andrew, but she was still a powerful storm.

"Callie," Noel called, "do you play poker? Lisa says she'll play if you do." Noel's wife grimaced at me, and I shook my head, mock regretfully. "Nope, I sure don't," I said, and Lisa gave me a surreptitious thumbs up.

"Are you making any progress?" Lily said, under her breath as she speared a cherry out of her drink and chomped on it. She grimaced, and dug into her bag until she found the packet of celery.

I took a sip of my drink while I thought. Could I trust Lily? "Am I right in thinking that all three chefs do the ordering?" I asked, carefully.

Lily glanced at me sharply. "Darryl asked me that not long before he left. Yes, it's true, any of them can order. Usually, Noel orders for his functions and Jerry orders for the restaurant. Chef oversees."

I pondered. Was there any way I could find out who did most of the ordering from Smith's Seafood, and would it prove anything if I did?

"Can you tell me anything about Smith's Seafood?" I said, throwing caution to the winds. There was no way I was going to find out the information I needed if I didn't ask the questions.

Lily pounded a passing housekeeper on the back. "Hey Nell," she boomed. And then to me, "I've met Frank Smith. We've been doing business with him for years, before Chef took over. Never had any problem with him." She looked at me from the corner of her eye. "Anything I should know?"

"What about Darryl and Frank? Did you have any indication that they might have known each other before they met here at the hotel?"

Lily frowned. "Well, Darryl was asking me similar questions about Frank before he left. And I *do* remember Darryl asking Frank if he had ever lived in Miami. It was a weird question, out of the blue, since as far as I knew Darryl had never been to Florida except for that stupid trip to see the Miami Dolphins he was always talking about. Frank looked at him funny and said no."

"He said no?" I was surprised. Janet had said Frank had lived in Florida. But that didn't necessarily mean he had lived in Miami. But why had Darryl wrote "Frank-Miami???" on the back of the folder?

"Is there something you want to tell me?"

I shrugged. "There's nothing definite, just a few ideas," I said, which was nothing but the truth.

Lily patted me on the back. "Go mingle," she ordered me, and I wandered off, already thinking longingly of my bed. It had been a long day.

I mingled for a while, growing steadily more tired, but knowing I would be unable to sleep.

Chef stopped me as I headed for the balcony. "Callie, girl, how you doing? Can I get you a Stoli, drugs, or me? No one ever said I wasn't the perfect host. I stand ready to go that extra mile. What does your little heart desire?"

I held up my drink. "I'm fine, thanks."

"Are you sure? Is there anything I can do to help your state of mind?" He blinked at me and swayed.

It was too good of an opportunity to pass up. "Well, now that you mention it, I've been thinking about Darryl."

"Tore out of here like a whirl wind," Chef commented. "Didn't even say goodbye. Never did like him anyway. Trivial little man."

"Did he talk to you about Easter brunch?"

Chef squinted at me and took a swig of his drink. "We talked about the menu some. He was upset the price had gone up, said we could get the seafood cheaper. Kept going on and on about food costs being high, and we weren't doing anything about it. Caught him going through my desk, like a damned spy. The man was coming unhinged, let me tell you." He leered at me with drug-hazed eyes. Before I could say anything else, he pounced on the passing head of housekeeping. "Oh, Nell, you sweet luscious thing, you! Give me a kiss!"

So, Darryl was worried about food costs, and the high price of the Easter Brunch menu had set him to snooping through the food invoices. He had obviously discovered that Smith's prices were higher than the competition, but what else had he discovered as he looked through the invoices?

I continued on my way to the balcony, and as I came out, Noel and Lisa greeted me warmly.

"We were just talking about Mac," Lisa told me. Lisa had the tendency to mother the kitchen guys, bringing them cookies and magazines, and they all adored her.

"What about him?" I asked.

"Well, he's not shown up for work for the last two days," Noel said, and I could hear the concern in his voice. Noel had always looked on Mac like his son, always trying to steal him away from Jerry into banquets. "He called in yesterday, but he didn't call today."

I looked out over the parking lot. The wind had stiffened a bit, and dead pampas grass skidded around on the pavement. I could hear the constant roar of the surf in the background.

"He probably left town because of the hurricane," I said.

"Maybe," Lisa said. "Jerry said he hasn't been home for two days either."

There were only about fifteen cars in the parking lot, all

parked close to the hotel for safety, plus the trucks from the news stations with satellites extended. My Jeep, hard top in place, was gleaming brightly in the lights of the parking lot.

"I just hope something hasn't happened to him," said Lisa.

Two cars down from my Jeep was a dark green Explorer.

"Who's Explorer is that?" I asked, pointing.

Lisa leaned over the railing, her black hair fluttering in the wind. "I thought I saw Janet driving it when we came. Remember, honey, she waved?" She looked at her husband.

Noel nodded. "Yep, she was driving it this afternoon."

"I thought she had a Cavalier," I said. "Did she get a new car?"

Noel frowned, and shrugged.

Lisa said, "I know," and Noel elbowed her sharply. She turned and looked at him. "I'm sure Callie already knows that Janet has a beau," she said and turned back to me. "I bet Frank from Smith's Seafood lent it to her. She was talking about having trouble with her alternator, and he probably let her borrow his car. He's pretty good about that. Why, last year, he even lent it to—"

I was so occupied with my thoughts that I didn't notice when she trailed off. Frank Smith had lent Janet the green Explorer. The same Explorer, as far as I could tell, that the person watching my house last night had driven.

CHAPTER SEVENTEEN

Back to the Beginning

As I followed Lisa and Noel back into the hotel room, Chef was holding up an empty Stoli bottle in dismay. "The night cannot go on without more vodka!" he announced. "It's only one o'clock, the night has barely begun."

No one paid him any attention

"We've got beautiful women," he said, louder this time, "wonderful company, and no vodka! This won't do."

"I've got a bottle in my room," Jerry said, looking up from his cards, the baseball hat slipping dangerously low over his heavy-lidded eyes. He dug in his pocket and tossed Chef the key. "Room one twenty-nine. Don't let Jesse out."

Chef left, looking as if he were concentrating on putting one food in front of the other.

A few minutes later, the lights blinked a couple of times, and went out. After a few moments, they came back on, and we all cheered in relief.

Janet was sitting on the bed and I went over to sit beside her. She seemed to be in a good mood tonight, humming softly and smiling.

"Callie," she said, "what's up?" She smiled at me, slowly, as if her face was made from melting rubber and she was forcing it into shape.

She was drunk, but so was almost everyone else.

"Nothing," I said, stretching. "I'm not looking forward to getting up at six a.m."

"Ouch," Janet said. "That doesn't sound very appealing."

"So is that a new car you're driving?"

Janet smiled her secret smile. "No, a friend lent it to me."

The phone rang.

"You mean Frank?" I had to shout because someone had turned up the music and everybody was singing along to "American Pie," at the top of their lungs.

The phone rang again. "Where's Chef?" Noel roared over the singing and snatched up the phone.

Janet gazed at me and smiled drunkenly. "I guess it's no big secret. I really like him, Callie. We've been real casual, he just broke up with this other woman so we're keeping it pretty low key. But he makes me so happy. I hope he feels the same way. Sometime I wonder..."

"Wrong number! CNN is staying down the hall!" Noel yelled into the phone and slammed it down, but no one heard him because the Chevy was to the levee.

"I gotta pee," Janet announced and got up. I stared after her thoughtfully. She sounded like a woman in love, the poor thing.

As she came back, the phone started to ring again and she grabbed it up. She listened and said, "I'll call you back." She put down the phone and winked at me as she made her unsteady way to the door.

I went over to watch the poker game which was interrupted several times as people went to the bathroom and then Jerry answered the phone and spent several minutes reassuring Chef's mom that we were all okay.

"It's the third time she's called," Jerry said, shaking his head and putting the phone down. "And my own mother hasn't called once."

I stuck my head outside and saw that the wind was blowing steadily, the flags lining the shops across the street whipping madly.

"Can you feel the energy?" Lisa asked, standing beside me, and allowing the wind to whip through her raven hair.

"Yes," I said, and I could feel it. Electrical energy fairly sizzled in the gusting wind, and in the thick low clouds lit from below by the parking lot lights.

"I'm going to have a heck of a time getting to sleep tonight," Lisa said, resting her head against the doorsill. "I'm tired but I can never get to sleep in strange places. Or when there's too much light, or too much noise, or Noel isn't home... Okay, I just plain have trouble sleeping." She laughed.

"I do too," I said. "I don't even try to get to sleep unless I'm exhausted."

Lisa nodded. "You know they always say that in every relationship you've got the heavy sleeper and the light sleeper. Well, both Noel and I are light sleepers. It can be a real pain, sometimes, let me tell you. I've got our sleeping pills so hopefully we'll be able to just pass out tonight." Lisa yawned and gazed out at the night. "It's hard sometimes, with Noel working such long hours, and never getting to see him on holidays."

"He seems happy," I said, thinking about Noel and his bright red Suburban, and rushing out to be the first at a fire. I looked around.

"Hi girls, did you miss me?" Noel boomed. He came up behind Lisa and put his arms around her.

"Did you find the candy?" Lisa asked him, kissing his cheek affectionately.

Noel held up a big bag of candy. "How could we ever forget Lisa's Teddy Grahams Candy?"

"Teddy Grahams covered with white chocolate," Lisa told me with a laugh.

"Yum," I said.

I ate some of the elaborate hors d'oeuvres which the chefs had prepared for the party and started to think serious bed thoughts. It was almost two o'clock, and I had to be up at six a.m. I looked around the room and realized that Jerry, Lily and myself were the only ones left. Noel and Lisa had left fifteen minutes before, both smothering yawns, and Janet soon afterward.

As I put my drink down and headed for the door, Lily yelled after me, "You're not leaving, are you?"

Jerry gazed at me from under his baseball hat, his eyes all but closed. "You can't leave yet," he said, but it came out sounding like "oooh-can-eat-that."

I waved at them both and let myself out the door. I was only two doors down the hall when I heard the door open and close and looked around to see Lily following me.

"I've got to be up at seven," she said. "I just didn't want to go. But if you're being such a good girl, I guess I will too." She teetered down the hall toward me on her bright pink heels.

We walked in companionable silence and I hit the button to call the elevator. It opened almost immediately and Chef stood wavering in the doorway. He peered at us and smiled.

He was obviously messed up; his eyes dilated and wide, his face slipping uncontrollably from the smile to puzzled bewilderment.

He walked by us very carefully, and Lily and I got into the elevator.

"Mac must be back," Lily said cynically.

I kept my mouth shut. I didn't ask how Lily knew that Mac was Chef's supplier, because I didn't want to admit that I knew.

The dog and cat were waiting for me, meowing and grunting in happiness. I turned the TV on– not to the Weather Channel– and noticed that my message light was blinking. I picked up the phone and dialed the code to access the voice mail.

"Callie, it's Mac. I've got to blow town. Things have got too hot. I just wanted to tell you to watch your back. Gotta go."

I replayed the message and then put the phone down. Mac had sounded... well, he had sounded scared. What had scared Mac, and did it have something to do with his being AWOL the last couple of days? When I had told him about someone trying to push me off the roof, he had said he was going to "make sure it didn't happen again." Had he talked to his partner, and had his partner threatened him? The timing fit, since Mac had disappeared the day after I had talked to him about the roof incident.

The dog started making circles at the door and whining deep in his throat.

"Ugh," I said. "You actually want to go out now?"

He did. Ice sat and washed his paws, smirking at me.

"You shut up," I told him and he looked at me innocently.

I grabbed my mace and my heavy flashlight and whistled the dog outside. My room faced the parking lot, and I had a door to both the inside of the hotel and a door to an outside patio which fronted the parking lot. I felt much safer taking the dog onto the highly-lit parking lot then into the dark blowing sand of the beach.

I sat on the edge of the concrete patio and let my feet dangle over the four-foot drop to the parking lot pavement. The dog ran around the almost empty parking lot, sniffing at the waving bushes that lined the separate rows of parking spaces, and shaking his head madly as the wind whipped his ears around his head.

He suddenly took off for the side of the hotel, ignoring my shrill whistles. I hefted my flashlight and jumped to the pavement, cursing the convenient deafness of animals and men.

But when I got around the side of the hotel and saw that the dog had found the sandy-grassy area the hotel dogs used for a toilet, I forgave him. He finished and we walked back to the room. He made the four-foot leap to the patio easily and I praised him as I shut the door.

I caught a glimpse of brake lights out of the corner of my eye and turned around in my doorway.

The green Explorer turned quickly onto the Beach Road and disappeared out of sight.

Six o'clock came entirely too early. The dog groaned and the cat purred as I sleepily hit the alarm clock with the palm of my hand and lay staring at the ceiling, wishing that I would look at the clock and it would say that I had another couple of hours of sleep.

No such luck. I got up to face the day.

"Going shopping," or going down to the walk-in refrigerators to stock cartons of milk, butters, cream cheese and Danishes is not my idea of fun at six o'clock in the morning. In fact, I could not wait for this hurricane scare to be over so I could go back to my normal life.

As I came out of the refrigerator I glanced down the hall at the freezer, and noticed that the freezer was unlocked. The padlock hung on its peg, the metal bar not attached. I put down the box of butters and cream cheese on the cart and went to swing the metal bar up across the freezer door and lock it. I glanced at the foggy window, and felt a small tickle of fear sneak across my neck. There was something about this freezer...

There was a small empty shrimp box lying against the freezer door, but I left it, suddenly feeling the need to get away, and pushed my cart at almost a run toward the elevator.

The sun didn't rise that morning, at least not that anybody could see. The fifth floor windows of the Seahorse Cafe offered a panoramic view of waves whipped to a froth by the gusting wind, and low scudding clouds. Small squalls were passing over the Outer Banks, delivering quick hard rain showers and flinty punches of wind.

Out beyond the breaking surf, at least ten wet-suited bodies lay flat on boards, waiting for the perfect wave. Every time one of those graceful bodies would rise to his feet on the curling edge of a wave, I would watch, waiting for him to fall, which he inevitably did. Once he fell, I held my breath until I saw his head bobbing in the foam-flecked waves. The wide windows were splattered with salt and rain and it wasn't always easy to make out the head when it reappeared.

I soon stopped watching the suicidal surfers.

From the Weather Channel I learned that a weak stationary front off the coast of North Carolina had slowed down the hurricane, well within striking distance of the coast. Now she sat, swirling over the warm moist waters of the Gulf Stream, gathering strength and waiting for the moment to strike.

That's how I felt, stuck in this hotel with someone who wanted me dead.

Breakfast was busy with just the two of us working, as the hotel staff straggled in, followed by the news media, dripping wet from their news reports delivered out on their balconies. As Lily had warned, I was asked to do an interview, which I refused.

The young woman reporter studied my face. "You look familiar," she said, and I smiled wanly, but she was too busy with her first big assignment to worry about me.

The media were arriving by the truckload, and there were rumors that the bridges to the Outer Banks would soon be closed. The bridges crossed wide expanses of sound and were very vulnerable to high wind and the waterspouts that the hurricane was already kicking up.

All in all, however, the weather was nasty but not yet terrifying. We waited, as Carrie swirled off the coast.

I waited until that afternoon, after everybody had finished in the F&B office and disappeared. Janet was the last to go, and when she did, I closed and locked the door, something that was never done. I closed the blinds on the wet stormy parking lot and drenched reporters and turned to the chefs' file cabinets.

The file wasn't hidden, it was clearly marked "Smith's Seafood." I pulled the thick folder from the file cabinet and carried it over to my desk. Inside were copies of weekly food invoices, listing what food was delivered, stapled together with a copy of the monthly bill which was paid by the accounting department.

I wasn't sure what I was looking for, but I suspected that Darryl had been going through these files right before he had left. What had he discovered? I knew that he had been concerned about the price increase on the banquet he had been working on in Janet's absence. He had been "snooping" in the chefs' files, probably looking into the price increase. Presumably, he had found something, because he had asked Lily questions about Smith's Seafood, and had kept a folder with Smith's Seafood invoices.

I idly flipped through the invoices. Crab legs and lobster and shrimp, oh my, salmon and flounder and scallops, oh my. Lots of seafood. A lot of money paid to Smith's Seafood every month. No surprise there. Seafood wasn't cheap. The hotel had paid them over ten thousand dollars last month. The month before that had been almost eleven thousand. No wonder Frank Smith appreciated our business.

I thought of something else. Was it relevant that Darryl had discovered a discrepancy while he was working on a banquet function? Could this mean that Janet, as banquet manager or Noel, banquet chef, was Mac's accomplice? Or did it mean that Darryl, holding the dual role of restaurant manager and banquet manager for the two weeks during Janet's absence, had had a unique insight into what was going on in the food and beverage department?

I heard somebody go by in the hall outside, and I tensed until he or she had passed.

I looked back at the invoices. In May, the hotel had ordered 9,864; in April 8,371; in March, 10,421. I continued flipping back to the first of the year. In January, the hotel had ordered 8,611.

Wait a minute. I fumbled in my briefcase for the empty Easter folder. On the back was the string of numbers:

430-j
4899-j
6591-a
7542-s
8289-o
7845-n
9102-d
8611-j
9680-f

10421-m

Yep, 8,611 was January, and 10,421 was March. I checked through the invoices to see if the monthly total for February was 9,680, and it was. So why in the world had Darryl been writing down how much the hotel ordered from Smith's Seafood every month?

Unfortunately, the chefs kept last year's invoices somewhere else, so I couldn't check the monthly totals from last year. Or could I?

I suddenly remembered the closet across the hall and the large, ancient file cabinets that I had never seen anybody use. Unlocking the door, I looked both ways and then hurried across to the narrow closet. Opening up one of the huge file drawers, I hurriedly rifled though its contents: menus and schedules dating back five years, old applications, and an assortment of other junk. I tried the next drawer and hit the jackpot. Smith's Seafood with last year's date was snuggled next to Sysco and PYA Monarch folders, and a variety of other purveyors.

I pulled it out and retreated to the office, locking the door behind me once again. I went through the folder, and saw that I had been right; Darryl had been listing monthly totals for some reason. He had gone back to June, when the monthly order total had been a measly 430 dollars. A big hop down from 4,899 in July. I continued back to the beginning of last year. For the first six months of last year, the monthly totals of the food that the hotel ordered from Smith's had been under five hundred dollars. And then in July, the total had jumped to almost five thousand, and had continued to climb to almost eleven thousand a year later. What had happened a year ago?

Darryl had had an idea. But then, he knew something about Frank Smith that I didn't, or why else would he have written, "Frank-Miami???"

That reminded me that I had not heard back from Debbie, and I picked up the phone and dialed her number. While a fresh young voice told me Debbie was unavailable (I had forgotten it was nap time in Debbie's world), my gaze was caught by a number: 16/20.

I had forgotten about that. I left a message with the young woman and looked at the invoice more closely. Fifty-pounds of shrimp: 16/20 p/d, or peeled and de-veined. Hmmm.

Darryl had written 16/20 on the back of the Smith's Invoices folder. I had suspected it had something to do with shrimp, but what?

Oh Lord, I remembered something. I scuffled through the invoices, working my way back from the most recent invoices back. The shrimp was all 16/20, peeled and de-veined.

Now that was strange. Just the other day, I had seen a box of Smith's seafood with 31/35 shrimp. But, according to the invoices, the hotel hadn't ordered any 31/35 shrimp for months. Where had it come from?

I put the folders back in the appropriate file cabinet and opened the door and the window shade. I sat back down at my desk and stared thoughtfully out the window at the pampas grass whipping at the window, and the raindrops slicing across the parking lot.

Well, this wasn't getting me anywhere. I had work to do. I picked up a pen and wrote the date at the top of a memo I planned to write about tardiness— it was July 9th. I stopped and stared at the paper until the lines blurred together. After a while I pulled out my briefcase and flipped it open to my appointment calendar. A few days ago, as I talked to Debbie, I had written in a phone number under today's date.

Picking up the phone, I dialed the number.

He answered.

"Dave," I said. "It's me."

Silence. Then, incredulously, with joy in his voice. "Laurie? Is that you?"

"Yes," I said, and was unable to say anything else.

"Where are you? Are you staying with Debbie? I had the feeling you've been with her all along, down there in the Keys." His voice was rich and warm like hot chocolate, just like I remembered it. It was hard not to fall under its spell, and easy to forget all that had happened. I closed my eyes, and clenched my hand whitely around the phone.

"No," I said, and my voice sounded calm. "I'm not staying with Debbie. As a matter of fact, I'm in North Carolina."

"North Carolina," he repeated. "What are you doing there? You know, I've had reporters calling me because of that article in *People*. Give me your phone number and I'll give it to them—"

"Dave," I said, "if you ever loved me, please don't tell anybody what I just told you. I don't want to talk to them."

Silence, as he tried to grasp what he had not been able to after the shooting. That I was not flattered by the publicity, that I didn't want to give interviews or sign autographs. *I don't un-*

derstand! He said it by his silence, but he had at least learned enough not to say it out loud.

"How are you, hon?" he asked, and the concern and love washed bright and warm over me.

"Just fine," I said. "Are you still with Justine?" It was amazing how easily the name rolled off my tongue, as if I were in the practice of inquiring about my husband's lover every day.

Several months after the shooting, unable to cope with my constant depression and jealous of the media attention, my husband had begun an affair with a coworker. It was true that wounds healed over time, but the remembered pain was just as severe.

Now he was uncomfortable. "No, we– no," he said and coughed.

"Oh," I said brightly. "And here I thought she was the reason you had called Debbie. I guess there's no reason to hurry the lawyer along with the divorce papers."

"You know why I called you, Lor," he said.

"Don't call me that," I said. "I've got to be going." Bright and cheery. "And Dave?"

"Yes?" Misery, pure and undiluted, flooded the line, and I almost cried for the love we had had, so idealistic, so reckless, damn the consequences, we had vowed to live on love alone.

"Happy anniversary," I said, and put the phone gently in the cradle.

For a moment I let the memories wash over me, the happiest ones at first because Dave and I had been happy for a long time. We had told one another everything, we had loved and laughed, and I had been happy. I was singing too, then, something I had wanted to do all my life but had been too shy to pursue. But a local San Francisco band had heard me singing, Karaoke of all things, and had asked me to sing back up for them. I thought I had everything, and I did.

The shooting had changed all that.

When Henry Gray and Andy had attended one of our shows after I had healed, the tabloids had again brought up the specter of romance between Henry and me, and they raked me cruelly in a review of the local band. They hounded me mercilessly, and I had given up singing. I just wasn't able to handle the attention, which had nothing to do with my singing and everything to do with whose son I had saved.

The media had staked out my house during the trial, and had discovered something else about me as well. I remember coming out of the courthouse, and the reporter had shoved the microphone in my face and asked me, "Ms. McKinley, what do you think of your husband's affair?"

I had said nothing, and had let myself into Dave's car and sat there in stunned silence as he drove away, his face stricken and petrified.

"Is it true?" I had asked numbly.

"Laurie, I wanted to tell you, it really means nothing, believe me, but you have been so distant lately..."

I tuned him out, and I think that was the moment that I realized that I had to get away.

I had left Dave and California, and my budding singing career and never looked back.

That night, the people were lined up at the doors when Kate and I opened them at five. The media had been put in an awkward position. Hurricane Carrie was not going to make landfall tonight. She might not make landfall for several days. But she was sitting off the coast, producing nasty, if not disastrous weather.

The Media Bigwigs could think of better things for their reporters to do than sit in a hotel and film a hurricane which at the moment was only kicking up high surf and gusting winds. However, the bridges were only a telephone call away from being closed, and once that happened the media would not be able to get back on the beach if the hurricane suddenly changed her mind and devoured the Outer Banks. So the reporters waited, enjoying an unexpected vacation.

And using their expense accounts.

"Where is everybody?" I said to Chef as the first orders started flowing in, and I went back to the kitchen. He was by himself.

"Jerry and Noel are helping maintenance board up windows. Mac was supposed to be here, and I told them I would be fine." Already perspiration was running down his cheeks as the orders continued to beep through on the kitchen printer.

"He hasn't been here for two days. What made you think he would show up now?"

Chef shook his head. "I can't believe he did this to me," he said.

But I was too busy to worry about Chef. Soon people were waiting at the door as Kate and I zipped around the restaurant, taking orders, delivering food, seating people. Lily came into the restaurant and immediately came over to me.

"What can I do?" she asked, quickly. I took in her fresh emerald green skirt and rose-colored coat, all very clean and very vulnerable to grease.

"Look," I said. "Chef needs help. We're really getting behind on the orders. If you can help Kate for a few minutes, I'll go back and help him. We can't find Jerry or Noel. As it is, table forty-three is waiting on a coke, ice tea and sprite, table thirty-one needs bread, table twenty needs another fork, ketchup and cocktail sauce..." I recited over my shoulder as I ran toward the kitchen.

"What do you need?" I yelled at Chef.

Without looking up, he barked, "A million dollars and a shot of tequila. Oh, and plates would be nice. I'm so weeded, I couldn't find my way out with a lawn mower and a weed eater."

I dove behind the dish line and started feeding plastic racks full of plates through the clanking mouth of the dish machine. I had to spray the plates first, and soon I was soaked with dirty dishwater. I picked up the stack of steaming plates and ran them over to Chef.

"Four fried shrimp, two clam strips, five side fries," he said without preamble as I arrived behind the line. In silence I dropped four orders of shrimp into one fryer and the fries into the other. I turned and helped Chef set up plates until the shrimp were floating on top of the oil. I brought out the basket and shook the oil from the shrimp, and deposited them on four plates.

"Six orders of fries, two hushpuppies, three scallops..."

In frantic silence, I dropped the clam strips, dumped the fries into a metal bowl with some salt, shook them, poured them onto the plates, and dropped two orders of scallops into the hissing oil. I reached into the freezer for another bag of fries, but there wasn't one.

"Fries?" I asked.

"Downstairs," Chef said, and wiping the sweat from his forehead. "I didn't get a chance to stock from the freezer this afternoon. Didn't get a chance to give myself a frontal lobotomy when I could have, either."

"I'll go get them. Watch the scallops!" I ducked behind him, running full speed for the freezer and a box of French fries.

"Run Forrest, run!" Chef cried after me.

And this is where you came in.

CHAPTER EIGHTEEN

The Dead Man is *Still* in the Freezer

I kicked aside the empty shrimp box which lay against the feezer door and unlocked the padlock, letting the bar swing down and hit the side of the door with a loud metallic gong.

There was a dead man in the freezer.

It was Mac.

I stopped in shock, my mouth working soundlessly. Jesus Christ, why did things like this always happen to me? And why the hell hadn't I just told the journalists we were out of French fries?

Hot tears burned my eyelids, and I blinked them back ruthlessly.

I stepped forward into the swirling mist of the sub-zero freezer and leaned down to feel the side of the frozen neck, but it was way too late. He was dead. There were bloody icicles hanging from his nose, for God's sake, and I choked back the feeling of nausea that crowded my throat.

"Mac," I said sadly, and moved back, wincing as I accidentally kicked one of his legs and it came unstuck from the floor with a crackling sound.

The back his head was bloody and mushy looking, under the thick coat of ice. He wore a dirty white chef's coat and looked very, very young as he lay with his eyes and mouth wide open. His nose ring had come out and a trickle of blood had frozen on his cheek. His hand touched an upturned steak box lying beside his head, and individually wrapped steaks lay scattered around the body.

Mac, who wrote me love poems and constantly propositioned me, Mac of the tattoos and body rings, Mac was dead. I felt an alarming rush of anxiety, and closed my eyes until it passed.

My first reaction was to run to my office and call the police. But a storm was raging outside, and it would take forever for them to get here, and Chef was upstairs by himself.

Mac was dead and there was nothing I could do to help him. I considered my options and then I did what any good restaurant manager would do, and reached up and grabbed the box of French fries.

Maneuvering with the bulky box, I pulled the metal arm up into place and carefully locked the freezer door.

And then I went upstairs to face my hungry, demanding customers.

At ten o'clock, as soon as we shut the doors, we called the police.

"Yes," Lily said. "This is Lily Thomas at the Holiday House Hotel. We have a dead man in the freezer. Yes, I said a dead man. No lights and sirens, please."

She hung up, and looked at me. We had just trooped en masse, myself, Lily, Chef, Noel and Jerry to look at the body.

"Jesus Christ," Chef had muttered and put a hand to his haggard face.

"Oh God, *Mac,*" Jerry said, and he left the freezer.

"He's dead all right," Lily said, looking up from where she was kneeling beside the body. "Looks like he hit his head." She stood up, and kicked one of the frozen steaks that lay beside the body.

Chef was frowning. "It looks like he was trying to get that steak box down and slipped and fell backward. He probably hit his head on that shelf. Do you think he slipped?" His voice was hopeful, and Lily and I studied the shelf, and then the back of Mac's head. It looked very possible that the metal shelf could have done the damage to the back of Mac's head.

"I sure as hell hope so," Lily said. "This is bad enough with all these reporters in the hotel. This is *not* the kind of publicity I was looking for. But I thought Callie said she *unlocked* the padlock. How could Mac have locked himself in the freezer?"

"The door was locked?" Noel said. "How could Mac—"

"I've been thinking about that," I said. "*I* locked the freezer. This morning at six. Mac was probably in here." I shook my head, trying not to think about Mac lying on the freezer floor, maybe still alive, when I locked the padlock.

"You didn't know," Lily said gently.

We stared at Mac's body, and the box of steaks lying on the floor beside him. Mac had died for a couple of steaks.

We had carefully locked the padlock and went back upstairs to call the police. Jerry had disappeared, but Chef was recovering.

"Why would he steal steaks, for God's sake? Why would he do that?" he asked, but he didn't expect an answer.

On the way up the stairs, Noel's beeper went off, he peered at it and turned it off. "God, I'm going to hate having to tell Lisa about this."

Half an hour later, representatives from what seemed like every fire department on the Outer Banks were milling around the lobby. Reporters were filming the assorted police cars, fire trucks and ambulances from their balconies as the rain streamed down.

"I said no lights, no sirens," Lily boomed. "It looks like World War Three just broke out. Come this way, please." She led a troop of heavy-booted firemen, paramedics and policemen through the offices to the back hall.

I collapsed on a lobby couch and ignored the young reporter's attempt to question me. Around the lobby, staff people were huddled, whispering, and smiling whenever a camera aimed their way.

Dowell, at the front desk, was ecstatic that something was going on. He was talking to a reporter, demonstrating something on the phone, smiling widely for the camera. I got up and went over to the desk.

"He came in last night. I saw him. Mac Tims," he was saying. "M-A-C, T-"

"Uh, Dowell," I said, and tugged at his arm. He turned to me, and I turned my head quickly as the camera panned in my direction. "I don't think you should be talking to the press," I said quietly.

His big face looked baffled, but understanding crept slowly across. "Yeah, right. No comment," he said to the reporter, waving him off.

"What's this about Mac?" I asked Dowell as he wrote carefully in the log book: "10:36– Police arrive to investigate dead man in freezer."

"Oh," Dowell said, opening a pack of M&Ms and stuffing five into his mouth. "Mac called last night, looking for Jerry. I patched him through to Jerry's room, but later, I got to thinking, ya'll were all up in Chef's room. He came in a while later, not through the lobby, he must have come in the door at the end of the first floor. I saw him 'cause I went to get a Coke out of the machine on the first floor. I tried to tell him that everybody was up in Chef's room, but he ducked into one twenty-nine so quick he didn't hear me. So I started thinking–"

God forbid. I kept my expression neutral. "One twenty-nine is Jerry's room, right?"

"Yep. So I called up to Chef's room and told Chef to tell Jerry that Mac was looking for him, and that he was in his room. I was kind of worried, see, 'cause Mac didn't sound too good on the phone."

"What do you mean?"

"He just sounded– odd. Usually he'll talk and kid with me, but this time he didn't even acknowledge me. He sounded like he was in a hurry."

"How did he know Jerry's room number?"

A particularly hard gust of wind beat at the windows of the lobby and Dowell looked around nervously. "He asked, and I don't tell room numbers usually, you know, except that I knew it was Mac, and–"

"I'm sure it's no big deal," I assured him, eyeing a reporter who was creeping closer with notebook and pen in hand. "So you gave him a key to Jerry's room?"

"No! I didn't say that! I don't know how he got into Jerry's room!"

I smiled at Dowell. "Thanks. Just be careful not to talk to the reporters until Lily tells us it's all right," I said, and ducked through the door leading to the hotel offices.

The authorities were tromping around the back, and I went upstairs to the restaurant to finish cleaning. The lights were still on and the Weather Channel still blared from the TV. Carrie dominated the weather map, as the meteorologists tried to decide how long she would be stalled by the stationary front.

I had told Kate to go to bed because she would be working the next morning. I bussed tables, and mindlessly completed the myriad small tasks while my mind was elsewhere. After I finished, I went to my room and romped with the animals, trying not to think of dead bodies or hurricanes or anything much at all. I had just settled down to watch *Cocoon* when the phone rang.

"Callie, would you please come down to my office? Thank you," Lily said, and hung up before I could say anything.

"Sure," I said to the dead receiver.

I put my shoes back on and went down to Lily's office. She was sitting in the office with a rugged looking man in his late forties, graying around the edges and wearing what looked like black combat fatigues.

"Callie," said Lily, "this is Dale Grain, a detective for the Nags Head Police Department. Dale, this is my restaurant manager, Callie McKinley."

Dale offered his hand, a horny, callused handshake. "You're new, aren't you?" he asked pleasantly.

"I've been here two months," I answered.

Dale smiled. "Lily says you were the one to find the body. At about seven, was it?"

I nodded. Uh-oh, here it comes.

But he said nothing about the discrepancy between the time I found the body and when we called the police. Evidently Lily had cleared it up.

Dale took out a note pad and asked me routine question, my name, address, phone number and social security number. Then he took me through my discovery of Mac's body, asking careful, probing questions. I answered as best I could.

"And you say the freezer door was locked?" Dale asked with no expression.

"Yes. But like I already told Lily, I locked the padlock at six this morning. I thought it was strange that it was unlocked, but I didn't think too much about it."

Dale nodded, and I could tell that Lily had passed this along to him.

"It doesn't look like anyone else went into the freezer all day until you found the body," Lily said. "Jerry locked the freezer at ten o'clock last night, and that was the last person who was in the freezer until you found Mac."

"So Mac died between ten o'clock last night and six this morning," I said.

"Well, it makes sense, doesn't it?" Lily said. "He wouldn't be stealing in the middle of the day. So we're thinking that he went in the freezer late last night, to steal some steaks, and slipped and hit his head on the shelf. He had some cocaine on him, and knowing Mac, he was probably drunk as well."

"So it was an accident?"

"At this juncture, it does appear that way," Dale answered easily. "The funeral home will take his body to the medical examiner in Greenville for an autopsy, and we'll know more then. But at this point, it does appear to be an accident."

I nodded. I was relieved to hear that Mac's death was an accident.

"Well, at least we know who's been stealing from us for the last several months," Lily said.

Was it as simple as that? Simple thievery? "I talked to Mac on Thursday, and I think he had an accomplice in the hotel," I volunteered.

Dale and Lily said "Oh?" at the same time.

"I had no proof, but I told him I suspected him, and he admitted that someone else helped him," I said. "He also called me last night and said things were getting too hot and he was leaving town."

"Not surprising if you confronted him about the stealing on Thursday," Lily said dryly.

Dale sighed. "Well, after the hurricane passes, we'll come back and look into the theft," he said. "Right now, we need to get back outside. The storm's getting worse. We should be about done taking pictures, so as soon as the funeral home collects the body, you can have your freezer back."

"That's all?" I asked, a little incredulously. It had been just a little more than two hours since they had arrived.

"We're in a state of emergency, Ms. McKinley," Dale said gently. "Right now, I don't see anything to indicate that this is not an accident. We need to get back out into the storm as soon as possible. As soon as we get the autopsy, we'll know more."

"I have a question," I said slowly.

They both looked at me in surprise. "Yes, Ms. McKinley?" the detective asked.

"What keys did he have on him?"

"He had a key to the freezer, if that's what you're asking," Lily said. "I identified it for Dale."

"But did he have a master room key?"

"No. I saw his key chain. Why?" Lily answered. Dale was listening with interest.

"Because I'm pretty sure Mac must have had a master room

key with him last night. But you said he didn't have it, and that's strange." When no one said anything right off, I said, "You might want to talk to Dowell, the front desk clerk. He saw Mac go into Jerry's room last night."

"Maybe Jerry gave Mac his room key. What does it matter, anyway?" Lily asked impatiently.

I shook my head. "I don't think so. Mac didn't know which room Jerry was staying in when he called about a half hour before he came to the hotel. I'm sure Jerry would have told him which room he was staying in if he had given Mac a key. And Mac didn't come up to *get* the key, because we would have seen him."

Lily nodded. "You're right, Mac didn't come to the party last night."

"And I think I saw the master key on his key ring when I caught him with the new food and beverage key a couple of days ago. But I was so pissed he had the F&B key, I didn't pay any attention. All I'm saying is that Mac probably had a master key. I'm surprised you didn't find it with the body."

"We'll look into it," Dale said. His beeper went off and he stood up. "I'll be right back, Lily. Thank you for your help, Ms. McKinley. I might have some more questions later."

I looked at Lily as Dale went out.

"They've got a lot more important stuff than this to occupy their time right now. You know, the hurricane?" Lily said and shrugged. "I don't see anything to make us think it was anything more than an accident, do you?"

I thought about it. Something was bugging me, but what?

"No, I guess not," I said slowly. Rubbing the side of my glasses, I thought about all I knew. I had Darryl's word that he had been locked in the freezer. I had almost been pushed off the roof of the hotel. Were any of these things relevant to Mac's death?

Almost certainly. I couldn't kid myself. Then I thought about the reporters. And decided to keep my mouth shut, at least for now. If the autopsy revealed murder, then I would tell what little I knew. Until then, for the sake of the hotel, and myself, I would keep my mouth closed.

I got up, glancing down at my watch. "Tell Detective Grain that I will be in my room if he needs me," I said, suppressing a yawn. My body was just fooling with me. As soon as I got to my room I would feel wide awake again.

"Okay Callie," Lily said sweetly, not looking tired at all,

though I knew she had had as little sleep as I had, and had been going all day. "Sweet dreams."

I gave her a dirty look and went up to bed.

Even though I didn't have to work breakfast, I was up at seven. If I didn't watch out my body would start getting used to this early morning thing. I took the dog outside, holding my raincoat against me as I watched him run around the wind-swept parking lot. Thunder rumbled, and lightening forked the sullen sky. The wind had definitely gotten worse; as I watched, the sign across the street began waving madly back and forth and toppled over. I whistled to the dog, and had to fight the wind to shut the door.

I went upstairs to the restaurant where Kate and Margie were jumping like water on a sizzling flat top. I moved around the restaurant, pouring coffee and water, bussing tables. Many of the reporters were talking about Mac, but they didn't sound suspicious. A couple of them were wondering if they could fit his death into the body count, as in, Hurricane Carrie has already claimed the life of a surfer, a heart attack victim who couldn't receive emergency treatment in time because of the flooding, and a dead man in the freezer. Everybody thought it would work out nicely, and make the hurricane sound even more dangerous.

During a lull in the action, I studied the TV. Hurricane Carrie was overcoming the stationary front and slowly pushing north-west. If she speeded up, which she showed signs of doing, she would hit the Outer Banks by midnight.

I shuddered and went into the kitchen.

"I've been covering for you for almost a year, and you don't want to talk about it. You've got to get off the stuff, man, it's messing with you, it's messing with your job. You can't even say you saw Mac last night because you'd have to admit what you two were doing. You saw him last," Jerry was saying as I came in. "I know you did."

"It was an accident," Chef said, "You heard what the police said. And if anybody had a motive to kill him, you—"

They broke off as they saw me. I unplugged the syrup machine and started wiping down the counters. The two chefs stared at me sullenly and went back to breaking down the line. I could smell the alcohol leaking from pores from where I stood.

You saw him last and *If anyone had a motive to kill him, you—* The accusations were starting to fly fast and furious. I remembered that Lily and I had seen Chef the night of Mac's death, stumbling out of the elevator as we left the party.

Mac must be back, Lily had said.

Had Chef seen Mac the night of Mac's death? Dowell said that he had called Chef and told him to tell Jerry that Mac was in Jerry's room. And Chef had gone to Jerry's room for a bottle of Stoli. *You saw him last...*

On the other hand, Chef said Jerry had a motive to kill Mac. What was it?

I finished cleaning and went downstairs. In the downstairs break room, Dowell was holding court among a few house-keepers and maintenance men.

"'Dowell,' he said, 'I'm not in too good of shape. I need to see Jerry.' And I said, 'Mac, I'm your friend, tell me what's bothering you.' But he wouldn't tell me." Dowell sighed dramatically, the Holiday House shirt stretched tight over his considerable belly. Obviously, the story of his brief conversation with Mac had grown larger with each telling. "If only he would have told me, maybe I could have helped him. As it was–" Dowell made a slicing motion across his throat.

"I bet it wasn't an accident. I bet someone killed him," said one of the housekeepers.

I stopped outside the door and listened.

"Could have been one of the chefs," Dowell said, enjoying his instant celebrity. "Or do you think someone came in from outside, one of his drug buddies, and offed him?" Dowell was starting to sound like one of those hard core TV detectives, and I was starting to feel nauseous. "Someone could have come through the loading dock if they had a key. I know they were locked because I always check them early in the night, because a lot of times I think I hear things in the back hallway. But Lily don't pay me enough to go walking back there by myself in the middle of the night."

"Well, he was stealing stuff, right? Maybe one of the chefs caught him at it and..." one of the maintenance men said.

"And terminated him," Dowell said solemnly.

It was almost funny how badly the hotel staff wanted to believe that one of the chefs was a murderer. The chefs did make a lasting impression. I had witnessed the fiasco at meal times when the housekeepers and front desk staff and maintenance men trooped into the kitchen for their one-dollar employee meals. I'd seen Jerry and Chef turn out all the lights and pretend they were holding a seance at five o'clock in the afternoon. I'd seen them carefully pack toilet paper and toothpicks in Styrofoam containers and give them out as employee lunches.

Gorgeous Ray, sculptured arms bulging from his tight shirt came up behind me.

"Hey Callie," he said. "You poor thing, I heard you found Mac's body."

"Hey Ray, hey Callie, who do *you* think offed Mac?" Dowell called out.

"It was an *accident,*" Ray said sharply. "Why are you talking all this trash? There's no reason to think it wasn't an accident."

Or was there?

"The box," I said.

"What?" Ray asked.

"I just remembered something," I said, and left him in puzzled silence.

I walked down the hall and stuck my head into Lily's office. She was sitting at her desk, munching celery, and staring out at the pounding rain.

"Lily," I said. "I think Mac *was* murdered."

CHAPTER NINETEEN

Sticks and Stones May Break my Bones, but Words Hurt Too

Lily turned and stared at me. For the first time I saw signs of exhaustion in her face. She was wearing a neat lemon pants suit, but her hair was springing wild and curly around her face as if she hadn't had time to really comb it, and her makeup had been applied in a hurry. I resisted the urge to brush the extra powder off the end of her nose.

"What?"

"I forgot about the shrimp box. I saw an empty five-pound shrimp box on the floor in front of the freezer at six o'clock in the morning. It was still there when I opened the door at seven that night and found Mac. Mac couldn't have dropped the box going into the freezer, it wouldn't have been up against the door like that; somebody must have dropped it going *out.*"

Lily and I stared at each other.

"That means," I said slowly, "there had to be another person with Mac the night he died. Mac couldn't have dropped the box going in, so someone dropped the box *after* Mac went in."

"Wait a minute. Anybody could have dropped that box by the freezer door. It doesn't mean they went *inside* the freezer and killed Mac."

"Somebody was in the hall by the freezer in the middle of the night dropping five-pound shrimp boxes? Remember, the box couldn't have been there when Mac went in, he would have dislodged it."

"But what in the world would Mac's killer be doing with a five-pound shrimp box? What did he do with the shrimp?"

Lily sounded genuinely puzzled, but it could be an act. Somebody in the hotel had killed Mac, and had already tried to kill me once. And I didn't know who it was. I hoped it wasn't Lily, but how did I know?

Lily sighed, and drummed her fingers on the desk. "What I'd like to know is how that boy worked for us so long and no one knew what a thief he was. The police searched his Suzuki in the parking lot. They found glassware and silverware, bags of dirty linen, *dirty* linen, mind you, and lamps and clock radios. All out of this hotel. So, not only did he have a food and beverage key, he had a master key for the rooms."

"Chef made himself a copy of the food and beverage key, it apparently wasn't hard to check out the food and beverage key and run up to Ace Hardware to make a copy."

"Oh, Chef made himself a copy?" Lily asked, but she didn't sound surprised. "So, where is the master key? Any bright ideas?"

I looked at her.

"Oh Jesus. You think the killer has got it? Great. Now, not only do we have a Category Four hurricane just a hop, skip and a jump off the coast, we have a deranged murderer running around the hotel with a key to everyone's room. That's just wonderful."

Lily looked at me shrewdly and took a bite from her celery stick. "You're not telling me everything, are you?"

I was silent. Finally I said, "I think there are things that everybody's not telling. And by the way, the entire staff thinks Mac's death wasn't an accident. You may want to talk to them about it, or the reporters are going to hear."

Lily chomped on her celery viciously. "When you come out of your little shell you do it with a vengeance, don't you?" she asked bitingly. "Should I just make you general manager now and get it over with?"

She sighed and pushed back in her chair.

"I'm going to call a meeting, this afternoon, one o'clock. Does that make you happy? We'll get things out in the open. I'll call Dale Grain and tell him what you've told me. The shrimp box is pretty flimsy, to tell you the truth. I'm not sure it proves that Mac was killed. But we'll see what he thinks. To tell you the truth, I'm not sure there's anything they can do until this hurricane passes."

I thought about Mac, lying frozen on the floor.

"By then it might be too late," I said, and the wind shrieked through the cracks in the window.

At one o'clock, the skeleton staff remaining in the hotel had gathered in the Heron conference room on the fourth floor. Rain lashed the windows, and the waves were pounding the dunes so hard that even four stories up we could hear the crash. The light was dim and watery until Janet snapped on the overhead lights.

She came over and sat beside me. "I don't know what the point of this is," she said, surveying the motley crew. "I can't believe everybody is so ready to jump to the conclusion that Mac was murdered."

I didn't say anything.

"All right," Lily said, coming into the room. All traces of exhaustion had been scrubbed from her face, and the glaring red lipstick contrasted cheerily with the lemon of her pantsuit. She stood and surveyed the staff sitting at the bare tables, many of them smoking cigarettes.

"I know this is a very trying time for all of us," she began. "I just got off the phone. Hurricane Carrie is expected to make landfall around Hatteras, and move north over Nags Head by midnight. The worst damage will be from the storm surge, which will be between thirteen and eighteen feet. We'll also need to worry about the wind, which is sustained well over a hundred miles an hour. Since we have our nice thirty-foot sand dune and a sturdy concrete building, we should be just fine. The hurricane is still a Category Four, and is a powerful storm, but this old hotel has seen worse." She patted the wall next to her affectionately. "Why, we've seen nor'easters worse than this little storm!"

Everybody laughed dutifully.

"In addition, I've just been informed that the bridges to the mainland are now closed. So if you were planning on leaving, you missed your chance."

More nervous laughter. The wind howled monotonously, shaking the glass as stronger gusts hit the window.

"As a precaution, we have moved everybody who had an ocean front room to street side. This is just a safety precaution. In addition, I've talked to Callie and the chefs and we've decided to close the restaurant at seven o'clock tonight. We de-cided the restaurant was just a tad bit too vulnerable perched up there on the fifth floor with all that glass."

She stopped and low murmurs erupted around the room. Everybody was sick of the hurricane. They were waiting to hear about Mac.

"Okay," Lily said briskly. "I know you've all heard about Mac Tims. Mac was a good guy, and we'll miss him. As soon as we get the details on his funeral, we'll pass them along for those of you who want to attend. This was a very nasty accident to have happen at any time, much less during a hurricane."

Angry buzzing rose like a swarm of bees.

"Accident?" Nell, the head of housekeeping, said. "That ain't what we heard. We heard it was murder. And I'm telling you, I'm scared to be sleeping in my bed if we got some murder-er running around!" She settled her considerable bulk back in her seat and crossed her delicate ankles. She peered around the room through her thick glasses, her ebony face worried and a bit angry.

"That's for the police to decide," Lily said firmly. "Right now, they are working on the assumption that it was an accident."

"I heard that boy was stealing, and someone pulped his head and locked him in the freezer to die," Nell said stubbornly and there was a hum of agreement.

"Mac was in Jerry's room that night," Dowell said loudly, not to be left out. He looked accusingly at the chefs' table.

"Oh no, here we go," Janet said softly.

"Let the mud slinging commence," I agreed. I looked over at Lily, but she seemed to have given up convincing the staff that the death was not a murder. Now she was listening as individual conversations started all over the room.

"Like I told the police," Jerry began, his voice breaking. He dashed angrily at his red-rimmed eyes with one hand. "Like I told the police," he repeated. "I never saw Mac. I wish to God I had," he said and tears abruptly spilled over onto his cheeks.

"But didn't Chef tell you Mac was in your room?" Dowell's voice was hard.

"I never–" "No, he didn't say–" Both Chef and Jerry said at the same time and stopped and looked at each other angrily.

"I never talked to you, Dowell," Chef said, his voice mildly condescending.

"He didn't tell me," Jerry finished.

"But I told you," Dowell said. "I called your room and told

you that Mac was in the hotel, in Jerry's room."

Chef shook his head. "You didn't talk to me."

Disbelieving muttering spread across the room, and angry looks flashed toward the chefs' table.

"What time did you call Chef's room, Dowell?" I called out.

"I don't know exactly, sometime before two o'clock, because I remember at two *Weekend at Bernie's* came on." His face colored a little, and I knew that he probably had turned the phone off at two, and maybe even caught a nap while watching the movie. "It was after the power went out and came back on, I do remember that."

"I saw Noel and Mac arguing pretty good a couple of days ago," said a maintenance man spitefully. "Came in the middle of the day to unplug the sink and they were yelling at each other."

Noel looked surprised. "He didn't clean the slicer," he said. "Mac sometimes was lazy about little stuff like that." His voice was apologetic. "Well, he was, sometimes. I got roast beef juice all over my onions. He got peeved at me for yelling at him about it."

"What about her?" someone said, pointing at me.

"Me?" I looked around at the housekeeper who was gazing at me malevolently.

"She's new, no one knows her. Maybe she killed him."

"She ain't no killer," Nell said scornfully. "You just sit your butt down and shut up."

The meeting disintegrated into individual accusations and mud slinging, and I listened with interest. Everybody had something to say, and in the close confines of a hotel, everybody had dirt on his or her coworkers.

Lily let this go on for a few minutes and then said loudly, "That's enough!"

To her credit, everybody stopped talking, many looking abashed at what they had just been saying.

"Listen to yourselves," Lily said sharply. "Listen to what you've been saying. We need to be coming together now, not turning on each other. We have absolutely no proof that Mac was murdered, and if he was, that he was killed by one of us. You should be ashamed of yourselves." She looked around the room, and like a class full of recalcitrant children, no one met her gaze.

"Okay, here's what we're going to do. Whether Mac was murdered or not, I'm sure he would not have wanted his death to stain the hotel's reputation. So, for his sake, we must not talk about his death as a murder until we know for sure from the police. The press would have a field day with this. We need to keep quiet until we know for sure what's going on. Is that understood?" She looked around the room, shamelessly using Mac's memory to get her own way.

Hesitation, and then nods began fluttering around the room.

"All right, everybody, we've all got things we need to be doing. Thank you all for coming."

Lily gestured to me, and I joined her in the back prep kitchen as everybody filed out of the room.

"Not exactly what I was hoping for," Lily said, "but at least we got some information. And I don't think they'll be talking to the press. I tried calling Dale, but just got his voice mail. Everybody's out in the storm. I thought about calling nine-one-one, but decided against it."

Jerry and Noel came through the door.

"Hey Lily, me beauty," Noel said. "Can we go into the freezer? Jerry and I already stocked from the refrigerator walkins, but we still need to get food from the freezer if you want to feed this starving lot."

"What's going on?" Janet said as she came through the swinging door. "I thought the police said we could have the freezer back. Though I personally don't want to go in there until someone cleans up the blood."

"No, none of us needs to be going into the freezer. Make do with what you have," Lily said. "That means everybody." She looked at me sharply. I nodded, and tried to look innocent, though I had every intention of going into the freezer. I needed to check something.

"Well, how we're supposed to feed this ravenous horde, I don't know..." Noel said.

"Jesus," Janet said, "I guess I'm starting to believe Mac was actually murdered. And we're trapped here in this hotel. I wish we had a nice handsome policeman with a gun here right now."

"Well, I can't help you with the handsome part," Lily said, "but..."

"Lily! You've got a gun?" Janet was impressed.

"I can take care of myself. Have been since my husband died."

"Big, bad, Lily the Kid!" Noel chortled, and everyone laughed.

"Will you people just stop it?" Jerry said in a choked voice, and our laughter died. "Mac is dead! How can you laugh?" He glared around at all of us, and then stomped out of the room.

"Poor guy, he's taking this hard," Noel said sympathetically. "Well, I gotta go help maintenance clean up some leaks."

"I want to talk to you later," Lily said to me. "I've got to meet with Chef right now, but come to my room, four twenty-six, in about an hour." Lily walked briskly down the hall toward the elevator.

I pushed through the swinging door back into the conference room. I saw Dowell gathering his stuff together and went over to him.

"Dowell," I said. "When you called Chef's room that night, asking for Jerry, are you sure you talked to Chef?"

"Sure," Dowell said indignantly, but a look of indecision flickered across his wide, pale pudding face. "I don't know why he doesn't remember."

"He said he was Chef? You recognized his voice?" I prompted.

"Well, no," Dowell said. "I really couldn't hear him too good. There was loud music in the background. Everybody was singing something."

"But he said, 'This is Chef?'"

"No," Dowell said slowly. "I really didn't even hear him say hello. The phone was answered and I heard someone say something, hello, I guess. And I said, 'Chef?', and then I told him to tell Jerry about Mac. I mean, it was his room, who else would have answered the phone?"

"Did the person say anything else?"

"I don't think so. Like I said, it was really hard to hear. I just hung up."

"Could it have been a woman who answered the phone?" I asked.

"No!" Dowell said, seeing that his credibility was going down the drain. But then, he looked at me uncertainly. "I don't think so," he said.

"One more thing," I said. "Can you pinpoint the time you called up there?"

"I really don't know what time it was," Dowell said, screwing his forehead up in concentration.

"But sometime after the lights went out, and before *Weekend at Bernie's* came on at two?" I prompted.

"Oh, yeah. I forgot about the lights. They went out as I was going back to the desk, and I bumped my shin on a flower pot. But then they came right back on."

"Thanks, Dowell," I said, and walked toward the elevator.

Whoever had taken the call from Dowell had known that Mac was in the hotel, in Jerry's room. What made the most sense was that Chef himself had taken the call, and then contrived a need for vodka to give himself a reason to go down to Jerry's room.

Except for one thing.

Chef had already left when the lights went out.

I thought about it as I rode the back service elevator down to the first floor. If Chef hadn't answered the phone, someone else had. Someone else had known that Mac was in the hotel. I had the feeling that the exact wrong person had answered the phone that night.

Mac's killer had discovered that Mac was in the hotel, and had killed him. Though why in the freezer and not in Jerry's room?

The first answer seemed obvious, because Chef had been in Jerry's room with Mac.

Then why had Mac gone to the freezer after he left Jerry's room? Just to steal steaks?

I had a theory I wanted to check out, something I had been wanting to do since I had spoken with Lily this morning. But someone had always been around, and I needed privacy for what I wanted to do.

There was no one in the downstairs main hallway. I hurried down the short hall to the walk-in freezer. I looked around once again, but I was alone. I used my key to unlock the padlock and entered the walk-in, taking the padlock with me. I was really beginning to hate the freezer. I glanced down at the floor where a Rorschach bloodstain still sprawled. No one had gotten around to cleaning it up, though the steaks had been piled back in the box and put back up on the shelf.

I stepped carefully around the bloodstains and walked to the back of the freezer, and looked up at the top shelf where the Smith's Seafood boxes were stored.

There it was. The fifty-pound shrimp box with "Cater" and a date a week from now was written on the side. The red dot was not visible from where I stood.

Gritting my teeth, I grasped the metal shelf with my hands, ignoring the burning cold metal, and hoisted myself up so I was standing on the first shelf. Goose pimples were running up and down my arms.

I pulled the box to me, and turned it around to make sure it was the one with the red dot. It was. I folded back the flaps. Inside were five-pound boxes of shrimp. Except one was missing. I could tell that right away.

I pulled out all nine of the boxes, but there was nothing amiss. Nothing amiss except that one five-pound box was missing out of a box that was destined for a cater next week.

My fingers were becoming numb, and I dropped down to the floor of the freezer, my shoe dislodging a box of hamburger tubes, which rolled across the floor. Shivering, I bent down to pick up the tubes of hamburgers. The second one I picked up had a dent in the side.

I bent to put it back in the box, but something caught my eye. A hair. A short bleached white hair.

I caught my breath and looked at the tube more closely. It was over a foot and a half long, three inches across and as hard as concrete. It didn't look like it would be easy to dent. I looked at the hair, and my stomach turned. The hair looked like the bleached white hair of Mac's mohawk.

Without warning the lights went out, and I yelled in surprise and fright and dropped the tube of hamburger. Looking out the window, the hall was pitch black as well. Had the power gone off?

I felt my way over to the door, trying to step around the bloodstain on the floor. I put my hands to the door and pushed, but the door wouldn't budge.

I pushed harder, feeling my head go light and my vision swim as the door would not open.

Somebody had locked me in the freezer.

CHAPTER TWENTY

Sojourn in the Freezer

I cursed my stupidity. The mace I carried in my pocket would do me no good now.

I closed my eyes in expectation of an anxiety attack, waiting for the waves of fear to engulf me. But surprisingly, my mind stayed clear, and though I was shaking almost uncontrollably, I was not about to disintegrate into an abysmal pit of fear.

I straightened. My anxiety attacks had abated over the last year. I had had so much to think about I didn't have time for them. Or maybe I was healing.

I pounded on the door, and yelled, but didn't expect anybody to hear me. The freezer was down at the end of a short hall, and the only way anybody would hear me is if they happened to be in the main hall directly opposite the hall with the walk-ins. Finally, I stopped pounding because the edges of my hands were numb with the cold. I had a flashback to Darryl's horror-stricken answer when I had asked him what had happened to his fingers.

The freezer.

I stuck my hands in my armpits, trying to ignore the knocking of my knees in my thin linen culottes.

I concluded by pressing my face to the single foggy, cold window that the lights had been turned off in the freezer and in the hall with the walk-ins, but not the main hallway. The person had evidently not wanted to raise suspicions. The thought of people walking along the main hallway gave me hope, and I started yelling again, feeling self-conscious even though it was an emergency.

I thought about how the killer had done this to me. How had the person locked the door when I carried the padlock? Had the person followed me down from the conference room with the intention of locking me in? Or had the person just happened along while I was in here?

That would imply a chef, but considering that the murder weapon had been left in the freezer, perhaps the person had come back to search for the weapon, and had seen me instead.

The very cold feet of tiny mice tiptoed up my spine. Had the murderer seen me find the murder weapon? I thought about the foggy window, which had prevented me from seeing the person as he or she locked me in the freezer. No, the person had probably not seen me. But I had left my keys in the hallway on a shelf, as I always did, to prevent my accidentally locking the keys in the freezer. Anybody who knew me would recognize the distinctive "I love cats, even mine" key chain.

So the killer had known I was in here, but presumably hadn't known what I had found. So perhaps locking me in the freezer was another scare tactic, not attempted murder, similar to what had happened to Darryl Menden. Darryl had been locked in this very same freezer, though I couldn't see why he hadn't just let himself using the emergency lock-in mechanism.

The emergency exit!

"Think, Callie, think," I muttered impatiently. How could I have forgotten the emergency exit?

Cursing my numb fingers, I felt along the door, and then beside the door to find the emergency lock-in mechanism. I was grateful that I had looked at it earlier in the week when I was trying to figure out how Darryl had been locked in the freezer, so I knew how it worked.

In the dark, my fingers fumbled over the wall, and I found the pin that needed to be rotated and pulled. I turned it, felt the tension release, and pulled it completely out, trying to ignore the searing cold metal on my fingertips. The pin dropped to the floor and I pushed at the door, expecting to hear a resounding clang as the metal bar dropped under the pressure.

Nothing happened.

I pushed at the door, and then kicked it, and still nothing

happened. Before long, I was shouting again, beating at the door with my fists and feet, my mind swirling into panic.

Stop it, stop it, stop it!

I forced myself to step back from the door, shaking with fear and exertion. I shoved my hands under my shirt, trying to ignore their cold, dead feeling on the flesh of my stomach.

The door had been locked in such a way that the emergency exit did not work. There was no getting around that. There was no getting out.

I bent my head and shoved my hands deeper under my shirt. My teeth were starting to chatter. I immersed myself in thought, trying not to think about how long it took for a person to freeze to death in sub-zero temperatures.

I thought about the progression from law-abiding citizen to murderer. I started with the assumption that this person had never killed before. He or she concocted some scheme to make money, never mind what the scheme was, since I only had a vague idea myself. Several months ago Darryl Menden began to figure it out. He learned too much, and started talking about food costs and cover-up. The schemer panicked a little, and locked Darryl in the freezer to shut him up. Darryl capitulated easily and agreed to leave.

At this point, how did the would-be murderer feel? Powerful and triumphant, I postulated. It was amazing what a little bit of threatening could accomplish.

Then I came along, and I started to take over where Darryl had left off. I called Darryl and started asking him questions. How had the murderer discovered that? Anyway, the person called Darryl and threatened him again; Darryl left town. Once again, a little bit of violence worked wonders.

But despite Darryl's disappearance, I kept poking around, and the killer decided to a) kill me or b) scare me badly. I thought maybe the person had decided to kill me, to push me off the roof in such a way that it would look like an accident. What had changed his or her mind? Because the person hadn't killed yet, and hadn't been ready to take that step?

But rapidly, this person had lost all grip on his or her humanity. He or she was being pushed into a corner and was fighting back in desperation. Whatever objections to murder the killer might have entertained had been overcome where Mac was concerned. He or she had been pushed to the limit and had hit Mac on the head with the frozen ten-pound tube of hamburger meat. Even if the intention had not been murder, leaving Mac to freeze to death on the cold freezer floor had been.

And now. Why had the person locked me in the freezer? It only proved that Mac was murdered. Why take that chance, when more likely than not I would be found before I died, though maybe not before I lost fingers or toes or ears to frostbite?

I took comfort in the fact that the chefs would have to come down to stock food before the evening shift. And then I remembered what Noel had said minutes before I came down to the freezer: *Jerry and I already stocked from the refrigerator walk-ins, but we still need to get food from the freezer if you want to feed this starving lot.*

The chefs had already stocked for the night. And Lily had told them, told *me* specifically, that the freezer was off-limits.

The chefs would have no reason to come down here for the rest of the night. I prayed that they would run out of heavy cream or romaine lettuce. If they went into one of the refrigerator walk-ins, surely I could attract their attention by yelling and banging on the door. Someone would have to hear me.

If they came down here.

Otherwise no one would find me until tomorrow.

The killer had no reason to stop short of murder. He had already gone there, and I had always heard it was easier the second time around. So what was the plan? Would the killer wait for me to freeze to death, and then remove my body and hide it somewhere where it would never be found, or simply throw it into the ocean? Or would he/she just leave me here, and tomorrow there would be one more unexplained body in the freezer?

I fully believed that this person had lost all vestiges of humanity and was cold-hearted enough to let me freeze in here to save his or her hide. I couldn't believe that any of my coworkers could do that, didn't *want* to believe that one of them could do that to me.

I began jumping up and down, trying to keep myself warm. Before long, I tired, and crouched on my heels, because there was no place to sit; steel walls and floor surrounded me, ready to steal any warmth from me. So I crouched on my heels and wrapped my arms around my knees and pressed my face to my knees, my warm breath thawing my knees and my face. The steel padlock seemed to be burning through the thin cloth of my culottes, and I fumbled for it with one hand, accidentally dropping it on the floor.

My back and thighs began to ache unmercifully, but I sank to a place where the cold and pain and fear were an abstract, sharp and shiny cubes to be taken out and examined with interest, but removed from my actual self.

I had lost feeling in my toes and fingers a long time ago.

When help came, I was so out of it that at first I didn't even hear the sound of someone fumbling with the door. Once I heard it, fear struck through me. What if it was the killer?

The door was pulled open, and a rush of warm air and light washed over me, and I toppled over backward, trying to stand up. As I looked up, I saw the lemon mirage that was Lily standing over me.

"Jesus Jumping Christ," she breathed and hurried to me, her heavy floral scent engulfing me as she picked me up bodily and put me on my feet. "Come on," she said briskly, guiding my faltering steps out the door.

She helped me down the hall to the main corridor, and the few steps required to make it to the service elevator. Once inside the elevator, Lily grabbed my hands and briskly rubbed them between her own.

"Callie," she said, smacking my face lightly but I didn't feel it. "Look at me."

I raised frost-encrusted eyelashes to gaze at her.

"Who locked you in? Do you know?"

I shook my head wordlessly, and she kept rubbing my lifeless hands.

We got off at the fourth floor, banquets, but the rooms were unlocked and empty from the meeting that afternoon. Lily led me through the echoing banquet rooms to the door that led to the main hotel hall, and down the hall to her room. By the time I reached her room, I was beginning to feel tingling in my hands and toes, but it was an unpleasant itchy, searing tingling and I rubbed my hands continually against the front of my shirt, trying to ease the ache.

Once inside her room, Lily went into the bathroom and began running water. I stood in the middle of the room and shivered, something I had not been able to stop doing. Lily came in and guided me to the bathroom, where she helped me into the tub, clothes and all. The water felt searing hot, though Lily said it was barely warm. I soaked in the water, and shut my mind to the pain that was shooting through me as frozen flesh began coursing with life-giving blood. Lily kept adding warmer water to the tub, and my convulsive shaking threw geysers of water over her pants suit.

Finally, I was able to get out of the tub on my own. I still was cold, but my flesh was a rosy, speckled pink. Lily handed me a bathrobe, and I peeled away my sodden culottes set and underwear and cuddled in the soft cotton of the robe. When I came out of the bathroom, Lily handed me a pair of warm socks and pointed at the bed where she had heaped three or four blankets and comforters.

"Get in," she said. "You're still shivering."

"I've got to work," I protested faintly.

Lily snorted. "Yeah right. Get in bed. I'll call Kate for you."

I sat on the edge of the bed, but reached for the phone myself, my hand shaking so badly I could barely hold the phone. I dialed Kate's room.

"Kate."

"Callie, is that you?"

"I'm not feeling real good," I said thickly. "Call Janet or Margie to come in tonight."

"Sure, Callie," Kate said. "You don't sound so good. Get some rest, okay?"

I hung up the phone and let Lily pull the covers up to my neck.

"Independent little cuss, aren't you," I heard her say as I drifted down, down, down. And a minute later, realization dawning in her voice. "And I guess you don't want anybody knowing where you are."

When I woke, it was dark in the room. As my eyes adjusted, I realized that it wasn't night dark, but the gray, under-the-water light of thick clouds and driving rain. I glanced at the clock. It was almost six o'clock. I sat up and switched on the light, amazed at how weak I felt. On the bed stand by the phone, I noticed a scrap of paper and a familiar telephone number scrawled across it.

The toilet flushed. I looked up as Lily, changed into a violet raw cotton dress with a vivid red and orange scarf belt, came into the room.

"You're awake. Good. How are you feeling?"

"Better," I said, and was pleased to discover that my voice almost sounded normal.

"You look better." Lily switched on another lamp and sat at

the table. "Well, you're lucky that I figured you right."

"What?" The wind howled, and rain was leaking under the edge of the balcony door.

"When I told all of you to stay out of the freezer, I saw your mind start buzzing. I met with Chef in my office and then went up to my room to wait for you. When you didn't show up in my room when you were supposed to, I figured you were down in the freezer. I didn't expect that you'd been locked in. Did you know that someone had stuck a two by four between the door and the wall?"

"Oh, Jesus." I remembered the paint cans and boards that had been piled in the alcove across from the freezer. I had seen the board, but hadn't realized what it was. It had probably been lying there innocuously since Darryl had been locked in the freezer. Had someone cut it specifically to fit between the door and the wall, or did it just happen to be lying there when Mac and his accomplice needed it to lock Darryl in the freezer?

I looked around Lily's room. It was ocean front, and on the fourth floor. "I thought you said everybody had been moved to street side for their own safety."

"They were. Everyone but me. I don't want to be stuck on the other side of the hotel, unable to see if a tidal wave of water comes rushing over the hotel."

"Good thing your staff didn't hear you say that," I said wryly.

Lily shrugged.

We were silent. I found myself vaguely embarrassed to be sitting in my boss's bathrobe.

"So you didn't get a look at the person?"

I shook my head. "The window was foggy and I had just found– oh my God, Lily, I found the murder weapon!"

"You what?"

"I found a frozen tube of hamburger meat with a dent and Mac's hair on it. I think it was used to kill Mac."

"You stay here," Lily said. "I'm going to go down and see if I can find it."

"I'm coming with you," I said, throwing back the covers and looking down in dismay at the bathrobe I wore.

"Well, I guess it's a good thing I went down to your room and petted that crazy looking dog of yours, and found this," Lily said, getting up and pulling one of my dresses from the rack.

I took the dress thankfully and went into the bathroom and changed. My shoes were still dry, as Lily had taken them off for me before I had gotten in the bath.

We headed down the hall, and without speaking chose to take the back way through banquets, to avoid running into anybody.

The freezer was locked.

Lily frowned. "I didn't lock it when I found you."

"I dropped the padlock on the floor inside the freezer," I said.

Several boards and paint cans were in the alcove. "Someone put the board back," Lily said, pointing at the board that lay on top of the pile, just the right size to fit between the freezer door and the wall.

My keys were still on the shelf beside the freezer door, and Lily used them to let us into the freezer. I stood outside as Lily stepped around the blood spot and stopped in front of where the hamburger tubes were stored.

"It's right in front," I said, taking a deep breath and stepping over the threshold of the freezer.

I kneeled down and pulled out all the hamburger tubes.

But the tube with the dent and Mac's hair on it was gone.

CHAPTER TWENTY-ONE

Conversations with a Killer

"Of course I brought up a tube of hamburger meat," Noel said. "Two in fact. We were completely out of hamburger meat. And a couple of steaks and some more French fries. Callie, you really have got to be more careful with your keys. They were right beside the door. Anybody could have unlocked the freezer and gone in."

It was after seven, and the chef and Lily and I were in the bar, partaking in an illegal drink from the bar, as all bars and liquor stores were required to close when a state of emergency was declared. But it wasn't likely that the Alcohol Law Enforcement would be coming by, considering that the winds were blowing seventy miles an hour and gusting higher. Carrie was coming, and she was coming with a vengeance. The lights were flickering fitfully, and we all wore green glow sticks around our necks, prepared for the inevitable power outage.

Though we had power, the cable was out, so we sat listening to news reports on the radio.

It felt very strange to be sitting here with the chefs and Lily and Janet, not knowing who had tried to lock me in the freezer.

"Noel, I told you not to go in the freezer," Lily said wearily.

"I know, I know, I'm sorry. But Chef had absolutely no food, and since the police said it was okay, I figured..." Noel looked sheepish.

"Don't blame him," Chef said. "I asked him to get me some stuff. We were out of everything."

"Was the freezer door locked when you went down there?" I asked Noel, rubbing my hands. Tiny purple blood vessels shot through the back of my hands, and I wondered if my sojourn in the freezer had done permanent damage.

Noel nodded. "Of course; it always is."

"And no board lying on the floor?"

Noel shook his head, and looked puzzled, as did everybody else except Lily. What was I expecting, someone to jump up and scream, all right, all right, I'm guilty, just stop talking about the damned board!

No such luck.

"What time did you go down there?"

"Probably four-thirty or so."

Lily had gotten me out of the freezer around three fifteen. That gave the killer over an hour to clean up the board and lock the freezer back. *And* steal the tube of hamburger meat. But it was just as likely that Noel had, in all innocence, taken the murder weapon for Chef to cook.

"Did you notice anything strange about the hamburger tubes?"

"Strange?" Noel looked mystified.

"What is this all about?" Chef said. "Tubes of hamburger meat? Boards? I'm starting to have some funny ideas about you, my dear. We need to get together later."

"Callie was locked in the freezer this afternoon. While she was in there she found a tube of hamburger meat with a dent and Mac's hair on it. We think it was used to hit Mac. When we went back to look for it, the tube was gone."

I looked at Noel. He had had the perfect opportunity to pick up the board and snag the tube when he went to the freezer to stock. On the other hand, anybody could have gone down there in the hour between my leaving the freezer and Noel arriving, and cleaned up the scene. And yet, a maintenance man had overheard Noel and Mac arguing. Had they been arguing about the slicer or something more sinister?

Everybody was making sounds of horror and disbelief at Lily's announcement and I wished very much that she hadn't said it. But she had her reasons.

"So now we know for sure that someone killed Mac, the same someone who locked Callie in the freezer."

"And tried to push her off the roof," Jerry said leadenly.

Lily shot me a look but continued smoothly as if she had known all along. "Yes, and tried to push her off the roof. So, I've got a few questions for everybody."

"Noel, did you use the tubes of hamburgers you brought up?"

Noel looked at Chef, who answered. "I was working the line, and yes, I used one of the tubes. I had to quick thaw the sucker, it was as hard as a brick and I needed it yesterday. And no, I didn't notice anything strange about it, except the label, but I was busy." He looked around. "What label, you ask? Why the one that said, use me quick, I'm the murder weapon!" He lounged back in his chair, and sipped from his drink, once more the suave and debonair chef. But his hand was shaking as he brought the drink to his lips, and he had been drinking far too much.

Jerry sat hunched over in his chair, holding a shot of tequila between his hands. He had been closest to Mac, and seemed to be most affected by his death. He also seemed to have developed an antipathy toward Chef, unexplained but tangibly real as he raised his head and glared at Chef with red-rimmed eyes. Chef seemed not to notice. I wondered what had happened between the two close friends.

At Lily's insistence, Chef and I went in the back and he showed me the remaining tube of hamburger. There was no dent or hair on it.

"Did the other one have a dent on it?"

"I'm sure I didn't notice," Chef said.

Either he had cooked the murder weapon, or the murderer had gotten it when he or she had put the board back and locked the freezer door. We would never know.

"Chef, why were you gone for so long the night of your party? The night Mac was killed. You were gone for about an hour," I said as we walked back toward the door to the bar.

Chef looked at me and raised his eyebrows. "Oh, so you think maybe I left my own party, ran downstairs and killed Mac in the freezer?"

"Did you?"

Chef laughed, and patted my cheek. I twisted my face away from the condescending gesture. "No dear girl. I merely went downstairs to Jerry's room for a bottle of Stoli. I may have fallen asleep for a time, watching the Weather Channel. But then I came back. Never went near the freezer, I promise you."

"Was Mac in Jerry's room?"

He didn't say anything, and then we were back at the bar.

"Find anything, Cal?" Janet asked. I was surprised at the depth of concern in her voice.

"No," I said.

Lily poured herself another drink and came around the side of the bar. "I have to say it; I can only assume that Mac's killer is someone staying in the hotel. It would have been damn near impossible for anybody to have fought their way through the storm and happen to be in the right place both to kill Mac and lock Callie in the freezer, *and* clean up the evidence after I got Callie out of the freezer."

I was sincerely glad that Lily did not see fit to tell everybody in what condition she found me. In fact, I would be happiest if the killer thought that Lily had let me out right after I was locked in. I didn't want the person to know how frightened I had been, how helpless I had felt. It was something that I vowed I would never feel again.

"So that means it's someone staying in the hotel. I think we can probably rule out the reporters, so that leaves the eighteen members of staff staying here." Lily took a deep breath. "I would really prefer not to think that one of our coworkers is a murderer, and if someone has evidence to the contrary please speak up now."

Silence filled with the gleeful howling of the wind. Everybody in the room avoided each other's eyes. So many secrets brewed in this room, and the silence was deafening.

Somebody knocked on the front door of the restaurant and Lily went to the door. "We're closed–" she started to say, and then, "hold on a minute, Lisa." She unlocked the door and Noel's pretty wife came in, looking around in confusion at all the people in the room. "Noel, I was just wondering–"

"Come on in, hon," Noel said. "It'll only be a minute. We're talking about Mac."

Lisa looked startled, but she sat down in a chair beside her husband and he put his arm around her shoulders.

"Callie, you have some questions?" Lily turned to me. We had talked about this before calling this meeting, but I still was uncertain. Lily had gotten hold of Dale Grain just before we had left to come to the restaurant. He had said to sit tight and that he would come as soon as the storm was over. But I didn't want to sit tight. I wanted to know who was trying to kill me. Lily was all for the idea.

"We'll get all the likeliest suspects together and look them in the eye while you ask your questions. Someone will react."

I looked around the room, at the concerned and antagonistic faces around me. "I'm going to ask everybody a question or two, so as not to single anybody out."

"And can we ask you a question?" Chef asked.

"I really don't think—" Lily said.

"You never know, maybe she faked the attempts on herself, just to look innocent," Jerry said suddenly.

"Oh, she managed to lock herself in the freezer all by herself," Lily said sarcastically. "What reason would she have to kill Mac, anyway?"

I tried to speak, but Noel said angrily, "What reason would any one of us have to kill Mac? We all liked him."

Finally, I was able to speak. "I would be more than happy to answer any questions put to me," I said.

"Let her get on with this already," Janet said irritably. "It's nerve-wracking enough knowing we've got a killer in our midst without everybody screaming at each other."

I took a deep breath and looked down at the list I had been compiling. "First, I have a question for everybody. Did anyone talk to Dowell on the phone the night of the party? Dowell says he called and told someone who he thought was Chef that Mac was in Jerry's room. But Chef said he never talked to Dowell."

"I didn't," Chef said quickly.

Everybody else shook their heads.

"Why is it important who Dowell talked to?" Jerry asked irritably. "Let's just get this over with, can we?"

"Can everyone tell me where they were this afternoon around three or so?"

The answers were varied and creative, but for the exception of Lily and Chef, who had been meeting in her office, everybody had been alone.

"Okay, let me start with Chef," I said, and Chef raised lazy eyes to me and smiled. "Where were you between ten p.m. and six a.m. the night of Mac's murder?"

Chef raised his eyes to the ceiling. "I was having a party. I seem to vaguely recall that you were there."

"You left around one."

"I left for a few minutes to go get vodka from Jerry's room. Sue me."

"A few minutes?" I raised my eyebrows. "I'm pretty sure it was a good hour."

Chef shrugged. "Whatever."

"Did you see Mac in Jerry's room? Dowell said he saw him go in there right about that time."

Chef was silent for a moment. "He must have left by the time I got down there," he said finally.

"I heard Jerry say that you were the last one to see Mac. What did he mean?"

Chef's smile didn't falter. "I worked with Mac his last night before he didn't show up for two days," he said. "I guess I was the last one to talk to him." He didn't flinch when Jerry made a choking sound.

"So," I said. "What did you mean when you said Jerry had a good reason to kill Mac?"

"I loved Mac like a brother!" Jerry said fiercely.

"I was just angry," Chef said, his gaze slipping away from mine.

"But what did you mean?"

"All I meant was that Mac owed Jerry a lot of money, and that he even stole some money from Jerry when he left."

"He didn't steal it," Jerry said. "He just didn't get a chance to tell me he was taking it. If only I–" He broke off and sank back in his chair.

"Jerry," I said gently, and Jerry looked up at me with hate-filled eyes. "Why are you so angry at Chef? Ever since the murder you've been angry at him. Why?"

Jerry was silent.

"Jerry?" Lily prompted.

Finally Jerry stirred and turned to stare at Chef, who visibly lost his composure as the stare lengthened.

"I know he was in that room, Michael," Jerry said directly to Chef. "I found his hat, the one with the pot leaf on it, in my bedroom when I went to my room after the party. Was he waiting for me when you went down to my room to get the vodka? He got you high, I know, because I saw how messed up you were when you came back."

I met Lily's eyes. We had both seen Chef when he came back to his room that night. Definitely messed up.

"Did you follow him down to the freezer and kill him before coming back to the party?" Jerry's voice dripped with hate.

"You really think I killed Mac?" Chef asked bitterly. "As long as we've been friends, all that we went through in college, and you really believe that?"

"I wish you'd never come here," Jerry said, and gulped the

shot of tequila.

Silence, and Chef said nothing to defend himself against what Jerry had said.

"Real quick, Jerry," I said. "Where were you between ten and six?"

"I took some things down to the walk-ins at about ten," he said, desultory.

"You went into the freezer?"

He nodded. "Then I went to Chef's party until about two-thirty, then I went down to my room and slept until ten in the morning." He spoke in a monotone, as if he didn't care what anybody thought about what he said.

"And Mac wasn't in your room when you got back?"

"No. Just his hat."

"Did you give Mac a key to your room?"

"No."

"Janet," I said, moving on. Janet looked at me in surprise. "Were you driving the green Explorer between two-thirty and three the night of Mac's murder?"

"What?" She leaned forward, the tip of her blond ponytail falling over her shoulder. "No, of course not. Why?"

"I saw a green Explorer the night of the murder being driven out of the parking lot."

Janet shook her head. "You must be mistaken," she said. "I went out to the Explorer the next morning, early, because I had left my tennis shoes in the back seat. It was there."

"I know it's there now," I said. "But someone drove it some-where the night of Mac's murder. Are you sure it hadn't been moved when you went out to it in the morning? Did you leave the keys in it?"

"No, of course not. I've been real careful to lock it. I guess I'm even a little paranoid about it."

"So it was in the same spot that you left it?"

Janet nodded her head slowly, but she looked troubled. "You know, it was funny, because I could have sworn I left my tennis shoes on the back seat, and when I went out the next morning they were on the floor."

I swallowed hard. "Janet, am I correct in thinking that the Explorer belongs to Frank Smith from Smith's Seafood?"

She nodded, her cheeks pinking a little with embarrass-ment.

"Do you think anyone else has keys to the car?"

Janet frowned, and then shrugged. "Frank keeps the Explorer at his beach house in Kitty Hawk. He uses it to go four-wheeling when he comes to the beach. I'm sure he's lent it out before. I think I saw Jerry drive it once."

Jerry looked up blearily. "He lent it to me when I wanted to take a couple of friends out to Oregon Inlet to go surf fishing. He's lent it to about everyone one time or another."

"And when was the last time you saw Frank?" I asked Janet.

"He left for Virginia Friday night."

Friday night. That was the night that someone had been on my deck and I had seen the green Explorer down the street. Wait a minute. Hadn't I seen Frank Saturday afternoon? Why had he lied to Janet?

"Do you know where Frank is now?"

"In Virginia," she said.

Dead end on that one. If Janet hadn't driven the Explorer and Frank was in Virginia, who had driven the car on the night of the murder? Was Janet telling the truth?

"Where were you between ten and six?"

"You saw me. At the party. Then I went to bed."

"You got a phone call that night. Was it Dowell asking for Jerry?"

"No," Janet said, frowning. "It was Frank. I told him I would be in Chef's room if he wanted to call."

Moving on, I turned my attention to Noel. He gave me a small grin, and I sorted through my notes. "Noel, how well do you know Frank Smith?"

Noel rubbed a big hand over his stubbly cheeks. "I've known him for a couple of years. He's a nice guy, and he's got a good company. I think you're way off base if you think Frank's involved in this, Callie. All he's interested in is preserving his father's company and supporting his family. He's got two little girls you know. He's a good family man, not like those bastards in Mary-land." He flicked an ash toward an ashtray on the bar and missed. Cursing, he swept it off the counter.

"And where were you–"

"Oh honey, you know where I was. I was at the party until almost two, and then Lisa and I went to bed. She fed us some sleeping pills, and we knocked right off. We have trouble sleeping in hotels."

"The wind wouldn't stop howling," Lisa said. "Noel and I took two pills instead of one, or we would never have gotten to sleep."

"But you left the party to go get candy from your room?"

Noel nodded. "It just took me five minutes."

Lisa nodded.

"And you didn't see anything out of place when you went down to the freezer to stock this afternoon?"

"Nope."

Silence, as we all stared at one another.

"All right," Lily said. "That's everybody. Does anybody have any questions for Callie?"

"Wait a minute," I said quietly. "I wasn't done."

Lily looked at me inquiringly.

"I've got one for you," I said directly to Lily.

She looked surprised but said, "Go on."

"Why did you have Darryl Menden's phone number in your room?"

CHAPTER TWENTY-TWO

Charts, Motives
and Phone Calls

Lily and Noel walked me back to my room, and waited
while I let the dog out into the howling wind on the patio. He
peed quickly and darted back in the door, which I struggled to
close.

"Are you sure you won't come stay in my room?" Lily asked.

"I've got some thinking to do, and I want to be alone. I'll put
a chair in front of the door, no one will be able to get in."

"I'm in room two eleven if you need some help. Just call,"
Noel said. "Me and Lisa'll be down here in a heartbeat. I'll stand
back and let Lisa finish 'em off. I know who wears the pants in
my family."

I laughed, thinking of tiny Lisa beating up the murderer.

Noel left and Lily paused in the door. "I was just curious
why you had called him. I saw your Rolodex flipped to his number the other day, and decided to call him, that's all," Lily said, a
little defensively.

She had already explained once.

"The number in my Rolodex was his disconnected number
from when he lived on the Outer Banks," I said. "So I guess you
didn't get hold of him in Virginia Beach." I looked at her sharply.

"Nope, I didn't get hold of him," Lily said innocently, then
her expression grew more serious. "There's something else,

Callie." She hesitated. "I can't find my gun anywhere. I think someone stole it this afternoon."

After she left I breathed a sigh of relief. My door shook as the wind beat on it, and the spreading pool of water leaking under the door had turned into a pond.

I plopped down on the bed, and the dog and Ice jumped up on either side of me. I rubbed both of their heads. "At least I know I can trust you two," I told them. Because I didn't know who to trust, and I felt very alone.

I glanced at the clock. Almost eight o'clock. The hurricane was getting closer and closer by the hour and I had a funny feeling in my chest that I thought might be due to the dropping pressure. Both of the animals were uneasy as well. They circled the room, avoiding each other with a growl and a slash of claws (Ice) and settled down only to pop up and start circling the room again.

"Let me guess, you've got cabin fever." They glanced at me, and then went back to circling.

I understood. I longed to get out of the hotel, to escape the interminable howl of the wind. The outside door shook against the hinges.

"All right guys," I said, grabbing a piece of paper out of my briefcase and settling back against the headboards. "Let's figure this out."

The guys ignored me.

I thought a minute and then listed all the managers in the food and beverage department, plus Lily. I thought a minute and then also added Frank Smith. I looked at the names: Chef, Jerry, Noel, Janet, Lily and Frank.

One of these six people were responsible for Mac's death and the attacks on me. I didn't have any definite proof, just a lot of coincidences, but in my gut I knew it was one of them.

I hoped with all my heart it was Frank Smith, though I didn't see how it was possible that he locked me in the freezer or tried to push me off the roof. Still, the alternative, that one of my coworkers had tried to kill me, was almost unthinkable.

Down one side of the paper, I wrote "July 4", "10 p.m.-2 a.m." and "2 a.m.-6 a.m." and "Today 2 p.m."

Mac had probably been killed between ten p.m., which was when Jerry had taken stuff down to the freezer, and six a.m. in the morning, which was when I had seen the empty shrimp box lying against the door, and had locked the freezer. I had split the night up because I had been in Chef's room until two a.m., and was able to verify alibis on my own. After two, I had to take my suspect's words for where they were. Unfortunately, Mac was probably killed after two, because all of my suspects, except Chef, had been in Chef's room until two.

"July 4" was when I had almost been pushed off the roof. I put "Today 2 p.m." on there, even though I couldn't verify what anybody had told me about where they had been when I had been locked in the freezer.

I was assuming that the incidents were all related, and that one person had been responsible for trying to push me off the roof, locking me in the freezer and killing Mac.

I filled in the chart with the whereabouts of the suspects at different times, starring those that I knew for a fact. When I was done, I looked at the chart.

I was working on the assumption that Mac had been killed after two in the morning, which was the time that the party broke up. I suspected that the deed had been done by two forty-five when the Explorer was driven out of the parking lot, but I couldn't prove that. Still, I was pretty sure that nobody had left the party for long enough to kill Mac before two a.m.

Except Chef, who had been gone for almost and hour between one and two. And who most probably had talked to Mac in Jerry's room, though he denied it. Why would he lie? And if he had killed Mac, how had he come to kill him in the freezer?

I clasped my aching head, and tried another tact. Dowell had called up to the room after the lights had gone out and told Chef that Mac was in Jerry's room. However, if I remembered correctly, Chef had already left for Jerry's room when the lights went out. Could Dowell be confused? Was it as easy as that? He actually called right before the lights went out, talked to Chef, and then Chef went down to Jerry's room to find Mac.

But Dowell had said very clearly that he had called *after* the lights went out, which would mean Chef wasn't there. Dowell couldn't have spoken to Chef, had in fact talked to someone else completely. Someone who was not admitting that he or she had talked to Dowell. Why would they lie? Unless it was the murderer and Dowell's phone call had been the tip off to him or her that Mac was in the hotel.

Chef said Mac had stolen money from Jerry. Had he gone to Jerry's room to steal more money? Did he have a master key which would let him into all the rooms? It would seem so, since

Jerry said he had not given Mac a key.

That thought made me shiver because if Mac had had a master key (and he had every other key to the hotel on his key ring) he hadn't had it when he died. That meant it was very possible that the murderer took it from Mac, which meant the murderer could get in any room he wanted. I looked at my door, with the chair braced in front of it. My mace was on the table beside me.

And then I thought about Lily coming into my room to get my clothes while I slept in her room. It made sense that the general manager would have a copy of the master key, but knowing that anyone had access to my room made me nervous. Even Lily.

Well, I knew one thing. Dowell had seen Mac going into Jerry's room a little before one. At least that was the time that Dowell had called up to the room. But had he called right after he had seen Mac, or had he waited a while? I needed to ask Dowell, and I jotted the question down.

I looked back at my chart. Mac had probably been alive shortly before one. Was it possible that someone had left the party between one and two and killed Mac? I had assumed not, but I took it person by person. Chef would have had plenty of time to kill Mac between one and two. Janet had left for about ten minutes right after she had gotten the call from Frank. Was it really Frank? Or had it been Dowell, and Janet had said it was Frank? It fit. Janet got the phone call, found out Mac was in the hotel, and then left to go kill him.

But Janet had not been gone for more than ten minutes tops. That was barely enough time to go downstairs to the freezer and come back. Would she really have had time to kill Mac and set up the scene to look like an accident? And Dowell had said Mac was in Jerry's room. Why would she have gone to the freezer to find Mac?

Lily had been in the room the entire time, as had Jerry. That left Noel, who had left for about five minutes to get the Teddy Grahams candy. He had left after the lights went out, and he had answered the phone, a wrong number, he had said. He had left shortly after that to get the candy, so maybe the phone call hadn't been a wrong number and had been Dowell. But Noel had only been gone for five minutes tops. Surely not enough time to kill Mac.

With the exception of Chef, no one had time to kill Mac before two a.m. After two a.m., everybody had the time. This was getting me nowhere.

I changed tracks again. Who had known that Mac was in the hotel? Or did it matter?

I thought it did. Though the murder looked hurried and unplanned (who would choose to use a ten-pound tube of frozen hamburger as a weapon?), I thought the murderer must have been waiting for Mac. Why else would he or she be down at the freezer in the middle of the night? So the killer had known that Mac was coming to the hotel, and knew somehow that Mac would go to the freezer. Or maybe, the person had followed Mac when he left Jerry's room.

Assuming the murderer had known Mac was in the hotel, how had he/she known? The murderer could have arranged a meeting with Mac. But Mac had been hiding for two days before his death, and had snuck into the hotel the back way so no one would see him. I had the distinct feeling that Mac had been scared of his accomplice. Scared enough to leave town; so why would he agree to a meeting?

That brought us to Dowell's phone call. He had called and told someone that Mac was in Jerry's room. Who had he told?

So again, who had known that Mac was in the hotel? Dowell, of course. And Dowell had called Chef's room and told somebody that Mac was in Jerry's room. Had he told anyone else? I wrote the question down.

Then there was Chef. He had denied it, but had he seen Mac in Jerry's room? Or seen the hat and known that he was around? And Jerry had known that Mac had been there when he saw the hat. Any of these people may have known that Mac would go to the freezer, waited for him and killed him.

I went back to the telephone call. The phone had been ringing a lot the night of the party. While I was in the room, I remembered Janet had answered a call from Frank, and had gone to her room to call him back. Had it been Frank?

Noel had answered one call and told the caller that CNN was down the hall. This was the hardest call to check. Had it truly been a wrong number, or had it been Dowell?

Finally, Jerry had answered a call from Chef's mother. He had chatted for almost ten minutes. Was it possible that he had faked the conversation to cover up the fact that Dowell had called and what he had said?

I was starting to get a serious headache. I jotted another question for Dowell on my note pad, and added another column to my chart, and labeled it "Phone calls."

Once more I came at the problem from another direction. Who had the motive to kill Mac?

Mac supplied Chef with his drugs.

Mac had stolen money from Jerry.

Noel had argued with Mac about something.

I thought. The problem with motive was that the probable reason that Mac had been killed was because he knew too much about whatever was in the Smith's boxes. He had been helping someone do something illegal, that much had been clear from what he had said about the black-market seafood, and locking Darryl in the freezer. So if the motive was that Mac knew too much, I knew far too little.

I added "Motive" to the bottom of the chart anyway and filled it in.

I looked down at the chart. If I had expected the answer to jump out at me, it wasn't.

I took it person by person.

Chef: Fourth of July, he was on the roof. He had been the one to save me, though that didn't necessarily mean anything, except that he was very close to me when I was pushed. He had most probably seen Mac in Jerry's room the night of Mac's murder (which he denied) and had been gone for an hour from one to two, the night of the murder. He was by himself after two-thirty that night.

However, Chef did have an alibi for today, when I was locked in the freezer. Lily had been talking to him in her office. She had said that they were together the entire time. Did that rule out Chef completely?

Jerry: He had also been on the roof when I was pushed. He had been at the party until at least two when I left, and said he had been there until two-thirty. He hadn't left at any time before two. Jerry had answered a phone call from Chef's mother, which may or may not have been Dowell, and he had been by himself in the kitchen when I had been locked in the freezer.

Janet: She had not been on the roof the night of July 4th (that I knew of). She had known I would be on the roof, because she had heard Mac ask me if I was going to be on the roof. Had she hidden up there? She had received a phone call from Frank (she said) the night of the murder and had left the room for ten minutes. She said she was in her room resting when I had been locked in the freezer.

Noel: He had also not been on the roof the night I was almost pushed off as far as I knew. Though he could have hidden up there beforehand, waiting for me. How would he have known I would be up there? He had been at the party until shortly before two, at which time he had left with Lisa and gone to sleep with her. He had answered a phone call that had been a wrong number (supposedly) and had left for five minutes after that to get Lisa's candy. He said he had been helping maintenance with mopping up water when I had been locked in the freezer.

Lily: She had not been on the roof, that I knew of. She had been at the party the entire time, and had left with me. She could have easily gone down to the freezer after leaving me and killed Mac. She and Chef alibied one another for the time I had been locked in the freezer.

Frank: I had no idea how he was related to all of this, but I had put him on the chart because I knew he was linked to this somehow. But the only revealing information on the chart was that I thought I had seen him outside the hotel, the day after I had seen the green Explorer outside my house, when, according to Janet, he had gone back to Virginia.

I stretched against the pillow, nudging the dog who had fallen asleep at my feet and Ice who was curled against the side of my leg. I knew that everybody was gathering in Lily's room to wait out the storm together, and as the wind increased I was becoming more antsy.

I looked at the questions I had written down for Dowell:

Did Dowell call Chef's room immediately after seeing Mac?

Had Dowell told anybody else besides the person on the phone that Mac was looking for Jerry?

What calls did Dowell patch through to Chef's room the night of the murder (Frank for Janet, Noel's wrong number, Chef's mother for Jerry)?

I put the questions down and stared down at my chart, but the killer wasn't jumping off the page.

I sat back and closed my eyes. Somehow my thoughts kept going back to Smith's Seafood, and the numbers Darryl had written on the back of the Easter folder. Why had he written on a manila folder the amounts that the Holiday House owed Smith's Seafood for the last ten months that he had worked at the Holiday House?

Darryl was always scribbling on manila folders.

I grabbed my mace and the heavy flashlight and went to the door.

CHAPTER TWENTY-THREE

Blackout

I poked my head out the door and looked both ways. No one in sight. I closed the door behind me, hearing the reassuring click as the lock engaged. Then it wasn't so reassuring as I thought about the murderer probably having access to the master key.

I went down the hall and across the lobby to where Dowell sat behind the front desk in front of a battery-powered radio. The lights flickered, went out, and then came back on.

"Hey Dowell," I said. "I've got a couple of questions for you."

Dowell looked up. "The winds are gusting to a hundred miles an hour out there," he said in wonderment.

"Did you call up to Chef's room right after you saw Mac?"

Dowell shrugged. "The power went out when I was on my way back to the desk. It was only out for a minute or two, and it was back on by the time I made it to the desk. I called up there as soon as I got back."

So Mac had been alive shortly before one when the lights went out.

"And you don't know if you talked to a man or woman?"

"The music was loud." At least he was admitting he didn't *know*.

"Did you remember what calls you put through to Chef's room after that?"

"No," Dowell said unhelpfully.

"Come on, Dowell, think," I coaxed. "There weren't a whole

lot of people in the hotel, just us and the media."

"Well, Mac called before, I told you about that."

"Yes, he called before he came to the hotel, before the lights went out. But who called after the lights went out?"

"Let me think. Jesus, Callie, I have no idea. I know those media people have cell phones, but they're still getting tons of calls. I remember a couple of people calling for five fourteen, Chef's room, but I don't remember when or how many."

"These couple of people, were they men or women?"

Dowell buried his head in his hands. "Callie, you don't understand; transferring calls to the rooms is like completely automatic. I don't even think about it, unless I have to look up somebody's name. A lot of the times they just ask for the room number."

I thought about that. "So the people who called for room five fourteen just asked for the room number? Nobody asked for Chef's room, or for Janet, and you put them through to five fourteen?"

"No, I'm pretty sure that they just asked for five fourteen. Two people, I think, maybe three."

"And this was after the lights went out."

"Yes."

Which didn't prove anything. I couldn't tell which of the three phone calls that night had been legitimate. All I knew was that somebody answered the phone and talked to Dowell, and wasn't admitting it.

"So you don't remember if the people who called were men or women."

"No," Dowell said shortly. "I have no idea who I put through, or when or why."

We were definitely going backwards here.

"One more question, Dowell," I said soothingly. "Did you tell anyone else that Mac was in the hotel? That night, I mean."

Dowell brightened up, happy to be able to answer a question. "Nope. Sure didn't."

I thanked Dowell and went down the brightly-lit corridor to the food and beverage office. The door was closed and locked, as all the managers were done for the night. I unlocked the door and thought about keys. It was fairly obvious that Mac had been using all those keys to steal from the hotel. Was that what this was all about?

Minor theft didn't seem to warrant murder.

I sat down at my desk and looked at my office door, which I

had left open, so Dowell could hear me if I screamed.

Though I doubted he would be able to hear me over the thundering of the rain, sounding like heavy fists beating on the glass of the window, and the incessant moaning of the wind as it found its way in cracks and under doors. As I looked out the window, the pampas grass bush beside the window suddenly took flight and levitated out of sight. A few seconds later I saw it skidding madly across the parking lot and lodge under a car.

The Holiday House sign careened over, narrowly missing a red Camaro as it crashed to the pavement. A trash can and a beach chair that someone had forgot to secure went sliding merrily down the Beach Road as if they were racing. The beach chair was winning.

I reached under the desk and brought out a bunch of empty manila folders and started sorting through them, flipping each one over, studying both sides.

I thought about what Dowell had said as I went through the folders. He couldn't remember what calls he had put through to five fourteen after the lights went out, though he thought it was two or three. If it was three, then Janet, Noel and Jerry were off the hook. That meant I simply had missed the fourth phone call.

But what if it had been only two legitimate phone calls? Then somebody, either Janet, Noel or Jerry, was lying. Jerry probably wasn't. He had been on the phone for several minutes talking to Chef's mom, and it would be easy enough to verify if Chef's mom had called. But what about Janet? She had left the room immediately after her phone call. And if Frank and Janet were in cahoots, Frank would probably back up her story whether or not he had called. And finally, Noel. His phone call was the hardest to prove and could easily have been a fake. But wrong numbers happened, so who could say?

Did it really matter that someone had received a message meant for Jerry? It revealed to someone that Mac was in the hotel, but someone else had known he was in the hotel. Chef had probably seen him in Jerry's room.

And when Jerry got back to his room, he had seen Mac's hat. He had known that Mac was in the hotel.

There was no way I could track who knew Mac was in the hotel. As far as I could tell I was the only when who didn't know that Mac was in the hotel that night, with maybe the exception of Lily. I didn't see how she could have known, but then again, maybe I underestimated her.

My fingers, which had been automatically shuffling through the folders, stopped, and then continued. Darryl had scribbled notes on the back of several of the folders, but none that seemed to be related to Smith's Seafood. I reached the bottom of the stack and put them back on the floor.

Hmmm. Darryl had written numbers on the back of the Easter folder, numbers which I had discovered were the monthly totals that the hotel ordered from Smith's Seafood. On the back of an empty folder entitled "Smith's Seafood," had been the notation about Frank ("Frank-Miami???") and "16/20" which probably had something to do with the fact that boxes of 16/20 shrimp was ordered every month from Smith's, but weren't delivered.

I noticed that my message light was blinking and punched in the code to check my voice mail. Messages from employees saying they were leaving town, a message from my mother worried about my safety. As I listened, I opened the file cabinet and began thumbing through the folders. Fourth of July, Christmas, Thanksgiving, BAC's Easter Brunch....

Darryl had been working on two things his last two weeks: Easter in the restaurant and the Born Again Christian's Easter Brunch in banquets. Why hadn't I thought about that? I pulled the folder from the cabinet, but laid it on the desk unopened when I heard the last message on my voice mail.

It was a message from Debbie. I listened to her message with growing excitement.

Bingo.

I replayed the message: "Hi Callie, really wanted to talk to you, but I keep missing you. Hope you are weathering the hurricane okay. Just wanted you to know I think I found what you were looking for. I checked the Miami papers for the entire month of September four years ago, and I finally found that name. Frank Smith. He and a bunch of other people were found not guilty of a drug smuggling charge; it was on the front page with pictures and everything. I gathered a lot of people think they were all guilty, but they got off. Anyway, I hope this helps you. Call me soon, will ya? Bye."

It had been a long shot, but it had panned out. That explained the "Frank-Miami???" notation. Darryl had been in Miami four years ago in September. He had seen Frank's picture on the front page, and four years later when he met Frank he thought he recognized him.

I turned over the BAC Easter Brunch manila folder and wasn't surprised at what I saw. Light pencil had scraped neat letters on the back of the folder.

SS = Coke???

And that was all.

The lights chose that moment to blink once, and go out as a spectacular explosion of sparks shot from the transformer across the street. Darkness folded over me like a prickly wool sweater.

Moving very slowly, I pulled my flashlight out of one pocket, and the mace from the other. Turning the light on, I flashed it over the folder again as sparks fluttered and died in the rampaging wind and rain.

It all fell together with a click. Darryl's interest in how much money the hotel paid Smith's Seafood. Mac's role in all this. The rising food costs.

So Smith's Seafood was delivering cocaine with its seafood. And I would bet the box marked with the red dot held the coke. Most importantly, it looked like the smuggler was using hotel money to finance the drugs. Ten months ago, the monthly order from Smith's had jumped from $430 in June to $4899 in July, and continued to increase over the past eight months. The hotel paid Smith's for seafood, and Smith's delivered cocaine with the seafood. Obviously, the hotel was paying too much for the seafood that was actually being delivered. Thus, the rising food costs. It also explained the long waste report, and Mac's conversation with the black-market fisherman. The smuggler bought cut-rate seafood and put it in Smith's boxes to replace the seafood that was not delivered because of the cocaine.

Frank Smith had been arrested for smuggling drugs four years ago in Miami. He had gotten off. Presumably he had went straight for a couple of years, but when his father died two years ago, he must have seen his opportunity to smuggle drugs though his seafood company, probably with the help of his old buddies down in Miami.

But as much as Mac was involved, there had to have been someone else in the hotel. It had to be a manager. But who?

I heard a noise in the hall, and quietly slid back my chair and stood up, flicking the flashlight off and holding the mace at ready.

"Callie?" a worried voice said, and Dowell appeared in the doorway, holding a propane lantern. "I was worried about you back here by yourself."

"Thanks, Dowell," I said, resisting the urge to put a hand to my fluttering heart. "Would you do me a favor and walk me back to my room?"

"Sure, Callie. There's not much I can do, anymore. Lily is wandering around, making sure everyone has got candles and aren't freaking out in their rooms. She told me I can go upstairs with the others, if I want."

He walked me back to my room, and stood just inside the door as I picked a note up off the floor, looked in the shower and under the beds. Ice and the dog frolicked around me.

"I don't blame you," Dowell said as he watched me search the room. "Everybody's freaked out about this murder. Are you coming upstairs? Everybody's in Lily's room."

"I know," I said. "I'll be up in a little while."

He pulled the door shut and I quickly propped the chair against the door. Balancing the flashlight on the table, I pulled the note out of my pocket. It had been shoved under the door.

> Callie-
> I'd like to talk to you. Will you meet me in the kitchen?
> I want to tell you about Mac.
> Jerry

Now, I'm not stupid. I was aware that the note might be a fake, tricking me into a trap.

But on the other hand, it might be legitimate. Jerry had been very close to Mac. Maybe Mac had inadvertently told him who the murderer was. I would play it safe.

I pulled the chair aside and opened the door. Dowell was at the end of the hall, knocking on a door.

"Hey Dowell!" I called, and he turned around with the lantern. "Can you come back here?"

"I'll be there in a second," he called.

I ducked back in my room, and went to the desk. My sheet of suspects lay on top. I read over it, trying to fit the motive, which I now knew, to a suspect.

I came up blank. Any one of the chefs could order food, and they all had ordered from Smith's. Anyone could have written "cater" and a date on the box with the red dot, which would render it untouchable until the date of the function. Any of chefs would fit the bill. Janet was "special friends" with Frank, and had access to the freezer. And Lily was general manager of the hotel. She could damn well do anything she wanted to.

So who was Mac's accomplice? I turned my attention back to the suspect list. Who did most of the ordering? Who was the "big boss" in the F&B department? Who had seen Mac last? Who had a drug problem himself? And who had admitted to me that he had manipulated the pricing of the spring menu to lower the food costs? When had this all started? Ten months ago. Who had arrived at the hotel twelve months ago?

Chef.

I stuck my head out the door and saw Dowell coming down the hall, the lantern bobbing in front of him. The sight inexplicably reminded me of the story of how the town of Nags Head supposedly got its name. According to the colorful story, back in the days when lighthouses were just a dream, and the "Graveyard of the Atlantic" was earning its name with a vengeance, local pirates would run a pony up and down the beach with a lantern around its neck. To the unsuspecting ships at sea, the up and down motion of the lantern would look like a ship at sea and they would steer toward it. The ship would crash up onto shore where the band of blood-thirsty pirates would finish off anybody who was unlucky enough to survive the wreck.

The lantern bobbed down the hall toward me, Dowell's grinning face above the light.

"The reporter lady in one thirty-one was taking a bath when the lights went out," he said. "Taking a bath, can you believe that, with a hurricane coming. I had to help her out of the bath."

That explained the grin.

"Would you escort me upstairs to the restaurant?" I asked, and Dowell, feeling like Lancelot, the Front Desk Knight, agreed happily. You would have thought I had asked him to a Sunday afternoon picnic, instead of escorting me up five flights of stairs. Turning to go I patted the dog's head and rubbed Ice behind the ears. They were not happy with me at all. I had been neglecting them shamefully.

"As soon as the hurricane is over, we'll do something fun," I promised them. Ice huffed in disbelief, and the dog with no name looked at me quizzically.

We climbed the steps, Dowell gamely not complaining, though he started sounding like the little engine that couldn't by the time we got to the top.

"Stay here," I whispered to Dowell, and had him wait in the back hall as I crept along the hall to the kitchen, where I saw a light flickering. I peeked around the corner and saw Jerry busily chopping vegetables by candlelight.

I tiptoed back to Dowell.

"Will you do me another favor?" I whispered and Dowell nodded, though he looked as if he thought death might be preferable to climbing any more stairs.

"Can you find Lily for me? Tell her I need to talk to her, it's an emergency. Don't tell anyone else, okay? I'll meet her–" I thought quickly of all the people who were in Lily's room, including Chef. "Tell her I'll meet her here."

Dowell nodded his agreement and went off down the stairs.

I turned to face the kitchen.

CHAPTER TWENTY-FOUR

Callie and the Dealer
and a Dog Named Jake

"Hi Jerry," I said, stepping into the kitchen.

"Callie," Jerry said, not looking up from the zucchini he was furiously chopping with the precision of an automaton.

I leaned against the tile wall, watching Jerry chop in the flickering candlelight. The sound of the storm was muted here, though two buckets were positioned in the middle of the floor and slow drips from the ceiling tick-tocked into the bottoms.

I glanced at my watch. It was almost eleven o'clock. The hurricane was approaching its full fury. It seemed so peaceful here in the bowels of the sterile kitchen watching Jerry chop, chop, chop.

He was making me nervous. I put my hand into my suit coat and grasped the mace.

"So I got your note," I began encouragingly.

"No shit," Jerry said, pushing the thinly sliced zucchini aside and starting on a portabello mushroom, the blade glinting and flashing as his hand rose and fell.

"So what did you want to talk to me about?" I said finally, my patience at an end. Lily should be up soon, and I could tell her what I had discovered about the cocaine and Chef.

"Mac was–" Jerry said, and swallowed hard. His cherubic face was grim. Today he wasn't wearing the pink baseball cap, and instead wore his long and tawny hair fastened in a ponytail at the back of his neck. I noticed he wore a gold hoop in his right ear. I had never noticed that before.

"Mac was like my little brother," he said, pulling another flat, saucer-shaped mushroom out of the box. He moved his face so all I could see was the back of his head. I thought he was probably crying.

"Did he talk about what was going on?" I asked softly.

"He was always messed up," Jerry said woodenly. "He spent every dime he made on surfing, alcohol and drugs. He hasn't paid his part of the rent and bills for the last five months. But he was like my brother."

I was silent as he turned to his cart and pulled out a large red onion and mechanically started slicing.

"Something was going on. Oh, I don't doubt he was stealing plates and other things from the hotel. I never caught him at it, but he wouldn't think twice about something like that. He was a good kid, really, but it was like no one had taught him the difference between right and wrong." He took a deep breath, and swiped angrily at his eyes.

"Something strange was going on between Chef and Mac. Mac was always getting Chef high, always had a line of coke for him. I asked him to stop, because Chef was getting to the point where he couldn't function. But Mac would just grin and say, 'we're having a good time, man.' And keep giving him the drugs. He knew that Chef had a drug problem. I had told Mac that before Chef came, one night when I got drunk. So he *knew* Chef didn't need the stuff, but he kept giving it to him. I don't even know where Mac was getting it. The stuff's not cheap you know, and I'd swear Chef wasn't buying it, that Mac was just giving it to him. It started as soon as Chef arrived. He was okay for a couple of months, and then he started just going through the motions. I tried to help him, but he wouldn't let me this time."

"This time?"

"This happened to him in college. He's got an addictive personality, you know? So do I. I went through it with heroin, I knew what I had to do to get him off the coke. I helped him with his papers, got him up and made him go to class. Eventually he beat it. But this time he wouldn't let me help. And everything's been going to shit. Food costs rising, food missing, and he won't do anything."

"You know anything about Smith's Seafood?"

"Huh? Smith's Seafood?" Jerry turned to me, his blue eyes watery and luminescent in the light from the candle. I couldn't tell if he was faking the confusion or not. But, if he was guilty, why would he tell me all this? Unless he was just muddying the waters, unless he *had* killed Mac, but for more personal reasons, and he was trying to throw suspicion on someone else. I narrowed my eyes and waited for his answer.

"Smith's? Mac always acted weird around Frank Smith. I never understood it. What do you know about that?"

"So who do you think killed Mac?" I asked, ignoring his question.

"Jesus!" Jerry said, throwing down the knife and turning to face me completely. "Do I have to spell it out for you? He admitted to me that Mac was in my room when he went down there to get the vodka, and he outright lied to you when you asked him to his face. Mac had come to me for help, I know that, because he was in some serious shit. I overheard him talking on the phone the last day he was home. He was pissed, but he was scared. I figured it had something to do with the coke. He was in something deep. I think he may have had something to do with Darryl Menden leaving. Darryl hated Mac, and the feeling was mutual. When Darryl was being such a pain in the ass that last month, Mac said not to worry, that he'd be gone soon. If you could have seen the expression on his face, just like a little boy's, all defiant and excited and secretive."

Jerry shook his head.

"So did Chef admit to killing Mac?"

"Are you insane? Of course not. He said Mac left right around two, and that he came back up to the party. Chef said that was the last time he saw Mac until you found him in the freezer. He swears it, but he was so messed up that night, I don't think he can remember a damn thing."

Jerry picked up the cutting board and slid the contents into a half hotel pan. He carried the board and the knife over to the dish room, and put the vegetables on top of his cart. He went to the door and looked back at me.

"I wish to God he never would have come here. It's my fault, I told the Pete that Michael was really good, better than Noel, for the job. I wish I never would have done that. Mac might still be alive."

He walked out of the kitchen, and down the steps, leaving me alone in the kitchen as the wind raged and roared and the candle flickered wildly in the drafts.

I wandered over to the fridges and shone my flashlight at the gauges. The electricity had not been out for long, and the temperatures were remaining steady, though that would change the longer we were without power. I thought about all the food downstairs in the walk-ins, and fervently hoped the power was restored soon.

I wondered if Dowell had found Lily yet. I wanted to talk to her so we could figure out what to do. I thought I heard a dog barking, but it must have been an eddy of wind.

Jerry had confirmed what I had already thought. Chef was the smuggler and the murderer. It made sense. So why did it feel wrong?

Glass broke in the restaurant. Had the window blown in? I rushed to the door and was in the restaurant before I had a chance to think.

Silence. I shone the flashlight over the windows and saw that the windows were intact. I heard a faint noise down the back hall, and called out. "Lily? I'm in here."

A glimmer of light caught my attention, and I directed the flashlight to the floor.

A broken water glass lay on the carpet.

I turned and was running for the kitchen when the shot rang out, almost deafening me. The window beside me blew out in a screech of glass and a rush of wind and water. Then I was past the window and slamming into the kitchen, almost running into the dish counter, sliding on the tile floor as I spun around the steel counter and sprinted down the length of the kitchen for the back door that led down the stairs to people and safety. Behind me the kitchen door crashed opened and the candle that Jerry had been using fluttered and went out. I slammed into a closed door.

It had been open a few minutes ago, when Jerry had left.

I fumbled with the knob, but before I could get it unlocked I felt a rush of air and someone hit me from behind. We fell into the side of one of the fridges, and I heard a grunt of pain from my attacker. I kicked wildly, and knocked my heavy flashlight against the side of someone's head. The flashlight flicked on and off as I hit, and I caught a glimpse of purple, and then I was out from underneath my attacker's leg and scrambling crab-like underneath the prep table. The dead flashlight spun out of my grasp and slid across the floor hitting the edge of the ice cream freezer with a resounding clank.

My attacker heaved off the ground and dove toward where

the flashlight had hit. I reached into my pocket and pulled out my mace. The person was kicking the side of the ice cream freezer and I crawled slowly from underneath the table towards the door to the restaurant. I could hear a knocking noise and wondered what the hell the killer was doing now.

I had decided that if I made for the door to the stairwell, my attacker would hear me and would be close enough to squeeze off another shot. If I could make it to the restaurant without the person hearing me, I could go to the front door of the restaurant, where, please, please, please, the keys would be in the door, and I could let myself out while the killer stumbled around the kitchen.

A beam of light flicked on, swept under the prep table where I had just been.

The killer had found my flashlight.

I broke for the door, hit the swinging door with all my force and was through it as I heard Lily's muffled voice shout, "Callie!"

Lily! It was Lily trying to kill me! She had lied about the gun being stolen!

I heard the blast of the gun again and ran into a wall. I rolled off the wall and made for the front door, clumsily running into walls and chairs in the inky darkness. The wind was howling through the tables, from the broken window on the other side of the restaurant.

I reached the door, and felt for where the keys usually hung from the lock.

Nothing.

Shit. Behind me the door from the kitchen opened, and the beam of the flashlight pierced the darkness. I ducked, and dove for the steps leading up to the bar as the flashlight swept the front door, losing my mace in the process. I tore up the stairs and around the bar and crouched, hidden by the U-shape of the bar. The floor smelled like bleach, and above me glasses on the racks crashed together in the wind that rocked the restaurant.

I could not hear Lily. All I could hear was the unearthly howling of the wind. I looked up as the beam of the flashlight slid over the top of the bar, piercing the mote-filled darkness. I held my breath, straining to hear footsteps. Nothing. The light slid away over the bar and disappeared out of my sight.

Was it possible that Lily would decide I had run down the back hallway? Would she go down there to check, leaving me with the opportunity to try to escape out the front door again?

The keys would be nearby, on the hostess stand, or in the register. It would take me just few seconds to find them. Or would she search the room from end to end? Inevitably she would find me.

I tried not to think about why Lily was trying to kill me. I had begun to trust her, and it hurt that I had been so wrong. But she could have done everything. She could have hid on the roof and tried to push me off, she could have left me the night of the party and gone to the freezer and killed Mac, and she could have locked me in the freezer and had a change of mind. And she could have ordered the seafood, and used Mac to put the orders away. Chef was so messed up on drugs he was having trouble figuring out how to use toilet paper; he wouldn't have noticed what she was doing. Was Lily that pissed that Mr. Peterson would not give her control over the food and beverage department? It was a hell of a revenge. It would explain Darryl Menden's number, and Lily could've taken the tube of hamburger when she left me asleep in her room and went to get my dress.

My calves were sore from my squatting position, reminding me horribly of my time in the freezer. That memory stung me into action.

I stuck my head out from behind the bar. Immediately I saw the beam of the flashlight, running over the front door and the hostess stand as Lily tried to find the keys. So much for the idea of escaping out the front.

I sidled out the other side of the bar. The door to the back hallway was all of twenty feet away, but the most direct route to it was blocked by booths. I crawled on my hands and knees until I came to a place in the corral that wasn't blocked by booths, which put me halfway up the length of the restaurant. I scrambled under the bars and made for the hallway.

It was hellish. Wind and rain tore into me as I ran, zigzagging, expecting to feel a bullet in my back every step I took. Glass and silverware blew off the tables in a tinkle of breaking glass and clanking of silver.

I heard footsteps behind me, but I couldn't see anything, my eyes blinded by darkness and the driving rain. I ran into a table and did a somersault over it to land in broken glass and the tines of a fork. I turned over on my back and kicked the overturned table in the direction of Lily's approaching footsteps. A grunt as the table hit and she went down heavily. I scrambled to my feet and sprinted with all my might for where the door of the back hallway should be, crashing into tables and overturning chairs. I misjudged the door by about five feet and ran into the wall, smashing my nose and the fingers of one hand.

I felt along the wall for the door. It was closed, and it took precious moments to find the handle, unlock and open it. I knew the hallway was lined on one side by shelves filled with hotel pans, dishes, buckets, baskets and boxes of paper goods, though for all I could see, it could have been buckets of gold. As I slammed the door open a box of what was probably Styrofoam cups fell on my head. I shoved it off and ran full speed down the hall.

And ran squarely into someone.

"Callie," Lily said. "What were those noises? I've been knocking for five minutes. Did you know your dog is loose and–" She was shining a flashlight in my face, spotlighting me for the person who had appeared in the doorway, gun pointing at us.

"Noel!" Lily said. "What are you doing with that—is that my gun?"

Noel raised the gun, tears running down his face. "I don't want to do this, but I can't let you mess this up for me. I would have stopped soon, don't you understand? I just needed enough money for Lisa and me to live comfortable when I get too old to work. But you couldn't leave it alone." The gun was wavering as Noel squinted at us in the glare of Lily's flashlight.

"Noel, you can't do this. You won't get away with killing both of us. Put the gun down, Noel, listen to me." Lily was speaking soothingly, convincingly.

I was speechless. I couldn't move.

Time slowed, trickling along like honey through an hourglass.

All I could see was the barrel of the gun, and Noel's speckled finger trembling on the trigger in the daylight glare of the flashlight.

His finger twitched, and I stared as if mesmerized. I could not move. The switch between mind and body had been switched to off, and once again I was helpless to do anything as Noel raised the gun and sighted along the barrel.

Move, move, move, move. The familiar monotonous words, but I was mesmerized by that shiny black barrel, the finger squeezing the trigger...

I heard what sounded like the snarl of a dog, and something clicked in my head.

Not again.

"No!" I yelled, throwing myself backward as Noel pulled the trigger, bowling over Lily. The echo of the shot ricocheted off the pots and pans as Lily's flashlight spun crazily down the hall. I turned over in the darkness, and found Lily right beside me as we slithered down the hall on our bellies.

I heard the clickety-clack of nails on tile floor, and felt a warm tongue bathe my face and then a furry body had jumped over me and was loping down the hall.

And suddenly I was angrier than I could ever remember being. I was *pissed.* I pushed off the floor, and stood up, mistaking Lily's back and leg for the ground.

"Jesus Christ," she muttered.

The hall was like a wind tunnel, wind whistling down the narrow passage, pots clanging to the floor, and above it all, the growling and grunts of Noel and the dog. I charged down the hall, unmindful of the gun, until I ran into an outstretched leg, and started kicking with all my might.

A beam of light suddenly spotlighted Noel on the floor as Lily regained the flashlight and came toward us. The dog sat by Noel's head, tongue hanging out as he grinned. Noel lay sprawled, in a purple T-shirt, eyes shut, knocked out cold.

"What are *you* doing here, dog?" I asked the panting animal.

There was Della and the dealer and a dog named Jake... Crazily enough, the refrain from my favorite song was running through my head.

Suddenly I knew why. It was the name of *my* dog.

"Good boy, Jake," I told him, and his tail thumped.

"Callie," Lily said from behind me.

"Yes?" I turned and stare at her, purple dress askew, curls springing wildly around her head.

"What the hell is going on?"

CHAPTER TWENTY-FIVE

Finding Home

Sharkey's was full on this Thursday night. Lenny Marks was singing as I came in the door. He smiled at me and mouthed "Hi Kalamazoo," and I waved a thumbs up.

I made my way to the end of the bar, and slid into the seat beside Susan, who moved her custom stool aside to give me more room. Melissa gave me a Tanqueray and tonic and I thanked her.

"Did you hear the pool from the Sea Escape Inn was seen floating down by what's left of the Nags Head Pier?" Susan asked.

I shook my head. "Hadn't heard that one."

It was a week since the Outer Banks had suffered the near miss from the hurricane. At the last minute, the frisky hurricane had decided to take a turn up the coast, skim Virginia Beach and then head out to sea. The Outer Banks had still been dealt a heavy blow, many million dollars' worth of damage, but nothing as bad as it could have been.

"Everybody always says that nor'easters are worse than hurricanes," Susan said, her grandmotherly face smug.

I laughed.

Susan turned to other subjects, a sign that the hurricane was slowly receding from the Outer Banks collective consciousness.

"I heard you went and saw Lisa Landrum," Susan said.

I didn't ask how she knew that. The grapevine at work.

I nodded. Lisa had been calm, and resigned, and standing by her man. Noel was in the "Manteo Hilton," and might never see the light of day again, though his lawyer was talking senility and mental disintegration. I'm sure Noel would love that. Lisa had been sweet to me, but distracted, and completely heartbroken. She did not understand what had happened to Noel. She knew that his scheming had been for her, and that hurt her beyond words.

"Doesn't he realize I would love him no matter what?" Lisa kept saying to me. "I didn't need the money. I just wanted him."

"She holding up?" Susan asked.

"Yes," I said.

Lily came in and made her way to the end of the bar. "Hi beautiful girls," she said, plopping down beside me. Melissa handed Lily her special container with celery in it, but Lily waved it aside.

"No more celery," she said. "After my near death experience, I decided I'd rather start smoking again. But when I went to light up, all I could taste was celery. It was the damnedest thing. Haven't been able to smoke a cigarette in a week, and I *wanted* to." She accepted her drink and turned to me. "It looks like you were right, we're going to have to redo the entire floor in the restaurant. The Pete was pissed, he's got insurance."

"I've got some ideas about the restaurant," I said, thinking of polished wood floors and greenery and slowly whirling fans.

Lily sighed.

"Why am I not surprised? Come talk to me tomorrow." She took a swallow of her drink.

Kyle Taylor made his way through the crowd toward us, and I pretended not to notice how nicely his faded blue jeans fit or the way his hair curled damply along the side of his neck.

"Why if it isn't the heroine herself," he said. "Quick now, what year was Adolph Hitler born?"

"In Austria in 1889," I said. "Born to Alois and Klara."

"Ugh," Lily said. "Can't you two think of a more cheerful trivia game?"

"He started it," I said.

"Well, why not the history of the Outer Banks?" Susan asked.

I looked at Kyle and he shrugged. "You'll have to give me a couple of weeks to bone up," I said.

"Two weeks. Same time, same place," he said and waved as

he made his way to the front door where he greeted several customers.

I watched him, and realized for the first time in a long time I wasn't thinking of my ex-husband every time I looked at another man. Kyle was annoying and obnoxious, and, okay, more than a little sexy, but he most definitely didn't remind me of my ex-husband.

"Have you heard anything more about Noel Landrum?" Susan asked. "I know you haven't wanted to talk about it, Callie, but I'm dying to know what really happened. The rumors can't be all true."

It had taken me a week to come to terms with what had happened. It had been very hard to believe that Noel, the jolly, happy volunteer fire man, could really have been responsible for the distribution of cocaine on the Outer Banks, and who had wanted to kill me. "I'm all right with it, now," I told Susan.

"I heard from Dale Grain that they've found out Noel had embezzled money from that corporation he used to work for in Maryland, and instead of scaring their investors by revealing the embezzlement, the company fired him and told him to leave the state," Lily said.

"Noel was good with numbers," I said.

"Yes, he was, wasn't he?" Lily said without humor.

"So I still don't understand why he did it," Susan said.

"Retirement security," Lily said.

"For Lisa," I said.

Susan looked at us quizzically.

"Noel loved his wife more than anything in the world," I said. "But he was obsessed with their age difference, and was afraid he would not be able to provide for her like a younger man could. He realized he couldn't do it like he wanted to on his retirement pay. I guess that's why he was embezzling money from the corporation in Maryland, and why he did what he did at the Holiday House."

"So how long had he been scamming the hotel?"

"From what we can see, since last July, the bastard. Apparently Noel was pissed when Chef was hired over him last year, and that's when Frank Smith and he started conniving." Lily shook her head in disgust.

"Frank Smith had been involved with drug smuggling down in Miami. The charges didn't stick. Afterward he came back up to Virginia and helped his ailing father with Smith's. Once Frank's father died, Frank was free to do whatever he wanted with the business. And what he wanted was to smuggle drugs. Smith's was being put out of business by big corporations anyway, so he wasn't making much money off the business.

"Strangely enough, that was the connection between Noel and Frank. Hatred of big corporations. Noel blamed all his troubles on the big corporation in Maryland where he used to work. They made a natural team."

"So I thought Janet was dating Frank. Did she have something to do with all of this?"

Lily shook her head. "Nope. At least not knowingly. Frank was worried that Noel was close to being discovered. After what happened with Darryl, Frank started seeing Janet so he could have an inside track on what was going on at the hotel. He tried to keep his and Janet's relationship a secret, but it got out, and Noel was pissed."

"It sounds like it was all falling apart, anyway. Fighting among the ranks, and all that," Susan said.

"Well, Noel was under a lot of stress. I was poking around, talking to Darryl Menden, who had a pretty good idea what was going on. Darryl was in Miami four years ago when Frank was acquitted of smuggling drugs and Darryl saw his picture in the paper. So Darryl had an idea of what Frank might be involved in, which is how he stumbled on to this whole thing. He had been working a banquet function in Janet's absence and took it upon himself to look into a price increase. He started looking at food invoices, and noticed that Smith's Seafood was charging more for seafood than some of the other purveyors. That was the start, and the more Darryl looked into Smith's Seafood, the more suspicious he became. So Darryl knew too much, and Noel had to get rid of him. Then Noel removed the incriminating Smith's Seafood invoices from Darryl's desk, but he forgot that Darryl wrote notes on the back of manila folders.

"So when I started talking to Darryl, Noel knew it was a real possibility that I would uncover the whole scam. To add to his stress, one of the distributors that Mac and Noel used, the kitchen manager at the White Gull, got busted, and he could identify Mac. Then Noel found out Frank was spying on him." I took a swig of my drink and continued.

"But in the beginning Frank and Noel got along great. Frank was already delivering drugs to other restaurants in Virginia Beach. But it was Noel who came up with the whole scheme of the hotel paying Frank Smith for his drugs. Then

Noel would turn around and sell the cocaine for pure profit.

"In July of last year, Noel started ordering all of his seafood from Smith's Seafood, and encouraging Jerry to do the same. Most of the month, Smith's delivered straight seafood, but once a month, the cocaine was delivered." I explained about the red dot, and the cocaine packed at the bottom of a seafood box.

"Of course, because of the cocaine, Smith's wasn't delivering all of the seafood on the invoices. That's why Mac or Noel had to be there for the Smith's deliveries. They would mark off the food as delivered, even though it wasn't. Noel was actually ordering more food than he needed, which was evidenced by the high food costs. But he also replaced some of the food with black-market seafood. It was delivered to Frank's summer cottage in Kitty Hawk, and they would pack it in Smith's boxes. They would bring the boxes at night and put them in the freezer. Dowell actually heard them in the back hallway a couple of times, but he was always too scared to go check.

"It was neat and simple. The hotel paid Smith's, and Smith's delivered drugs. It would stay in the freezer for a couple of days, during which time Mac would deliver the stuff in the Holiday House Cater truck.

"There were two problems with the scheme. One was that the black-market seafood wasn't as good quality as it should have been. That's why the fiasco on New Year's Eve happened. Noel and Frank were lucky, because there were shrimp from a company called Deel's in the freezer, as well as the black-market shrimp labeled Smith's. Noel swore that he had used Deel's shrimp."

"He put them out of business to save his own hide," Susan said, shaking her head.

I nodded. "The other problem with the scheme was that the hotel was paying more money for less food, and food costs were going up. But Noel was working on that. He was making enough money to buy more black-market seafood. He made sure that the wastage report was filled out with bogus wasted food. Also, the hotel would pay Smith's for top quality seafood, and actually receive the cheapest seafood. That's why Darryl had written '16/20' on the folder. He had noticed that the Smith's invoices reflected that high quality, peeled and de-veined 16/20 shrimp had been paid for, when in fact it was the much cheaper 31/35 shrimp which was being delivered. And that was just one example."

"Chef was helping that along with his high menu pricing

and the padded waste report. Chef was too messed up to figure out why the food costs were rising. Noel made sure of that, by keeping him supplied with drugs through Mac. He had found out from Mac that Chef had been fighting a drug addiction all his life, and ruthlessly took advantage of it."

"So what about you, Callie?" Susan asked. "Why was Noel chasing you around the restaurant with a gun?"

"It started before that," I said. "Noel was feeling the pressure. The kitchen manager at the White Gull had been busted with some of Noel's cocaine. Then Noel found out I was snooping around. Mac told him he thought I might have seen him with the black-market dealer. I made the mistake of asking Frank Smith an indiscreet question about Darryl Menden, which Frank relayed to Noel, and clued Noel to the fact that I was interested in talking to Darryl. And finally he saw my Rolodex flipped to Darryl Menden's number. When he tracked Darryl down to his mother's house, he found out I was asking the right questions. He scared Darryl so badly that Darryl left town again.

"Then, Noel was passing by the F&B office when we were talking about going up on the roof to watch the fireworks, and he decided to hide on the roof before anyone else got up there and wait for me. He says he just meant to scare me."

"But when he locked her in the freezer, I think he was trying to kill her, though he says he was only trying to scare her. But what else would he say?" Lily took over the story. "But I messed up that plan," Lily looked affectionately at me. "What's weird is that he keeps telling the police how much he liked Callie, and that he didn't want to hurt her. She just kept getting in his way."

"He and Frank Smith came to my house, the night before we evacuated. Frank lied to Janet about going back to Virginia that night so he could accompany Noel. Jake scared them off, but who knows what they planned to do? And when Noel came looking for me the night of the hurricane, he meant to kill me," I said. "After locking me in the freezer didn't work, he used the master key that he had stolen from Mac to let himself in Lily's room and steal her gun. He was pretty far gone by that time. When the lights went out, he went to my room. I was gone. Unfortunately, I had left the note from Jerry asking me to meet him in the kitchen. Jake chased him out of my room, but he didn't pull the door all the way shut, which is how Jake got out a few minutes later and came looking for me."

"So Noel went upstairs and waited for Callie to finish talking to Jerry so he could kill her. He broke a glass in the restaurant to draw her into the restaurant, and then went around to lock the door to the kitchen so she was trapped. I got Callie's message through Dowell about that time and came upstairs to find the kitchen door locked. I was knocking and calling for Callie while Callie was running for her life, and when she heard my voice she actually thought I was the murderer!" Lily said, immensely amused.

"It was *very* dark," I said and took a sip of my drink. I regretted ever telling Lily that little piece of information.

"That crazy dog of hers went for Noel like a bat out of hell," Lily said with some satisfaction. "And Callie was no slouch herself."

"Well, Jake knew instinctively that Noel was threatening me. And Noel had kicked Jake for trying to steal some fish, which is why Jake was limping the first day I saw him."

"So why did he kill Mac?" Susan said, lighting up another cigarette.

"Mac had become somewhat of a liability. The manager from White Gull could identify him. Mac was stealing from the hotel, using the keys Noel had given him. Noel was afraid the minor theft would draw attention to his bigger scam. Then, Mac threatened to go to the police if Noel didn't leave me alone. I had told Mac that someone had tried to push me off the roof, and Mac had known it had been Noel. But Noel had too much to lose at this point. He had to stop me, and he wasn't going to let Mac get in his way. Noel threatened to kill him if he didn't leave town, and Mac believed him. A maintenance guy saw them arguing that day, and Mac went into hiding the next day. But Mac needed money, and he came to the hotel to ask Jerry for money to get out of town. Unfortunately, Dowell saw him and called up to Chef's room to tell Jerry, and got Noel. Noel pretended it was a wrong number.

"Then he left to go to Jerry's room, looking for Mac. Unfortunately for Noel, Chef was in Jerry's room too. However, Noel heard them talking about money; Mac was asking to borrow some money from Chef, but Chef didn't have any. Noel heard Mac say that he knew how to get some money, and Noel knew that Mac was talking about the Smith's boxes in the freezer, where bags of cocaine were nestled under a layer of ice and shrimp. So Noel went back to the party and he and Lisa and went to their room a while later. He pretended to take two sleeping pills with her and lay down. As soon as she was asleep, he got up and used his forged F&B key to go through the restaurant and down the back service elevator so Dowell at the front desk wouldn't see him. He waited in the utility closet across the hall from the freezer, until he saw Mac go in. Noel followed him in, and tried to talk to him, because he really didn't want to kill him. But Mac turned around and started taking down the box with the drugs in it, and Noel picked up the tube of hamburger and hit him in the back of the head.

"Noel then knocked the box of steaks on the floor, and put steaks in Mac's coat, to make it look like Mac had fallen while trying to steal steaks. He put the hamburger tube back with the others, not noticing the small dent and hair on it, and took the cocaine from the Smith's box. As he was leaving, he accidentally dropped the empty shrimp box outside the door. Then he took Frank's Explorer and took the cocaine to Frank's Kitty Hawk cottage. He didn't want to take the chance that the police wouldn't fall for the accident set-up, and search the freezer, and maybe everyone's rooms. Frank had given Noel a key to his Explorer a couple of months ago so Noel could run an errand for Frank.

"Noel had been wearing gloves, so he wasn't really worried about the hamburger tube, especially as he hoped Mac's death would be seen as an accident. But after he locked me in the freezer, he knew he had to get rid of it. Noel took the tube of hamburger when he came to check on me after he locked me in the freezer and I was gone. He gave it to Chef to use for dinner that night."

"So is it true, that Chef is in detox?"

Lily nodded. "I knew he was getting bad, but there was nothing I could do about it, not without the Pete's say-so. The Pete had a talk with him when he came down, and Chef volunteered to go into detox. The Pete even went and talked to Noel, to hear his side of it."

"It's sad in a way," Susan said. "That he did all that out of love."

"And greed," Lily said.

I took another sip of my drink and rolled my neck, feeling the miniature pops as my neck cracked.

"Noel just wasn't what he seemed," Susan said.

"A lot of people are like that," Lily said, and I turned to find both Susan and Lily staring at me.

"Is it time?" Kyle asked, walking by.

"Yeah," Lily said.

I was starting to feel uncomfortable.

"What do you think, Laurie?" Lily asked me.

"Huh?" It took me a moment to realize that she had called me by my real name.

Later they told me that they should have remembered to have a camera ready to take a picture of the expression on my face.

"Laurie McKinley," Susan said. "We've known who you were since you got here. Kyle recognized you right off, and Lily and I were talking about how familiar you looked one day and realized why."

"No one said anything," I said, feeling numb. Suddenly I felt cold and alienated.

"You didn't seem to want anyone to know," Susan said simply.

"But we decided that it was time you came out of your shell," Kyle said from behind me.

I turned slowly and saw that he was holding out a portable microphone to me.

"It's yours, from us at Sharkey's to you, just like Susan's got her chair and Elliot's got his wine," Kyle said.

"I would like to introduce a special friend of mine, Ms. Callie McKinley," Lenny Marks announced over the microphone. "She's a very talented young lady. I happen to know 'cause I've heard her singing when she thought nobody could hear her. Ya'll give Callie a hand. Come on up, Cal."

"How did you know that I sang?" I asked weakly.

"It was in the *People* article," Lily said.

I looked around at the smiling, supportive faces. "Okay," I said, feeling the familiar excitement of performing rising in me like a blooming flower. "Okay."

I got up and went to the front of the bar. I looked down the bar at the familiar faces, many of them who had been in on the secret.

I knew I was safe here. I knew I had found my home.

"What do you want to sing?" Lenny said.

"What do you think?" I asked.

He started the opening lines of "Della and the Dealer."

And I sang.

ABOUT THE AUTHOR

Wendy Howell Mills currently pursues the same profession as her book's heroine as manager of a hotel restaurant on the beautiful Outer Banks of North Carolina, where she lives with her husband, Eddie.

The author is a member of Sisters in Crime and Mystery Writers of America. She is currently hard at work on her next book. For more information, check out the author's website at www.wendyhowellmills.com.

CALLIE AND THE DEALER AND A DOG NAMED JAKE was co-winner of the Dark Oak Mystery Contest 2000.

ABOUT THE ARTIST

Mary Montague Sikes (Monti to her friends) has studied with such famed artists as Peter Saul and Diana Kurz, Jim La France and Elaine Harvey. Her art has been exhibited at Roanoke Museum of Fine Art, Virginia Museum of Fine Arts, Johns Hopkins University and Piedmont Arts Center, and other fine galleries.

In addition to this novel, Monti has provided the cover art for several Oak Tree books, including her own *Hearts Across Forever*, due in July 2001. Her art- and-narrative high concept large format book, *Hotels to Remember* is set for a Spring 2001 release.

Dark Oak 2001 Mystery Contest

Grand Prize Winner to be announced in
Fall 2001.

~

Visit our website at www.oaktreebooks.com for information on the winners, guidelines for the upcoming Dark Oak 2002, and details on our other fine books.

~

Oak Tree Press books are available at Barnes & Noble and other fine bookstores, Amazon.com and other internet booksellers, or direct from the publisher.

~

For more information, send SASE to:

Oak Tree Press
915 W. Foothill Blvd. #411
Claremont, CA 91711-3356
909/625-8400 Tel 909/624-3930

More *Dark Oak Mysteries* you will enjoy...

An Affinity for Murder
A Lake George Mystery
By Anne White

Ellen, a new resident of Lake George in upstate New York, hopes to interview a famed art critic, but instead is entangled in a dangerous and confusing situation involving paintings that just might be undiscovered works of Georgia O'Keeffe.

ISBN 1-892343-16-9 $8.50

TULSA TIME
By Letha Albright

Reporter Viv Powers confronts the challenge of her life when her love, Charley, is accused of murder and will do nothing to defend himself — not even declare his innocence to her. A firm believer in logic and facts, Viv learns to face the trials of faith as she pursues the truth and the reasons why Charley isn't talking.

ISBN 1-892343-12-6 $7.95

Available at Barnes & Noble and other fine bookstores, Amazon.com and other internet booksellers, or direct from the publisher.